Mysteries

The Man in the Brown
    Suit
The Secret of Chimneys
The Seven Dials Mystery
The Mysterious Mr
    Quin
The Sittaford Mystery
The Hound of Death
The Listerdale Mystery
Why Didn't They Ask
    Evans?
Parker Pyne Investigates
Murder Is Easy
And Then There Were
    None
Towards Zero
Death Comes as the End
Sparkling Cyanide
Crooked House
They Came to Baghdad
Destination Unknown
Spider's Web *
The Unexpected Guest *
Ordeal by Innocence
The Pale Horse
Endless Night
Passenger To Frankfurt
Problem at Pollensa Bay
While the Light Lasts

Poirot

The Mysterious Affair at
    Styles
The Murder on the
    Links
Poirot Investigates
The Murder of Roger
    Ackroyd
The Big Four
The Mystery of the Blue
    Train
Black Coffee *
Peril at End House

Lord Edgware Dies
Murder on the Orient
    Express
Three-Act Tragedy
Death in the Clouds
The ABC Murders
Murder in Mesopotamia
Cards on the Table
Murder in the Mews
Dumb Witness
Death on the Nile
Appointment with Death
Hercule Poirot's
    Christmas
Sad Cypress
One, Two, Buckle My
    Shoe
Evil Under the Sun
Five Little Pigs
The Hollow
The Labours of Hercules
Taken at the Flood
Mrs McGinty's Dead
After the Funeral
Hickory Dickory Dock
Dead Man's Folly
Cat Among the Pigeons
The Adventure of the
    Christmas Pudding
The Clocks
Third Girl
Hallowe'en Party
Elephants Can
    Remember
Poirot's Early Cases
Curtain: Poirot's Last
    Case

Marple

The Murder at the
    Vicarage
The Thirteen Problems
The Body in the Library
The Moving Finger

A Murder Is Announced
They Do It with Mirrors
A Pocket Full of Rye
4.50 from Paddington
The Mirror Crack'd
    from Side to Side
A Caribbean Mystery
At Bertram's Hotel
Nemesis
Sleeping Murder
Miss Marple's Final Cases

Tommy & Tuppence

The Secret Adversary
Partners in Crime
N or M?
By the Pricking of My
    Thumbs
Postern of Fate

**Published as Mary
    Westmacott**

Giant's Bread
Unfinished Portrait
Absent in the Spring
The Rose and the Yew
    Tree
A Daughter's a Daughter
The Burden

Memoirs

An Autobiography
Come, Tell Me How You
    Live
The Grand Tour

Play and Stories

Akhnaton
The Mousetrap and
    Other Plays
The Floating Admiral †
Star Over Bethlehem
Hercule Poirot and the
    Greenshore Folly

* novelized by Charles Osborne   † contributor

Agatha Christie®

They Came to Baghdad

HarperCollins*Publishers*

HarperCollins*Publishers* Ltd
1 London Bridge Street
London SE1 9GF
www.harpercollins.co.uk

This paperback edition 2017

6

First published in Great Britain by
Collins, The Crime Club 1951

A catalogue record for this book is available from the British Library

ISBN 978-0-00-819635-6 (PB)
ISBN 978-0-00-825600-5 (POD PB)

Set in Sabon LT Std by Palimpsest Book Production Limited, Falkirk, Stirlingshire
Printed and bound by
CPI Group (UK) Ltd, Croydon, CR0 4YY

To all my friends in Baghdad

CHAPTER 1

Captain Crosbie came out of the bank with the pleased air of one who has cashed a cheque and has discovered that there is just a little more in his account than he thought there was.

Captain Crosbie often looked pleased with himself. He was that kind of man. In figure he was short and stocky, with rather a red face and a bristling military moustache. He strutted a little when he walked. His clothes were, perhaps, just a trifle loud, and he was fond of a good story. He was popular among other men. A cheerful man, commonplace but kindly, unmarried. Nothing remarkable about him. There are heaps of Crosbies in the East.

The street into which Captain Crosbie emerged was called Bank Street for the excellent reason that most of the banks in the city were situated in it. Inside the bank it was cool and dark and rather musty. The predominant sound was of large quantities of typewriters clicking in the background.

Outside in Bank Street it was sunny and full of swirling dust and the noises were terrific and varied. There was the persistent honking of motor horns, the cries of vendors of various wares. There were hot disputes between small groups of people who seemed ready to murder each other but were really fast friends; men, boys and children were selling every type of tree, sweetmeats, oranges and bananas, bath towels, combs, razor blades and other assorted merchandise carried rapidly through the streets on trays. There was also a perpetual and ever renewed sound of throat clearing and spitting, and above it the thin melancholy wail of men conducting donkeys and horses amongst the stream of motors and pedestrians shouting, '*Balek—Balek*!'

It was eleven o'clock in the morning in the city of Baghdad.

Captain Crosbie stopped a rapidly running boy with an armful of newspapers and bought one. He turned the corner of Bank Street and came into Rashid Street which is the main street of Baghdad, running through it for about four miles parallel with the river Tigris.

Captain Crosbie glanced at the headlines in the paper, tucked it under his arm, walked for about two hundred yards and then turned down a small alleyway and into a large khan or court. At the farther side of this he pushed open a door with a brass plate and found himself in an office.

A neat young Iraqi clerk left his typewriter and came forward smiling a welcome.

'Good morning, Captain Crosbie. What can I do for you?'

'Mr Dakin in his room? Good, I'll go through.'

He passed through a door, up some very steep stairs and

along a rather dirty passage. He knocked at the end door and a voice said, 'Come in.'

It was a high, rather bare room. There was an oil stove with a saucer of water on top of it, a long, low cushioned seat with a little coffee table in front of it and a large rather shabby desk. The electric light was on and the daylight was carefully excluded. Behind the shabby desk was a rather shabby man, with a tired and indecisive face—the face of one who has not got on in the world and knows it and has ceased to care.

The two men, the cheerful self-confident Crosbie, and the melancholy fatigued Dakin, looked at each other.

Dakin said, 'Hallo, Crosbie. Just in from Kirkuk?'

The other nodded. He shut the door carefully behind him. It was a shabby looking door, badly painted, but it had one rather unexpected quality; it fitted well, with no crevices and no space at the bottom.

It was, in fact, sound-proof.

With the closing of the door, the personalities of both men changed ever so slightly. Captain Crosbie became less aggressive and cocksure. Mr Dakin's shoulders drooped less, his manner was less hesitating. If any one had been in the room listening they would have been surprised to find that Dakin was the man in authority.

'Any news, sir?' asked Crosbie.

'Yes.' Dakin sighed. He had before him a paper which he had just been busy decoding. He dotted down two more letters and said:

'It's to be held in Baghdad.'

Then he struck a match, set light to the paper and

watched it burn. When it had smouldered to ashes, he blew gently. The ashes flew up and scattered.

'Yes,' he said. 'They've settled on Baghdad. Twentieth of next month. We're to "preserve all secrecy".'

'They've been talking about it in the souk—for three days,' said Crosbie drily.

The tall man smiled his weary smile.

'Top secret! No top secrets in the East, are there, Crosbie?'

'No, sir. If you ask me, there aren't any top secrets anywhere. During the war I often noticed a barber in London knew more than the High Command.'

'It doesn't matter much in this case. If the meeting is arranged for Baghdad it will soon have to be made public. And then the fun—our particular fun—starts.'

'Do you think it will ever take place, sir?' asked Crosbie sceptically. 'Does Uncle Joe'—thus disrespectfully did Captain Crosbie refer to the head of a Great European Power—'really mean to come?'

'I think he does this time, Crosbie,' said Dakin thoughtfully. 'Yes, I think so. And if the meeting comes off—comes off without a hitch—well, it might be the saving of— everything. If some kind of understanding could only be reached—' he broke off.

Crosbie still looked slightly sceptical. 'Is—forgive me, sir—is understanding of any kind *possible*?'

'In the sense you mean, Crosbie, probably *not*! If it were just a bringing together of two men representing totally different ideologies probably the whole thing would end as usual—in increased suspicion and misunderstanding. But there's the third element. If that fantastic story of Carmichael's is true—'

He broke off.

'But surely, sir, it can't be true. It's *too* fantastic!'

The other was silent for a few moments. He was seeing, very vividly, an earnest troubled face, hearing a quiet nondescript voice saying fantastic and unbelievable things. He was saying to himself, as he had said then, 'Either my best, my most reliable man has gone mad: or else—this thing is *true* . . .'

He said in the same thin melancholy voice:

'Carmichael believed it. Everything he could find out confirmed his hypothesis. He wanted to go there to find out more—to get proof. Whether I was wise to let him or not, I don't know. If he doesn't get back, it's only my story of what Carmichael told me, which again is a story of what someone told *him*. Is that enough? I don't think so. It is, as you say, such a fantastic story . . . But if the man himself is here, in Baghdad, on the twentieth, to tell his own story, the story of an eyewitness, and to produce proof—'

'Proof ?' said Crosbie sharply.

The other nodded.

'Yes, he's got proof.'

'How do you know?'

'The agreed formula. The message came through Salah Hassan.' He quoted carefully: '*A white camel with a load of oats is coming over the Pass.*'

He paused and then went on:

'So Carmichael has got what he went to get, but he didn't get away unsuspected. They're on his trail. Whatever route he takes will be watched, and what is far more dangerous, they'll be waiting for him—here. First on the frontier. And if he succeeds in passing the frontier, there will be a cordon drawn round the Embassies and the Consulates. Look at this.'

He shuffled amongst the papers on his desk and read out:

'An Englishman travelling in his car from Persia to Iraq shot dead—supposedly by bandits. A Kurdish merchant travelling down from the hills ambushed and killed. Another Kurd, Abdul Hassan, suspected of being a cigarette smuggler, shot by the police. Body of a man, afterwards identified as an Armenian lorry driver, found on the Rowanduz road. All of them mark you, of roughly the same description. Height, weight, hair, build, it corresponds with a description of Carmichael. They're taking no chances. They're out to get him. Once he's in Iraq the danger will be greater still. A gardener at the Embassy, a servant at the Consulate, an official at the Airport, in the Customs, at the railway stations . . . all hotels watched . . . A cordon, stretched tight.'

Crosbie raised his eyebrows.

'You think it's as widespread as all that, sir?'

'I've no doubt of it. Even in our show there have been leakages. That's the worst of all. How am I to be sure that the measures we're adopting to get Carmichael safely into Baghdad aren't known already to the other side? It's one of the elementary moves of the game, as you know, to have someone in the pay of the other camp.'

'Is there any one you—suspect?'

Slowly Dakin shook his head.

Crosbie sighed.

'In the meantime,' he said, 'we carry on?'

'Yes.'

'What about Crofton Lee?'

'He's agreed to come to Baghdad.'

'Everyone's coming to Baghdad,' said Crosbie. 'Even Uncle Joe, according to you, sir. But if anything should happen to the President—while he's here—the balloon will go up with a vengeance.'

'Nothing must happen,' said Dakin. 'That's our business. To see it doesn't.'

When Crosbie had gone Dakin sat bent over his desk. He murmured under his breath:

'They came to Baghdad . . .'

On the blotting pad he drew a circle and wrote under it *Baghdad*—then, dotted round it, he sketched a camel, an aeroplane, a steamer, a small puffing train—all converging on the circle. Then on the corner of the pad he drew a spider's web. In the middle of the spider's web he wrote a name:*Anna Scheele*. Underneath he put a big query mark.

Then he took his hat, and left the office. As he walked along Rashid Street, some man asked another who that was.

'That? Oh, that's Dakin. In one of the oil companies. Nice fellow, but never gets on. Too lethargic. They say he drinks. *He*'ll never get anywhere. You've got to have drive to get on in this part of the world.'

'Have you got the reports on the Krugenhorf property, Miss Scheele?'

'Yes, Mr Morganthal.'

Miss Scheele, cool and efficient, slipped the papers in front of her employer.

He grunted as he read.

'Satisfactory, I think.'

'I certainly think so, Mr Morganthal.'

'Is Schwartz here?'

'He's waiting in the outer office.'

'Have him sent in right now.'

Miss Scheele pressed a buzzer—one of six.

'Will you require me, Mr Morganthal?'

'No, I don't think so, Miss Scheele.'

Anna Scheele glided noiselessly from the room.

She was a platinum blonde—but not a glamorous blonde. Her pale flaxen hair was pulled straight back from her forehead into a neat roll at the neck. Her pale blue intelligent eyes looked out on the world from behind strong glasses. Her face had neat small features, but was quite expressionless. She had made her way in the world not by her charm but by sheer efficiency. She could memorize anything, however complicated, and produce names, dates and times without having to refer to notes. She could organize the staff of a big office in such a way that it ran as by well-oiled machinery. She was discretion itself and her energy, though controlled and disciplined, never flagged.

Otto Morganthal, head of the firm of Morganthal, Brown and Shipperke, international bankers, was well aware that to Anna Scheele he owed more than mere money could repay. He trusted her completely. Her memory, her experience, her judgement, her cool level head were invaluable. He paid her a large salary and would have made it a larger one had she asked for it.

She knew not only the details of his business but the details of his private life. When he had consulted her in the matter of the second Mrs Morganthal, she had advised divorce and suggested the exact amount of alimony. She had not expressed sympathy or curiosity. She was not, he would have said, that kind of woman. He didn't think she had any feelings, and it had never occurred to him to wonder what she thought about. He would indeed have been astonished if he had been told that she had any thoughts—other, that is, than thoughts connected with Morganthal, Brown and Shipperke and with the problems of Otto Morganthal.

So it was with complete surprise that he heard her say as she prepared to leave his office:

'I should like three weeks' leave of absence if I might have it, Mr Morganthal. Starting from Tuesday next.'

Staring at her, he said uneasily: 'It will be awkward—very awkward.'

'I don't think it will be too difficult, Mr Morganthal. Miss Wygate is fully competent to deal with things. I shall leave her my notes and full instructions. Mr Cornwall can attend to the Ascher Merger.'

Still uneasily he asked:

'You're not ill, or anything?'

He couldn't imagine Miss Scheele being ill. Even germs respected Anna Scheele and kept out of her way.

'Oh no, Mr Morganthal. I want to go to London to see my sister there.'

'Your sister?' He didn't know she had a sister. He had never conceived of Miss Scheele as having any family or relations. She had never mentioned having any. And here she was, casually referring to a sister in London. She had been over in London with him last fall but she had never mentioned having a sister then.

With a sense of injury he said:

'I never knew you had a sister in England?'

Miss Scheele smiled very faintly.

'Oh yes, Mr Morganthal. She is married to an Englishman connected with the British Museum. It is necessary for her to undergo a very serious operation. She wants me to be with her. I should like to go.'

In other words, Otto Morganthal saw, she had made up her mind to go.

He said grumblingly, 'All right, all right . . . Get back as soon as you can. I've never seen the market so jumpy. All this damned Communism. War may break out at any moment. It's the only solution, I sometimes think. The whole country's riddled with it—riddled with it. And now the President's determined to go to this fool conference at Baghdad. It's a put-up job in my opinion. They're out to get him. Baghdad! Of all the outlandish places!'

10

'Oh I'm sure he'll be very well guarded,' Miss Scheele said soothingly.

'They got the Shah of Persia last year, didn't they? They got Bernadotte in Palestine. It's madness—that's what it is—madness.

'But then,' added Mr Morganthal heavily, 'all the world is mad.'

CHAPTER 2

Victoria Jones was sitting moodily on a seat in FitzJames
Gardens. She was wholly given up to reflections—or one might
almost say moralizations—on the disadvantages inherent in
employing one's particular talents at the wrong moment.

Victoria was like most of us, a girl with both qualities
and defects. On the credit side she was generous, warm-
hearted and courageous. Her natural leaning towards
adventure may be regarded as either meritorious or the
reverse in this modern age which places the value of security high. Her principal defect was a tendency to tell lies
at both opportune and inopportune moments. The superior
fascination of fiction to fact was always irresistible to
Victoria. She lied with fluency, ease, and artistic fervour. If
Victoria was late for an appointment (which was often the
case) it was not sufficient for her to murmur an excuse of
her watch having stopped (which actually was quite often
the case) or of an unaccountably delayed bus. It would
appear preferable to Victoria to tender the mendacious
explanation that she had been hindered by an escaped
elephant lying across a main bus route, or by a thrilling

smash-and-grab raid in which she herself had played a part to aid the police. To Victoria an agreeable world would be one where tigers lurked in the Strand and dangerous bandits infested Tooting.

A slender girl, with an agreeable figure and first-class legs, Victoria's features might actually have been described as plain. They were small and neat. But there was a piquancy about her, for 'little india-rubber face,' as one of her admirers had named her, could twist those immobile features into a startling mimicry of almost anybody.

It was this last-named talent that had led to her present predicament. Employed as a typist by Mr Greenholtz of Greenholtz, Simmons and Lederbetter, of Graysholme Street, WC2, Victoria had been whiling away a dull morning by entertaining the three other typists and the office boy with a vivid performance of Mrs Greenholtz paying a visit to her husband's office. Secure in the knowledge that Mr Greenholtz had gone round to his solicitors, Victoria let herself go.

'Why do you say we not have that Knole settee, Daddee?' she demanded in a high whining voice. 'Mrs Dievtakis she have one in electric blue satin. You say it is money that is tight? But then why you take that blonde girl out dining and dancing—Ah! you think I do not know—and if you take that girl—then I have a settee and all done plum coloured and gold cushions. And when you say it is a business dinner you are a damn' fool—yes—and come back with lipstick on your shirt. So I have the Knole settee and I order a fur cape—very nice—all like mink but not really mink and I get him very cheap and it is good business—'

Agatha Christie

The sudden failure of her audience—at first entranced, but now suddenly resuming work with spontaneous agreement, caused Victoria to break off and swing round to where Mr Greenholtz was standing in the doorway observing her.

Victoria, unable to think of anything relevant to say, merely said, 'Oh!'

Mr Greenholtz grunted.

Flinging off his overcoat, Mr Greenholtz proceeded to his private office and banged the door. Almost immediately his buzzer sounded, two shorts and a long. That was a summons for Victoria.

'It's for you, Jonesey,' a colleague remarked unnecessarily, her eyes alight with the pleasure occasioned by the misfortunes of others. The other typists collaborated in this sentiment by ejaculating: 'You're for it, Jones,' and 'On the mat, Jonesey.' The office boy, an unpleasant child, contented himself with drawing a forefinger across his throat and uttering a sinister noise.

Victoria picked up her notebook and pencil and sailed into Mr Greenholtz's office with such assurance as she could muster.

'You want me, Mr Greenholtz?' she murmured, fixing a limpid gaze on him.

Mr Greenholtz was rustling three pound notes and searching his pockets for coin of the realm.

'So there you are,' he observed. 'I've had about enough of you, young lady. Do you see any particular reason why I shouldn't pay you a week's salary in lieu of notice and pack you off here and now?'

Victoria (an orphan) had just opened her mouth to explain how the plight of a mother at this moment suffering a major operation had so demoralized her that she had become completely light-headed, and how her small salary was all the aforesaid mother had to depend upon, when, taking an opening glance at Mr Greenholtz's unwholesome face, she shut her mouth and changed her mind.

'I couldn't agree with you more,' she said heartily and pleasantly. 'I think you're absolutely *right*, if you know what I mean.'

Mr Greenholtz appeared slightly taken aback. He was not used to having his dismissals treated in this approving and congratulatory spirit. To conceal a slight discomfiture he sorted through a pile of coins on the desk in front of him. He then sought once more in his pockets.

'Ninepence short,' he murmured gloomily.

'Never mind,' said Victoria kindly. 'Take yourself to the pictures or spend it on sweets.'

'Don't seem to have any stamps, either.'

'It doesn't matter. I never write letters.'

'I could send it after you,' said Mr Greenholtz but without much conviction.

'Don't bother. What about a reference?' said Victoria.

Mr Greenholtz's choler returned.

'Why the hell should I give you a reference?' he demanded wrathfully.

'It's usual,' said Victoria.

Mr Greenholtz drew a piece of paper towards him and scrawled a few lines. He shoved it towards her.

'That do for you?'

*Miss Jones has been with me two months as a shorthand
typist. Her shorthand is inaccurate and she cannot spell.
She is leaving owing to wasting time in office hours.*

Victoria made a grimace.

'Hardly a recommendation,' she observed.

'It wasn't meant to be,' said Mr Greenholtz.

'I think,' said Victoria, 'that you ought at least to say
I'm honest, sober and respectable. I am, you know. And
perhaps you might add that I'm discreet.'

'Discreet?' barked Mr Greenholtz.

Victoria met his gaze with an innocent stare.

'Discreet,' she said gently.

Remembering sundry letters taken down and typed by
Victoria, Mr Greenholtz decided that prudence was the
better part of rancour.

He snatched back the paper, tore it up and indited a
fresh one.

*Miss Jones has been with me for two months as a
shorthand typist. She is leaving owing to redundancy of
office staff.*

'How about that?'

'It could be better,' said Victoria, 'but it will do.'

So it was that with a week's salary (less ninepence) in her
bag Victoria was sitting in meditation upon a bench in
FitzJames Gardens which are a triangular plantation of

rather sad shrubs flanking a church and overlooked by a tall warehouse.

It was Victoria's habit on any day when it was not actually raining to purchase one cheese, and one lettuce and tomato sandwich at a milk-bar and eat this simple lunch in these pseudo-rural surroundings.

Today, as she munched meditatively, she was telling herself, not for the first time, that there was a time and place for everything—and that the office was definitely not the place for imitations of the boss's wife. She must, in future, curb the natural exuberance that led her to brighten up the performance of a dull job. In the meantime, she was free of Greenholtz, Simmons and Lederbetter, and the prospect of obtaining a situation elsewhere filled her with pleasurable anticipation. Victoria was always delighted when she was about to take up a new job. One never knew, she always felt, what might happen.

She had just distributed the last crumb of bread to three attentive sparrows who immediately fought each other with fury for it, when she became aware of a young man sitting at the other end of the seat. Victoria had noticed him vaguely already, but her mind full of good resolutions for the future, she had not observed him closely until now. What she now saw (out of the corner of her eye) she liked very much. He was a good-looking young man, cherubically fair, but with a firm chin and extremely blue eyes which had been, she rather imagined, examining her with covert admiration for some time.

Victoria had no inhibitions about making friends with strange young men in public places. She considered herself

17

an excellent judge of character and well able to check any manifestations of freshness on the part of unattached males.

She proceeded to smile frankly at him and the young man responded like a marionette when you pull the string.

'Hallo,' said the young man. 'Nice place this. Do you often come here?'

'Nearly every day.'

'Just my luck that I never came here before. Was that your lunch you were eating?'

'Yes.'

'I don't think you eat enough. I'd be starving if I only had two sandwiches. What about coming along and having a sausage at the SPO in Tottenham Court Road?'

'No thanks. I'm quite all right. I couldn't eat any more now.'

She rather expected that he would say: 'Another day,' but he did not. He merely sighed—then he said:

'My name's Edward, what's yours?'

'Victoria.'

'Why did your people want to call you after a railway station?'

'Victoria isn't only a railway station,' Miss Jones pointed out. 'There's Queen Victoria as well.'

'Mm yes. What's your other name?'

'Jones.'

'Victoria Jones,' said Edward, trying it over on his tongue. He shook his head. 'They don't go together.'

'You're quite right,' said Victoria with feeling. 'If I were Jenny it would be rather nice—Jenny Jones. But Victoria needs something with a bit more class to it. Victoria Sackville-West for instance. That's the kind of thing one needs. Something to roll round the mouth.'

'You could tack something on to the Jones,' said Edward with sympathetic interest.

'Bedford Jones.'

'Carisbrooke Jones.'

'St Clair Jones.'

'Lonsdale Jones.'

This agreeable game was interrupted by Edward's glancing at his watch and uttering a horrified ejaculation.

'I must tear back to my blinking boss—er—what about you?'

'I'm out of a job. I was sacked this morning.'

'Oh I say, I am sorry,' said Edward with real concern.

'Well, don't waste sympathy, because I'm not sorry at all. For one thing, I'll easily get another job, and besides that, it was really rather fun.'

And delaying Edward's return to duty still further, she gave him a spirited rendering of this morning's scene, re-enacting her impersonation of Mrs Greenholtz to Edward's immense enjoyment.

'You really are marvellous, Victoria,' he said. 'You ought to be on the stage.'

Victoria accepted this tribute with a gratified smile and remarked that Edward had better be running along if he didn't want to get the sack himself.

'Yes—and I shouldn't get another job as easily as you will. It must be wonderful to be a good shorthand typist,' said Edward with envy in his voice.

'Well, actually I'm not a good shorthand typist,' Victoria admitted frankly, 'but fortunately even the lousiest of shorthand typists can get some sort of a job nowadays—at any rate an educational or charitable one—they can't afford to pay much and so they get people like me. I prefer the learned type of job best. These scientific names and terms are so frightful anyway that if you can't spell them properly it doesn't really shame you because nobody could. What's your job? I suppose you're out of one of the services. RAF?'

'Good guess.'

'Fighter pilot?'

'Right again. They're awfully decent about getting us jobs and all that, but you see, the trouble is, that we're not particularly brainy. I mean one didn't need to be brainy in the RAF. They put me in an office with a lot of files and figures and some thinking to do and I just folded up. The whole thing seemed utterly purposeless anyway. But there it is. It gets you down a bit to know that you're absolutely no good.'

Victoria nodded sympathetically—Edward went on bitterly:

'Out of touch. Not in the picture any more. It was all right during the war—one could keep one's end up all right—I got the DFC for instance—but now—well, I might as well write myself off the map.'

'But there ought to be—'

Victoria broke off. She felt unable to put into words her conviction that those qualities that brought a DFC to their owner should somewhere have their appointed place in the world of 1950.

'It's got me down, rather,' said Edward. 'Being no good at anything, I mean. Well—I'd better be pushing off—I say—would you mind—would it be most awful cheek—if I only could—'

As Victoria opened surprised eyes, stammering and blushing, Edward produced a small camera.

'I would like so awfully to have a snapshot of you. You see, I'm going to Baghdad tomorrow.'

'To Baghdad?' exclaimed Victoria with lively disappointment.

'Yes. I mean I wish I wasn't—now. Earlier this morning I was quite bucked about it—it's why I took this job really—to get out of this country.'

'What sort of job is it?'

'Pretty awful. Culture—poetry, all that sort of thing. A Dr Rathbone's my boss. Strings of letters after his name, peers at you soulfully through pince-nez. He's terrifically keen on uplift and spreading it far and wide. He opens bookshops in remote places—he's starting one in Baghdad. He gets Shakespeare's and Milton's works translated into Arabic and Kurdish and Persian and Armenian and has them all on tap. Silly, I think, because you've got the British Council doing much the same thing all over the place. Still, there it is. It gives me a job so I oughtn't to complain.'

'What do you actually *do*?' asked Victoria.

'Well, really it boils down to being the old boy's personal Yes-man and Dogsbody. Buy the tickets, make the reservations, fill up the passport forms, check the packing of all the horrid little poetic manuals, run round here, there, and everywhere. Then, when we get out there I'm supposed to fraternize—kind of glorified youth movement—all nations together in a united drive for uplift.' Edward's tone became more and more melancholy. 'Frankly, it's pretty ghastly, isn't it?'

Victoria was unable to administer much comfort.

'So you see,' said Edward, 'if you wouldn't mind awfully—one sideways and one looking right at me—oh I say, that's wonderful—'

The camera clicked twice and Victoria showed that purring complacence displayed by young women who know they have made an impression on an attractive member of the opposite sex.

'But it's pretty foul really, having to go off just when I've met you,' said Edward. 'I've half a mind to chuck it—but I suppose I couldn't do that at the last moment—not after all those ghastly forms and visas and everything. Wouldn't be a very good show, what?'

'It mayn't turn out as bad as you think,' said Victoria consolingly.

'N-no,' said Edward doubtfully. 'The funny thing is,' he added, 'that I've got a feeling there's something fishy somewhere.'

'Fishy?'

'Yes. Bogus. Don't ask me why. I haven't any reason. Sort of feeling one gets sometimes. Had it once about my port oil. Began fussing about the damned thing and sure enough there was a washer wedged in the spare gear pump.'

The technical terms in which this was couched made it quite unintelligible to Victoria, but she got the main idea.

22

'You think *he's* bogus—Rathbone?'

'Don't see how he can be. I mean he's frightfully respectable and learned and belongs to all these societies—and sort of hob-nobs with Archbishops and Principals of Colleges. No, it's just a *feeling*—well, time will show. So long. I wish you were coming, too.'

'So do I,' said Victoria.

'What are you going to do?'

'Go round to St Guildric's Agency in Gower Street and look for another job,' said Victoria gloomily.

'Goodbye, Victoria. Partir, say mourir un peu,' added Edward with a very British accent. 'These French johnnies know their stuff. Our English chaps just maunder on about parting being a sweet sorrow—silly asses.'

'Goodbye, Edward, good luck.'

'I don't suppose you'll ever think about me again.'

'Yes, I shall.'

'You're absolutely different from any girl I've ever seen before—I only wish—' The clock chimed a quarter, and Edward said, 'Oh hell—I must fly—'

Retreating rapidly, he was swallowed up by the great maw of London. Victoria remaining behind on her seat absorbed in meditation was conscious of two distinct streams of thought.

One dealt with the theme of Romeo and Juliet. She and Edward, she felt, were somewhat in the position of that unhappy couple, although perhaps Romeo and Juliet had expressed their feelings in rather more high-class language. But the position, Victoria thought, was the same. Meeting, instant attraction—frustration—two fond hearts thrust asunder. A remembrance of a rhyme once frequently recited by her old nurse came to her mind:

Jumbo said to Alice I love you,
Alice said to Jumbo I don't believe you do,
If you really loved me as you say you do
You wouldn't go to America and leave me in the Zoo.

Substitute Baghdad for America and there you were!

Victoria rose at last, dusting crumbs from her lap, and walked briskly out of FitzJames Gardens in the direction of Gower Street. Victoria had come to two decisions: the first was that (like Juliet) she loved this young man, and meant to have him.

The second decision that Victoria had come to was that as Edward would shortly be in Baghdad, the only thing to do was for her to go to Baghdad also. What was now occupying her mind was how this could be accomplished. That it could be accomplished somehow or other, Victoria did not doubt. She was a young woman of optimism and force of character.

Parting is such sweet sorrow appealed to her as a sentiment no more than it did to Edward.

'Somehow,' said Victoria to herself, 'I've *got* to get to Baghdad!'

CHAPTER 3

The Savoy Hotel welcomed Miss Anna Scheele with the *empressément* due to an old and valued client—they inquired after the health of Mr Morganthal—and assured her that if her suite was not to her liking she had only to say so—for Anna Scheele represented DOLLARS.

Miss Scheele bathed, dressed, made a telephone call to a Kensington number and then went down in the lift. She passed through the revolving doors and asked for a taxi. It drew up and she got in and directed it to Cartier's in Bond Street.

As the taxi turned out of the Savoy approach into the Strand a little dark man who had been standing looking into a shop window suddenly glanced at his watch and hailed a taxi that was conveniently cruising past and which had been singularly blind to the hails of an agitated woman with parcels a moment or two previously.

The taxi followed along the Strand keeping the first taxi in sight. As they were both held up by the lights in going round Trafalgar Square, the man in the second taxi looked out of the left-hand window and made a slight gesture

with his hand. A private car, which had been standing in
the side street by the Admiralty Arch started its engine and
swung into the stream of traffic behind the second taxi.

The traffic had started on again. As Anna Scheele's taxi
followed the stream of traffic going to the left into Pall
Mall, the taxi containing the little dark man swung away
to the right, continuing round Trafalgar Square. The private
car, a grey Standard, was now close behind Anna Scheele.
It contained two passengers, a fair rather vacant-looking
young man at the wheel and a smartly dressed young
woman beside him. The Standard followed Anna Scheele's
taxi along Piccadilly and up Bond Street. Here for a moment
it paused by the kerb, and the young woman got out.

She called brightly and conventionally:

'Thanks so much.'

The car went on. The young woman walked along
glancing every now and again into a window. A block held
up the traffic. The young woman passed both the Standard
and Anna Scheele's taxi. She arrived at Cartier's and went
inside.

Anna Scheele paid off her taxi and went into the jewel-
ler's. She spent some time looking at various pieces of
jewellery. In the end she selected a sapphire and diamond
ring. She wrote a cheque for it on a London bank. At the
sight of the name on it, a little extra *empressement* came
into the assistant's manner.

'Glad to see you in London again, Miss Scheele. Is Mr
Morganthal over?'

'No.'

'I wondered. We have a very fine star sapphire here—I

know he is interested in star sapphires. If you would care to see it?'

Miss Scheele expressed her willingness to see it, duly admired it and promised to mention it to Mr Morganthal.

She went out again into Bond Street, and the young woman who had been looking at clip earrings expressed herself as unable to make up her mind and emerged also.

The grey Standard car having turned to the left in Grafton Street and gone down to Piccadilly was just coming up Bond Street again. The young woman showed no signs of recognition.

Anna Scheele had turned into the Arcade. She entered a florist's. She ordered three dozen long-stemmed roses, a bowl full of sweet big purple violets, a dozen sprays of white lilac, and a jar of mimosa. She gave an address for them to be sent.

'That will be twelve pounds, eighteen shillings, madam.'

Anna Scheele paid and went out. The young woman who had just come in asked the price of a bunch of primroses but did not buy them.

Anna Scheele crossed Bond Street and went along Burlington Street and turned into Savile Row. Here she entered the establishment of one of those tailors who, whilst catering essentially for men, occasionally condescend to cut a suit for certain favoured members of the feminine sex.

Mr Bolford received Miss Scheele with the greeting accorded to a valued client, and the materials for a suit were considered.

'Fortunately, I can give you our own export quality. When will you be returning to New York, Miss Scheele?'

'On the twenty-third.'

'We can manage that nicely. By the clipper, I presume?'

'Yes.'

'And how are things in America? They are very sadly here—very sadly indeed.' Mr Bolford shook his head like a doctor describing a patient. 'No *heart* in things, if you know what I mean. And no one coming along who takes any pride in a good job of work. D'you know who will cut your suit, Miss Scheele? Mr Lantwick—seventy-two years of age he is and he's the only man I've got I can really trust to cut for our best people. All the others—'

Mr Bolford's plump hands waved them away.

'Quality,' he said. 'That's what this country used to be renowned for. Quality! Nothing cheap, nothing flashy. When we try mass production we're no good at it, and that's a fact. That's *your* country's speciality, Miss Scheele. What *we* ought to stand for, and I say it again, is *quality*. Take time over things, and trouble, and turn out an article that no one in the world can beat. Now what day shall we say for the first fitting. This day week? At 11.30? Thank you very much.'

Making her way through the archaic gloom round bales of material, Anna Scheele emerged into daylight again. She hailed a taxi and returned to the Savoy. A taxi that was drawn up on the opposite side of the street and which contained a little dark man, took the same route but did not turn into the Savoy. It drove round to the Embankment and there picked up a short plump woman who had recently emerged from the service entrance of the Savoy.

'What about it, Louisa? Been through her room?'

'Yes. Nothing.'

Anna Scheele had lunch in the restaurant. A table had been kept for her by the window. The Maître d'Hôtel inquired affectionately after the health of Otto Morganthal.

After lunch Anna Scheele took her key and went up to her suite. The bed had been made, fresh towels were in the bathroom and everything was spick and span. Anna crossed to the two light air-cases that constituted her luggage, one was open, the other locked. She cast an eye over the contents of the unlocked one, then taking her keys from her purse she unlocked the other. All was neat, folded, as she had folded things, nothing had apparently been touched or disturbed. A brief-case of leather lay on top. A small Leica camera and two rolls of films were in one corner. The films were still sealed and unopened. Anna ran her nail across the flap and pulled it up. Then she smiled, very gently. The single almost invisible blonde hair that had been there was there no longer. Deftly she scattered a little powder over the shiny leather of the brief-case and blew it off. The brief-case remained clear and shiny. There were no finger-prints. But that morning after patting a little brilliantine on to the smooth flaxen cap of her hair, she had handled the brief-case. There *should* have been fingerprints on it, her own.

She smiled again.

'Good work,' she said to herself. 'But not quite good enough . . .'

Deftly, she packed a small overnight-case and went down-stairs again. A taxi was called and she directed the driver to 17 Elmsleigh Gardens.

Elmsleigh Gardens was a quiet, rather dingy Kensington Square. Anna paid off the taxi and ran up the steps to the peeling front door. She pressed the bell. After a few minutes an elderly woman opened the door with a suspicious face which immediately changed to a beam of welcome.

'Won't Miss Elsie be pleased to see you! She's in the study at the back. It's only the thought of your coming that's been keeping her spirits up.'

Anna went quickly along the dark hallway and opened the door at the far end. It was a small shabby, comfortable room with large worn leather arm-chairs. The woman sitting in one of them jumped up.

'Anna, darling.'

'Elsie.'

The two women kissed each other affectionately.

'It's all arranged,' said Elsie. 'I go in tonight. I do hope—'

'Cheer up,' said Anna. 'Everything is going to be quite all right.'

The small dark man in the raincoat entered a public callbox at High Street Kensington Station, and dialled a number.

'Valhalla Gramophone Company?'

'Yes.'

'Sanders here.'

'Sanders of the River? What river?'

'River Tigris. Reporting on A. S. Arrived this morning from New York. Went to Cartier's. Bought sapphire and diamond ring costing one hundred and twenty pounds. Went to florist's, Jane Kent—twelve pounds eighteen shillings' worth of flowers to be delivered at a nursing home in Portland Place. Ordered coat and skirt at Bolford and Avory's. None of these firms known to have any suspicious contacts, but particular attention will be paid to them in future. A. S.'s room at Savoy gone through. Nothing suspicious found. Brief-case in suitcase containing papers relating to Paper Merger with Wolfensteins. All above board. Camera and two rolls of apparently unexposed films. Possibility of films being photostatic records, substituted other films for them, but original films reported upon as being straightforward unexposed films. A.S. took small overnight-case and went to sister at 17 Elmsleigh Gardens. Sister entering nursing home in Portland Place this evening for internal operation. This confirmed from nursing home and also appointment book of surgeon. Visit of A. S. seems perfectly above board. Showed no uneasiness or consciousness of being followed. Understand she is spending tonight at nursing home. Has kept on her room at the Savoy. Return passage to New York by clipper booked for twenty-third.'

The man who called himself Sanders of the River paused and added a postscript off the record as it were.

'And if you ask what I think it's all a mare's nest! Throwing money about, that's all *she's* doing. Twelve pounds eighteen on flowers! I ask you!'

CHAPTER 4

It says a good deal for the buoyancy of Victoria's temperament that the possibility of failing to attain her objective did not for a moment occur to her. Not for her the lines about ships that pass in the night. It was certainly unfortunate that when she had—well—frankly—fallen for an attractive young man, that that young man should prove to be just on the verge of departure to a place distant some three thousand miles. He might so easily have been going to Aberdeen or Brussels, or even Birmingham.

That it should be Baghdad, thought Victoria, was just her luck! Nevertheless, difficult though it might be, she intended to get to Baghdad somehow or other. Victoria walked purposefully along Tottenham Court Road evolving ways and means. Baghdad. What went on in Baghdad? According to Edward: 'Culture.' Could she, in some way, play up culture? Unesco? Unesco was always sending people here, there and everywhere, sometimes to the most delectable places. But these were usually, Victoria reflected, superior young women with university degrees who had got into the racket early on.

Victoria, deciding that first things came first, finally bent her steps to a travel agency, and there made her inquiries. There was no difficulty, it seemed, in travelling to Baghdad. You could go by air, by long sea to Basrah, by train to Marseilles and by boat to Beirut and across the desert by car. You could go via Egypt. You could go all the way by train if you were determined to do so, but visas were at present difficult and uncertain and were apt to have actually expired by the time you received them. Baghdad was in the sterling area and money therefore presented no difficulties. Not, that is to say, in the clerk's meaning of the word. What it all boiled down to was that there was no difficulty whatsoever in getting to Baghdad so long as you had between sixty and a hundred pounds in cash.

As Victoria had at this moment three pounds ten (less ninepence), an extra twelve shillings, and five pounds in the PO Savings Bank, the simple and straightforward way was out of the question.

She made tentative queries as to a job as air hostess or stewardess, but these, she gathered, were highly coveted posts for which there was a waiting-list.

Victoria next visited St Guildric's Agency where Miss Spenser, sitting behind her efficient desk, welcomed her as one of those who were destined to pass through the office with reasonable frequency.

'Dear me, Miss Jones, not out of a post *again*. I really hoped this last one—'

'Quite impossible,' said Victoria firmly. 'I really couldn't begin to tell you what I had to put up with.'

A pleasurable flush rose in Miss Spenser's pallid cheek.

'Not—' she began—'I do hope not—He didn't seem to me really that sort of man—but of course he *is* a trifle gross—I do hope—'

'It's quite all right,' said Victoria. She conjured up a pale brave smile. 'I can take care of myself.'

'Oh, of course, but it's the *unpleasantness*.'

'Yes,' said Victoria. 'It *is* unpleasant. However—' She smiled bravely again.

Miss Spenser consulted her books.

'The St Leonard's Assistance to Unmarried Mothers want a typist,' said Miss Spenser. 'Of course, they don't pay very much—'

'Is there any chance,' asked Victoria brusquely, 'of a post in Baghdad?'

'In Baghdad?' said Miss Spenser in lively astonishment.

Victoria saw she might as well have said in Kamchatka or at the South Pole.

'I should very much like to get to Baghdad,' said Victoria.

'I hardly think—in a secretary's post you mean?'

'Anyhow,' said Victoria. 'As a nurse or a cook, or looking after a lunatic. Any way at all.'

Miss Spenser shook her head.

'I'm afraid I can't hold out much hope. There was a lady in yesterday with two little girls who was offering a passage to Australia.'

Victoria waved away Australia.

She rose. 'If you did hear of anything. Just the fare out—that's all I need.' She met the curiosity in the other woman's eye by explaining—'I've got—er—relations out there. And I understand there are plenty of well-paid jobs. But of course, one has to get there first.

'Yes,' repeated Victoria to herself as she walked away from St Guildric's Bureau. 'One has to get there.'

It was an added annoyance to Victoria that, as is customary, when one has had one's attention suddenly focused on a particular name or subject, everything seemed to have suddenly conspired to force the thought of Baghdad on to her attention.

A brief paragraph in the evening paper she bought stated that Dr Pauncefoot Jones, the well-known archaeologist, had started excavation on the ancient city of Murik, situated a hundred and twenty miles from Baghdad. An advertisement mentioned shipping lines to Basrah (and thence by train to Baghdad, Mosul, etc.). In the newspaper that lined her stocking drawer, a few lines of print about students in Baghdad leapt to her eyes. *The Thief of Baghdad* was on at the local cinema, and in the high-class highbrow bookshop into whose window she always gazed, a new biography of Haroun el Rashid, Caliph of Baghdad, was prominently displayed.

The whole world, it seemed to her, had suddenly become Baghdad conscious. And until that afternoon at approximately 1.45 she had, for all intents and purposes never heard of Baghdad, and certainly never thought about it.

The prospects of getting there were unsatisfactory, but Victoria had no idea of giving up. She had a fertile brain and the optimistic outlook that if you want to do a thing there is always some way of doing it.

She employed the evening in drawing up a list of possible approaches. It ran:

Insert advertisement?
Try Foreign Office?
Try Iraq Legation?
What about date firms?
Ditto shipping firms?
British Council?
Selfridge's Information Bureau?
Citizen's Advice Bureau?

None of them, she was forced to admit, seemed very promising. She added to the list:

Somehow or other, get hold of a hundred pounds?

The intense mental efforts of concentration that Victoria had made overnight, and possibly the subconscious satisfaction at no longer having to be punctually in the office at nine a.m., made Victoria oversleep herself.

She awoke at five minutes past ten, and immediately jumped out of bed and began to dress. She was just passing a final comb through her rebellious dark hair when the telephone rang.

Victoria reached for the receiver.

A positively agitated Miss Spenser was at the other end.

'So glad to have caught you, my dear. Really the most amazing coincidence.'

'Yes?' cried Victoria.

'As I say, really a startling coincidence. A Mrs Hamilton Clipp—travelling to Baghdad in three days' time—has broken her arm—needs someone to assist her on journey—I rang you up at once. Of course I don't know if she has also applied to any other agencies—'

'I'm on my way,' said Victoria. 'Where is she?'

'The Savoy.'

'And what's her silly name? Tripp?'

'Clipp, dear. Like a paper clip, but with two P's—I can't think why, but then she's an American,' ended Miss Spencer as if that explained everything.

'Mrs Clipp at the Savoy.'

'Mr and Mrs Hamilton Clipp. It was actually the husband who rang up.'

'You're an angel,' said Victoria. 'Goodbye.'

She hurriedly brushed her suit and wished it were slightly less shabby, recombed her hair so as to make it seem less exuberant and more in keeping with the role of ministering angel and experienced traveller. Then she took out Mr Greenholtz's recommendation and shook her head over it.

We must do better than that, said Victoria.

From a No. 19 bus, Victoria alighted at Green Park, and entered the Ritz Hotel. A quick glance over the shoulder of a woman reading in the bus had proved rewarding. Entering the writing-room Victoria wrote herself some generous lines of praise from Lady Cynthia Bradbury who had been announced as having just left England for East Africa . . . *'excellent in illness,'* wrote Victoria, *'and most capable in every way . . .'*

Leaving the Ritz she crossed the road and walked a short way up Albemarle Street until she came to Balderton's Hotel, renowned as the haunt of the higher clergy and of old-fashioned dowagers up from the country.

In less dashing handwriting, and making neat small Greek 'E's, she wrote a recommendation from the Bishop of Llangow.

Thus equipped, Victoria caught a No. 9 bus and proceeded to the Savoy.

At the reception desk she asked for Mrs Hamilton Clipp and gave her name as coming from St Guildric's Agency. The clerk was just about to pull the telephone towards him when he paused, looked across, and said:

'That is Mr Hamilton Clipp now.'

Mr Hamilton Clipp was an immensely tall and very thin grey-haired American of kindly aspect and slow deliberate speech.

Victoria told him her name and mentioned the Agency.

'Why now, Miss Jones, you'd better come right up and see Mrs Clipp. She is still in our suite. I fancy she's interviewing some other young lady, but she may have gone by now.'

Cold panic clutched at Victoria's heart.

Was it to be so near and yet so far?

They went up in the lift to the third floor.

As they walked along the deep carpeted corridor, a young woman came out of a door at the far end and came towards them. Victoria had a kind of hallucination that it was herself who was approaching. Possibly, she thought, because of the young woman's tailor-made suit that was so exactly what she would have liked to be wearing herself. 'And it would fit me too. I'm just her size. How I'd like to tear it off her,' thought Victoria with a reversion to primitive female savagery.

The young woman passed them. A small velvet hat perched on the side of her fair hair partially hid her face, but Mr Hamilton Clipp turned to look after her with an air of surprise.

'Well now,' he said to himself. 'Who'd have thought of that? Anna Scheele.'

He added in an explanatory way:

'Excuse me, Miss Jones. I was surprised to recognize a young lady whom I saw in New York only a week ago, secretary to one of our big international banks—'

He stopped as he spoke at a door in the corridor. The key was hanging in the lock and, with a brief tap, Mr Hamilton Clipp opened the door and stood aside for Victoria to precede him into the room.

Mrs Hamilton Clipp was sitting on a high-backed chair near the window and jumped up as they came in. She was a short bird-like sharp-eyed little woman. Her right arm was encased in plaster.

Her husband introduced Victoria.

'Why, it's all been most unfortunate,' exclaimed Mrs Clipp breathlessly. 'Here we were, with a full itinerary, and enjoying London and all our plans made and my passage booked. I'm going out to pay a visit to my married daughter in Iraq, Miss Jones. I've not seen her for nearly two years. And then what do I do but take a crash—as a matter of fact, it was actually in Westminster Abbey—down some stone steps—and there I was. They rushed me to hospital and they've set it, and all things considered it's not *too* uncomfortable—but there it is, I'm kind of helpless, and however I'd manage travelling, I don't know. And George here, is just tied up with business, and simply can't get away for at least another three weeks. He suggested that I should take a nurse along with me—but after all, once I'm out there I don't need a nurse hanging around, Sadie can do all that's necessary—and it means paying her fare back as well, and so I thought I'd ring up the agencies and see if I couldn't find someone who'd be willing to come along just for the fare out.'

'I'm not *exactly* a nurse,' said Victoria, managing to imply that that *was* practically what she was. 'But I've had a good deal of experience of nursing.' She produced the first testimonial. 'I was with Lady Cynthia Bradbury for over a year. And if you should want any correspondence or secretarial work done, I acted as my uncle's secretary for some months. My uncle,' said Victoria modestly, 'is the Bishop of Llangow.'

'So your uncle's a Bishop. Dear me, how interesting.'

Both the Hamilton Clipps were, Victoria thought, decidedly impressed. (And so they should be after the trouble she had taken!)

Mrs Hamilton Clipp handed the two testimonials to her husband.

'It really seems quite wonderful,' she said reverently. 'Quite providential. It's an answer to prayer.'

Which, indeed, was exactly what it was, thought Victoria.

'You're taking up a position of some kind out there? Or joining a relative?' asked Mrs Hamilton Clipp.

In the flurry of manufacturing testimonials, Victoria had quite forgotten that she might have to account for her reasons for travelling to Baghdad. Caught unprepared, she had to improvise rapidly. The paragraph she had read yesterday came to her mind.

'I'm joining my uncle out there. Dr Pauncefoot Jones,' she explained.

'Indeed? The archaeologist?'

'Yes.' For one moment Victoria wondered whether she were perhaps endowing herself with too many distinguished uncles. 'I'm terribly interested in his work, but of course I've no special qualifications so it was out of the question for the Expedition to pay my fare out. They're not too well off for funds. But if I can get out on my own, I can join them and make myself useful.'

'It must be very interesting work,' said Mr Hamilton Clipp, 'and Mesopotamia is certainly a great field for archaeology.'

'I'm afraid,' said Victoria, turning to Mrs Clipp, 'that my uncle the Bishop is up in Scotland at this moment. But I can give you his secretary's telephone number. She is staying in London at the moment. Pimlico 87693— one of the Fulham Palace extensions. She'll be there any time from (Victoria's eyes slid to the clock on the mantelpiece) 11.30 onwards if you would like to ring her up and ask about me.'

'Why, I'm sure—' Mrs Clipp began, but her husband interrupted.

'Time's very short, you know. This plane leaves day after tomorrow. Now have you got a passport, Miss Jones?'

'Yes.' Victoria felt thankful that owing to a short holiday trip to France last year, her passport was up to date. 'I brought it with me in case,' she added.

'Now that's what I call businesslike,' said Mr Clipp approvingly. If any other candidate had been in the running, she had obviously dropped out now. Victoria with her good recommendations, and her uncles, and her passport on the spot had successfully made the grade.

'You'll want the necessary visas,' said Mr Clipp, taking the passport. 'I'll run round to our friend Mr Burgeon in American Express, and he'll get everything fixed up. Perhaps you'd better call round this afternoon, so you can sign whatever's necessary.'

This Victoria agreed to do.

As the door of the apartment closed behind her, she heard Mrs Hamilton Clipp say to Mr Hamilton Clipp:

'Such a nice *straightforward* girl. We really are in luck.'

Victoria had the grace to blush.

She hurried back to her flat and sat glued to the telephone prepared to assume the gracious refined accents of a Bishop's secretary in case Mrs Clipp should seek confirmation of her capability. But Mrs Clipp had obviously been so impressed by Victoria's straightforward personality that she was not going to bother with these technicalities. After all, the engagement was only for a few days as a travelling companion.

In due course, papers were filled up and signed, the necessary visas were obtained and Victoria was bidden to spend the final night at the Savoy so as to be on hand to help Mrs Clipp get off at 7 a.m. on the following morning for Airways House and Heathrow Airport.

CHAPTER 5

The boat that had left the marshes two days before paddled gently along the Shatt el Arab. The stream was swift and the old man who was propelling the boat needed to do very little. His movements were gentle and rhythmic. His eyes were half closed. Almost under his breath he sang very softly, a sad unending Arab chant:

'Asri bi lel ya yamali
Hadhi alek ya ibn Ali.'

Thus, on innumerable other occasions, had Abdul Suleiman of the Marsh Arabs come down the river to Basrah. There was another man in the boat, a figure often seen nowadays with a pathetic mingling of West and East in his clothing. Over his long robe of striped cotton he wore a discarded khaki tunic, old and stained and torn. A faded red knitted scarf was tucked into the ragged coat. His head showed again the dignity of the Arab dress, the inevitable *keffiyah* of black and white held in place by the black silk *agal*. His eyes, unfocused in a wide stare, looked out blearily over the river bend. Presently he too began to hum in the same key and tone. He was a figure like thousands of other figures in the Mesopotamian landscape. There was nothing to show that he was an Englishman, and that he carried with him a secret that influential men in almost every country in the world were striving to intercept and to destroy along with the man who carried it.

His mind went hazily back over the last weeks. The ambush in the mountains. The ice-cold of the snow coming over the Pass. The caravan of camels. The four days spent trudging on foot over bare desert in company with two men carrying a portable 'cinema.' The days in the black tent and the journeying with the Aneizeh tribe, old friends of his. All difficult, all fraught with danger—slipping again and again through the cordon spread out to look for him and intercept him.

'Henry Carmichael. British Agent. Age about thirty. Brown hair, dark eyes, five-foot-ten. Speaks Arabic, Kurdish, Persian, Armenian, Hindustani, Turkish and many mountain dialects. Befriended by the tribesmen. *Dangerous.*'

Carmichael had been born in Kashgar where his father was a Government official. His childish tongue had lisped various dialects and patois—his nurses, and later his bearers, had been natives of many different races. In nearly all the wild places of the Middle East he had friends.

Only in the cities and the towns did his contacts fail him. Now, approaching Basrah, he knew that the critical moment of his mission had come. Sooner or later he had got to re-enter the civilized zone. Though Baghdad was his ultimate destination, he had judged it wise not to approach it direct. In every town in Iraq facilities were awaiting him, carefully discussed and arranged many months beforehand. It had had to be left to his own judgement where he should, so to speak, make his landing ground. He had sent no word to his superiors, even through the indirect channels where he could have done so. It was safer thus. The easy plan—the aeroplane waiting at the appointed rendezvous—had failed, as he had suspected it would fail. That rendezvous had been known to his enemies. Leakage! Always that deadly, that incomprehensible, leakage.

And so it was that his apprehensions of danger were heightened. Here in Basrah, in sight of safety, he felt instinctively sure that the danger would be greater than during the wild hazards of his journey. And to fail at the last lap—that would hardly bear thinking about.

Rhythmically pulling at his oars, the old Arab murmured without turning his head.

'The moment approaches, my son. May Allah prosper you.'

'Do not tarry long in the city, my father. Return to the marshes. I would not have harm befall you.'

'That is as Allah decrees. It is in his hands.'

'Inshallah,' the other repeated.

For a moment he longed intensely to be a man of Eastern and not of Western blood. Not to worry over the chances of success or of failure, not to calculate again and again the hazards, repeatedly asking himself if he had planned wisely and with forethought. To throw responsibility on the All Merciful, the All Wise. Inshallah, I shall succeed!

Even saying the words over to himself he felt the calmness

and the fatalism of the country overwhelming him and he welcomed it. Now, in a few moments, he must step from the haven of the boat, walk the streets of the city, run the gauntlet of keen eyes. Only by *feeling* as well as looking like an Arab could he succeed.

The boat turned gently into the waterway that ran at right angles to the river. Here all kinds of river craft were tied up and other boats were coming in before and after them. It was a lovely, almost Venetian scene; the boats with their high scrolled prows and the soft faded colours of their paintwork. There were hundreds of them tied up close alongside each other.

The old man asked softly:

'The moment has come. There are preparations made for you?'

'Yes, indeed my plans are set. The hour has come for me to leave.'

'May God make your path straight, and may He lengthen the years of your life.'

Carmichael gathered his striped skirts about him and went up the slippery stone steps to the wharf above.

All about him were the usual waterside figures. Small boys, orange-sellers squatting down by their trays of merchandise. Sticky squares of cakes and sweetmeats, trays of bootlaces and cheap combs and pieces of elastic. Contemplative strollers, spitting raucously from time to time, wandering along with their beads clicking in their hands. On the opposite side of the street where the shops were and the banks, busy young *effendis* walked briskly in European suits of a slightly purplish tinge. There were

Agatha Christie

Europeans, too, English and foreigners. And nowhere was there interest shown, or curiosity, because one amongst fifty or so Arabs had just climbed on to the wharf from a boat.

Carmichael strolled along very quietly, his eyes taking in the scene with just the right touch of childlike pleasure in his surroundings. Every now and then he hawked and spat, not too violently, just to be in the picture. Twice he blew his nose with his fingers.

And so, the stranger come to town, he reached the bridge at the top of the canal, and turned over it and passed into the souk.

Here all was noise and movement. Energetic tribesmen strode along pushing others out of their way—laden donkeys made their way along, their drivers calling out raucously. *Balek—balek* . . . Children quarrelled and squealed and ran after Europeans calling hopefully, *Baksheesh*, madame, *Baksheesh. Meskin-meskin* . . .

Here the produce of the West and the East were equally for sale side by side. Aluminium saucepans, cups and saucers and teapots, hammered copperware, silverwork from Amara, cheap watches, enamel mugs, embroideries and gay patterned rugs from Persia. Brass-bound chests from Kuwait, second-hand coats and trousers and children's woolly cardigans. Local quilted bedcovers, painted glass lamps, stacks of clay water-jars and pots. All the cheap merchandise of civilization together with the native products.

All as normal and as usual. After his long sojourn in the wilder spaces, the bustle and confusion seemed strange to Carmichael, but it was all as it should be, he could detect no jarring note, no sign of interest in his presence. And yet, with the instinct of one who has for some years known what it is to be a hunted man, he felt a growing uneasiness— a vague sense of menace. He could detect nothing amiss. No one had looked at him. No one, he was almost sure, was following him or keeping him under observation. Yet he had that indefinable certainty of danger.

He turned up a narrow dark turning, again to the right, then to the left. Here among the small booths, he came to the opening of a khan, he stepped through the doorway into the court. Various shops were all round it. Carmichael went to one where *ferwahs* were hanging—the sheepskin coats of the north. He stood there handling them tentatively. The owner of the store was offering coffee to a customer, a tall bearded man of fine presence who wore green round his tarbush showing him to be a Hajji who had been to Mecca.

Carmichael stood there fingering the *ferwah*.

'*Besh hadha*?' he asked.

'Seven dinars.'

'Too much.'

The Hajji said, 'You will deliver the carpets at my khan?'

'Without fail,' said the merchant. 'You start tomorrow?'

'At dawn for Kerbela.'

'It is my city, Kerbela,' said Carmichael. 'It is fifteen years now since I have seen the Tomb of the Hussein.'

'It is a holy city,' said the Hajji.

The shopkeeper said over his shoulder to Carmichael:

'There are cheaper *ferwahs* in the inner room.'

'A white *ferwah* from the north is what I need.'

49

'I have such a one in the farther room.'

The merchant indicated the door set back in the inner wall.

The ritual had gone according to pattern—a conversation such as might be heard any day in any souk—but the sequence was exact—the keywords all there—Kerbela—white *ferwah*.

Only, as Carmichael passed to cross the room and enter the inner enclosure, he raised his eyes to the merchant's face—and knew instantly that the face was not the one he expected to see. Though he had seen this particular man only once before, his keen memory was not at fault. There was a resemblance, a very close resemblance, but it was not the same man.

He stopped. He said, his tone one of mild surprise, 'Where, then, is Salah Hassan?'

'He was my brother. He died three days ago. His affairs are in my hands.'

Yes, this was probably a brother. The resemblance was very close. And it was possible that the brother was also employed by the department. Certainly the responses had been correct. Yet it was with an increased awareness that Carmichael passed through into the dim inner chamber. Here again was merchandise piled on shelves, coffee pots and sugar hammers of brass and copper, old Persian silver, heaps of embroideries, folded *abas*, enamelled Damascus trays and coffee sets.

A white *ferwah* lay carefully folded by itself on a small coffee table. Carmichael went to it and picked it up. Underneath it was a set of European clothes, a worn, slightly flashy business suit. The pocket-book with money and credentials was already in the breast pocket. An unknown Arab had entered the store, Mr Walter Williams of Messrs Cross and Co., Importers and Shipping Agents would emerge and would keep certain appointments made for him in advance. There was, of course, a real Mr Walter Williams—it was as careful as that—a man with a respectable open business past. All according to plan. With a sigh of relief Carmichael started to unbutton his ragged army jacket. All was well.

If a revolver had been chosen as the weapon, Carmichael's mission would have failed then and there. But there are advantages in a knife—noticeably noiselessness.

On the shelf in front of Carmichael was a big copper coffee pot and that coffee pot had been recently polished to the order of an American tourist who was coming in to collect it. The gleam of the knife was reflected in that shining rounded surface—a whole picture, distorted but apparent was reflected there. The man slipping through the hangings behind Carmichael, the long curved knife he had just pulled from beneath his garments. In another moment that knife would have been buried in Carmichael's back.

Like a flash Carmichael wheeled round. With a low flying tackle he brought the other to the ground. The knife flew across the room. Carmichael disentangled himself quickly, leaped over the other's body, rushed through the outer room where he caught a glimpse of the merchant's startled malevolent face and the placid surprise of the fat Hajji. Then he was out, across the khan, back into the crowded souk, turning first one way, then another, strolling

51

again now, showing no signs of haste in a country where to hurry is to appear unusual.

And walking thus, almost aimlessly, stopping to examine a piece of stuff, to feel a texture, his brain was working with furious activity. The machinery had broken down! Once more he was on his own, in hostile country. And he was disagreeably aware of the significance of what had just happened.

It was not only the enemies on his trail he had to fear. Nor was it the enemies guarding the approaches to civilization. There were enemies to fear within the system. For the passwords had been known, the responses had come pat and correct. The attack had been timed for exactly the moment when he had been lulled into security. Not surprising, perhaps, that there was treachery from within. It must have always been the aim of the enemy to introduce one or more of their own number into the system. Or, perhaps, to buy the man that they needed. Buying a man was easier than one might think—one could buy with other things than money.

Well, no matter how it had come about, there it was. He was on the run—back on his own resources. Without money, without the help of a new personality, and his appearance known. Perhaps at this very moment he was being quietly followed.

He did not turn his head. Of what use would that be? Those who followed were not novices at the game.

Quietly, aimlessly, he continued to stroll. Behind his listless manner he was reviewing various possibilities. He came out of the souk at last and crossed the little bridge over the canal. He walked on until he saw the big painted hatchment over the doorway and the legend: British Consulate.

He looked up the street and down. No one seemed to be paying the least attention to him. Nothing, it appeared, was easier than just to step into the British Consulate. He thought for a moment, of a moustrap, an open mousetrap with its enticing piece of cheese. That, too, was easy and simple for the mouse . . .

Well, the risk had to be taken. He didn't see what else he could do.

He went through the doorway.

CHAPTER 6

Richard Baker sat in the outer office of the British Consulate waiting until the Consul was disengaged.

He had come ashore from the *Indian Queen* that morning and seen his baggage through the Customs. It consisted almost entirely of books. Pyjamas and shirts were strewed amongst them rather as an afterthought.

The *Indian Queen* had arrived on time and Richard, who had allowed a margin of two days since small cargo boats such as the *Indian Queen* were frequently delayed, had now two days in hand before he need proceed, via Baghdad, to his ultimate destination, Tell Aswad, the site of the ancient city of Murik.

His plans were already made as to what to do with these two days. A mound reputed to contain ancient remains at a spot near the seashore in Kuwait had long excited his curiosity. This was a heaven-sent opportunity to investigate it.

He drove to the Airport Hotel and inquired as to the methods of getting to Kuwait. A plane left at ten o'clock the following morning, he was told, and he could return the following day. Everything therefore was plain sailing. There were, of course, the inevitable formalities, exit visa and entry visa for Kuwait. For these he would have to repair to the British Consulate. The Consul-General at Basrah, Mr Clayton, Richard had met some years previously in Persia. It would be pleasant, Richard thought, to meet him again.

The Consulate had several entrances. A main gate for cars. Another small gate leading out from the garden to the road that lay alongside the Shatt el Arab. The business entrance to the Consulate was in the main street. Richard went in, gave his card to the man on duty, was told the Consul-General was engaged at the moment but would soon be free, and was shown into a small waiting-room to the left of the passage which ran straight through from the entrance to the garden beyond.

There were several people already in the waiting-room. Richard hardly glanced at them. He was, in any case, seldom interested by members of the human race. A fragment of antique pottery was always more exciting to him than a mere human being born somewhere in the twentieth century AD.

He allowed his thoughts to dwell pleasantly on some aspects of the Mari letters and the movements of the Benjaminite tribes in 1750 BC.

It would be hard to say exactly what awoke him to a vivid sense of the present and of his fellow human beings. It was, first, an uneasiness, a sense of tension. It came to him, he thought, though he could not be sure, through his nose. Nothing he could diagnose in concrete terms—but it was there, unmistakable, taking him back to days in the late war. One occasion in particular when he, and two others, had been parachuted from a plane, and had waited in the small cold hours of dawn for the moment to do their stuff. A moment when morale was low, when the full hazards of the undertaking were clearly perceived, a moment of dread lest one might not be adequate, a shrinking of the flesh. The same acrid, almost imperceptible tang in the air.

The smell of *fear* . . .

For some moments, this registered only subconsciously. Half of his mind still obstinately strove to focus itself BC. But the pull of the present was too strong.

Someone in this small room was in deadly fear . . .

He looked around. An Arab in a ragged khaki tunic, his fingers idly slipping over the amber beads he held. A stoutish Englishman with a grey moustache—the commercial traveller type—who was jotting down figures in a small notebook and looking absorbed and important. A lean tired-looking man, very dark-skinned, who was leaning back in a reposeful attitude, his face placid and uninterested. A man who looked like an Iraqi clerk. An elderly Persian in flowing snowy robes. They all seemed quite unconcerned.

The clicking of the amber beads fell into a definite rhythm. It seemed, in an odd way, familiar. Richard jerked himself to attention. He had been nearly asleep. Short—long—long—short—that was Morse—definite Morse signalling. He was familiar with Morse, part of his job during the war had dealt with signalling. He could read it

easily enough. *OWL*. F-L-O-R-E-A-T-E-T-O-N-A. What the
devil! Yes, that was it. It was being repeated. *Floreat Etona*.
Tapped out (or rather clicked out) by a ragged Arab. Hallo,
what was this? 'Owl. Eton. Owl.'

His own nickname at Eton—where he had been sent
with an unusually large and solid pair of spectacles.

He looked across the room at the Arab, noting every
detail of his appearance—the striped robe—the old khaki
tunic—the ragged hand-knitted red scarf full of dropped
stitches. A figure such as you saw hundreds of on the
waterfront. The eyes met his vacantly with no sign of
recognition. But the beads continued to click.

Fakir here. Stand by. Trouble.

Fakir? *Fakir?* Of course! Fakir Carmichael! A boy who
had been born or who had lived in some outlandish part
of the world—Turkestan, Afghanistan?

Richard took out his pipe. He took an exploratory pull
at it—peered into the bowl and then tapped it on an adja-
cent ashtray:*Message received*.

After that, things happened very fast. Later, Richard was
at pains to sort them out.

The Arab in the torn army jacket got up and crossed
towards the door. He stumbled as he was passing Richard,
his hand went out and clutched Richard to steady himself.
Then he righted himself, apologized and moved towards
the door.

It was so surprising and happened so quickly that it
seemed to Richard like a cinema scene rather than a scene
in real life. The stout commercial traveller dropped his
notebook and tugged at something in his coat pocket.

Because of his plumpness and the tight fit of the coat, he was a second or two in getting it out and in that second or two Richard acted. As the man brought the revolver up, Richard struck it out of his hand. It went off and a bullet buried itself in the floor.

The Arab had passed through the doorway and had turned towards the Consul's office, but he paused suddenly, and turning he ran swiftly the other way to the door by which he had entered and into the busy street.

The kavass ran to Richard's side where he stood holding the stout man's arm. Of the other occupants of the room, the Iraqi clerk was dancing excitedly on his feet, the dark thin man was staring and the elderly Persian gazed into space unmoved.

Richard said:

'What the devil are you doing, brandishing a revolver like that?'

There was just a moment's pause, and then the stout man said in a plaintive Cockney voice:

'Sorry, old man. Absolute accident. Just clumsy.'

'Nonsense. You were going to shoot at that Arab fellow who's just run out.'

'No, no, old man, not shoot him. Just give him a fright. Recognized him suddenly as a fellow who swindled me over some antikas. Just a bit of fun.'

Richard Baker was a fastidious soul who disliked publicity of any kind. His instincts were to accept the explanation at its face value. After all, what could he prove? And would old Fakir Carmichael thank him for making a song and dance about the matter? Presumably if he were on some hush-hush, cloak-and-dagger business he would not.

Richard relaxed his grasp on the man's arm. The fellow was sweating, he noticed.

The kavass was talking excitedly. It was very wrong, he was saying, to bring firearms into the British Consulate. It was not allowed. The Consul would be very angry.

'I apologize,' said the fat man. 'Little accident—that's all.' He thrust some money into the kavass's hand who pushed it back again indignantly.

'I'd better get out of this,' said the stout man. 'I won't wait to see the Consul.' He thrust a card suddenly on Richard. 'That's me and I'm at the Airport Hotel if there's any fuss, but actually it was a pure accident. Just a joke if you know what I mean.'

Reluctantly, Richard watched him walk with an uneasy swagger out of the room and turn towards the street.

He hoped he had done right, but it was a difficult thing to know what to do when one was as much in the dark as he was.

'Mr Clayton, he is disengaged now,' said the kavass.

Richard followed the man along the corridor. The open circle of sunlight at the end grew larger. The Consul's room was on the right at the extreme end of the passage.

Mr Clayton was sitting behind his desk. He was a quiet grey-haired man with a thoughtful face.

'I don't know whether you remember me?' said Richard. 'I met you in Tehran two years ago.'

'Of course. You were with Dr Pauncefoot Jones, weren't you? Are you joining him again this year?'

'Yes. I'm on my way there now, but I've got a few days to spare, and I rather wanted to run down to Kuwait. There's no difficulty I suppose?'

'Oh, no. There's a plane tomorrow morning. It's only about an hour and a half. I'll wire to Archie Gaunt—he's the Resident there. He'll put you up. And we can put you up here for the night.'

Richard protested slightly.

'Really—I don't want to bother you and Mrs Clayton. I can go to the hotel.'

'The Airport Hotel's very full. We'd be delighted to have you here. I know my wife would like to meet you again. At the moment—let me see—we've got Crosbie of the Oil Company and some young sprig of Dr Rathbone's who's down here clearing some cases of books through the customs. Come upstairs and see Rosa.'

He got up and escorted Richard out through the door and into the sunlit garden. A flight of steps led up to the living quarters of the Consulate.

Gerald Clayton pushed open the wire door at the top of the steps and ushered his guest into a long dim hallway with attractive rugs on the floor and choice examples of furniture on either side. It was pleasant coming into the cold dimness after the glare outside.

Clayton called, 'Rosa, Rosa,' and Mrs Clayton, whom Richard remembered as a buoyant personality with abounding vitality, came out of an end room.

'You remember Richard Baker, dear? He came to see us with Dr Pauncefoot Jones in Tehran.'

'Of course,' said Mrs Clayton, shaking hands. 'We went

to the bazaars together and you bought some lovely rugs.'

It was Mrs Clayton's delight when not buying things herself to urge on her friends and acquaintances to seek for bargains in the local souks. She had a wonderful knowledge of values and was an excellent bargainer.

'One of the best purchases I've ever made,' said Richard. 'And entirely owing to your good offices.'

'Baker wants to fly to Kuwait tomorrow,' said Gerald Clayton. 'I've said that we can put him up here for tonight.'

'But if it's any trouble . . .' began Richard.

'Of course it's no trouble,' said Mrs Clayton. 'You can't have the best spare room, because Captain Crosbie has got it, but we can make you quite comfortable. You don't want to buy a nice Kuwait chest, do you? Because they've got some lovely ones in the souk just now. Gerald wouldn't let me buy another one for here though it would be quite useful to keep extra blankets in.'

'You've got three already, dear,' said Clayton mildly. 'Now, if you'll excuse me, Baker. I must get back to the office. There seems to have been a spot of trouble in the outer office. Somebody let off a revolver, I understand.'

'One of the local sheikhs, I suppose,' said Mrs Clayton. 'They are so excitable and they do so love firearms.'

'On the contrary,' said Richard. 'It was an Englishman. His intention seemed to be to take a potshot at an Arab.' He added gently, 'I knocked his arm up.'

'So you were in it all,' said Clayton. 'I didn't realize that.' He fished a card out of his pocket. 'Robert Hall, Achilles

Agatha Christie

Works, Enfield, seems to be his name. I don't know what he wanted to see me about. He wasn't drunk, was he?'

'He said it was a joke,' said Richard drily, 'and that the gun went off by accident.'

Clayton raised his eyebrows.

'Commercial travellers don't usually carry loaded guns in their pockets,' he said.

Clayton, Richard thought, was no fool.

'Perhaps I ought to have stopped him going away.'

'It's difficult to know what one should do when these things happen. The man he fired at wasn't hurt?'

'No.'

'Probably was better to let the thing slide, then.'

'I wonder what was behind it?'

'Yes, yes . . . I wonder too.'

Clayton looked a little distrait.

'Well, I must be getting back,' he said and hurried away.

Mrs Clayton took Richard into the drawing-room, a large inside room, with green cushions and curtains and offered him a choice of coffee or beer. He chose beer and it came deliciously iced.

She asked him why he was going to Kuwait and he told her.

She asked him why he hadn't got married yet and Richard said he didn't think he was the marrying kind, to which Mrs Clayton said briskly, 'Nonsense.' Archaeologists, she said, made splendid husbands—and were there any young women coming out to the Dig this season? One or two, Richard said, and Mrs Pauncefoot Jones of course.

Mrs Clayton asked hopefully if they were nice girls who

were coming out, and Richard said he didn't know because he hadn't met them yet. They were very inexperienced, he said.

For some reason this made Mrs Clayton laugh.

Then a short stocky man with an abrupt manner came in and was introduced as Captain Crosbie. Mr Baker, said Mrs Clayton, was an archaeologist and dug up the most wildly interesting things thousands of years old. Captain Crosbie said he never could understand how archaeologists were able to say so definitely how old these things were. Always used to think they must be the most awful liars, ha ha, said Captain Crosbie. Richard looked at him in a rather tired kind of way. No, said Captain Crosbie, but how *did* an archaeologist know how old a thing was? Richard said that that would take a long time to explain, and Mrs Clayton quickly took him away to see his room.

'He's very nice,' said Mrs Clayton, 'but not quite quite, you know. Hasn't got any *idea* of culture.'

Richard found his room exceedingly comfortable, and his appreciation of Mrs Clayton as a hostess rose still higher.

Feeling in the pocket of his coat, he drew out a folded-up piece of dirty paper. He looked at it with surprise, for he knew quite well that it had not been there earlier in the morning.

He remembered how the Arab had clutched him when he stumbled. A man with deft fingers might have slipped this into his pocket without his being aware of it.

He unfolded the paper. It was dirty and seemed to have been folded and refolded many times.

In six lines of rather crabbed handwriting, Major John

Wilberforce recommended one Ahmed Mohammed as an industrious and willing worker, able to drive a lorry and do minor repairs and strictly honest—it was, in fact, the usual type of 'chit' or recommendation given in the East. It was dated eighteen months back, which again is not unusual as these chits are hoarded carefully by their possessors.

Frowning to himself, Richard went over the events of the morning in his precise orderly fashion.

Fakir Carmichael, he was now well assured, had been in fear of his life. He was a hunted man and he bolted into the Consulate. Why? To find security? But instead of that he had found a more instant menace. The enemy or a representative of the enemy had been waiting for him. This commercial traveller chap must have had very definite orders—to be willing to risk shooting Carmichael in the Consulate in the presence of witnesses. It must, therefore, have been very urgent. And Carmichael had appealed to his old school friend for help, and had managed to pass this seemingly innocent document into his possession. It must, therefore, be very important, and if Carmichael's enemies caught up with him, and found that he no longer possessed this document, they would doubtless put two and two together and look for any person or persons to whom Carmichael might conceivably have passed it on.

What then was Richard Baker to do with it?

He could pass it on to Clayton, as His Britannic Majesty's representative.

Or he could keep it in his own possession until such time as Carmichael claimed it?

After a few minutes' reflection he decided to do the latter.

But first he took certain precautions.

Tearing a blank half sheet of paper off an old letter, he sat down to compose a reference for a lorry driver in much the same terms, but using different wording—if this message was a code that took care of that—though it was possible, of course, that there was a message written in some kind of invisible ink.

Then he smeared his own composition with dust from his shoes—rubbed it in his hands, folded and refolded it—until it gave a reasonable appearance of age and dirt.

Then he crumpled it up and put it into his pocket. The original he stared at for some time whilst he considered and rejected various possibilities.

Finally, with a slight smile, he folded and refolded it until he had a small oblong. Taking a stick of plasticine (without which he never travelled) out of his bag, he first wrapped his packet in oilskin cut from his sponge-bag, then encased it in plasticine. This done he rolled and patted out the plasticine till he had a smooth surface. On this he rolled out an impression from a cylinder seal that he had with him.

He studied the result with grim appreciation.

It showed a beautifully carved design of the Sun God Shamash armed with the Sword of Justice.

'Let's hope that's a good omen,' he said to himself.

That evening, when he looked in the pocket of the coat he had worn in the morning, the screwed-up paper had gone.

CHAPTER 7

Life, thought Victoria, life at last! Sitting in her seat at Airways Terminal there had come the magic moment when the words 'Passengers for Cairo, Baghdad and Tehran, take your places in the bus, please,' had been uttered.

Magic names, magic words. Devoid of glamour to Mrs Hamilton Clipp who, as far as Victoria could make out, had spent a large portion of her life jumping from boats into aeroplanes and from aeroplanes into trains with brief intervals at expensive hotels in between. But to Victoria they were a marvellous change from the oft-repeated phrases, 'Take down, please, Miss Jones.' 'This letter's full of mistakes. You'll have to type it again, Miss Jones.' 'The kettle's boiling, ducks, just make the tea, will you.' 'I know where you can get the most marvellous perm.' Trivial boring everyday happenings! And now: Cairo, Baghdad, Tehran—all the romance of the glorious East (and Edward at the end of it) . . .

Victoria returned to earth to hear her employer, whom she had already diagnosed as a non-stop talker, concluding a series of remarks by saying:

'—and nothing really *clean* if you know what I mean. I'm always very very careful what I eat. The filth of the streets and the bazaars you wouldn't believe. And the unhygienic rags the people wear. And some of the toilets— why, you just couldn't call them toilets at all!'

Victoria listened dutifully to these depressing remarks, but her own sense of glamour remained undimmed. Dirt and germs meant nothing in her young life. They arrived at Heathrow and she assisted Mrs Clipp to alight from the bus. She was already in charge of passports, tickets, money, etc.

'My,' said that lady, 'it certainly is a comfort to have you with me, Miss Jones. I just don't know what I'd have done if I'd had to travel alone.'

Travelling by air, Victoria thought, was rather like being taken on a school treat. Brisk teachers, kind but firm, were at hand to shepherd you at every turn. Air hostesses, in trim uniform with the authority of nursery governesses dealing with feeble-minded children explained kindly just what you were to do. Victoria almost expected them to preface their remarks with 'Now, children.'

Tired-looking young gentlemen behind desks extended weary hands to check passports, to inquire intimately of money and jewellery. They managed to induce a sense of guilt in those questioned. Victoria, suggestible by nature, knew a sudden longing to describe her one meagre brooch as a diamond tiara value ten thousand pounds, just to see the expression on the bored young man's face. Thoughts of Edward restrained her.

The various barriers passed, they sat down to wait once

more in a large room giving directly on the aerodrome. Outside the roar of a plane being revved up gave the proper background. Mrs Hamilton Clipp was now happily engaged in making a running commentary on their fellow travellers.

'Aren't those two little children just too cute for words? But what an ordeal to travel alone with a couple of children. British, I guess they are. That's a well-cut suit the mother has on. She looks kind of tired, though. That's a good-looking man—rather Latin looking, I'd say. What a loud check that man has on—I'd call it very bad taste. Business, I guess. That man over there's a Dutchman, he was just ahead of us at the controls. That family over there is either Turkish or Persian, I should say. There don't seem to be any Americans. I guess they go mostly Pan American. I'd say those three men talking together are Oil, wouldn't you? I just love looking at people and wondering about them. Mr Clipp says to me I've got real yen for human nature. It seems to me just natural to take an interest in your fellow creatures. Wouldn't you say that mink coat over there cost every bit of three thousand dollars?'

Mrs Clipp sighed. Having duly appraised her fellow travellers she became restless.

'I'd like to know what we are waiting for like this. That plane's revved up four times. We're all here. Why can't they get on with things? They're certainly not keeping to schedule.'

'Would you like a cup of coffee, Mrs Clipp? I see there is a buffet at the end of the room.'

'Why, no, thank you, Miss Jones. I had coffee before I started, and my stomach feels too unsettled right now to take anything more. What are we waiting for, I'd like to know?'

Her question seemed to be answered almost before the words were out of her mouth.

The door leading from the corridor out of the Customs and Passport Department swung open with a rush and a tall man came through with the effect of a gust of wind. Air officials of the line hovered around him. Two large canvas sacks sealed were carried by an officer of BOAC.

Mrs Clipp sat up with alacrity.

'He's certainly some big noise,' she remarked.

'*And* knows it,' thought Victoria.

There was something of calculated sensationalism about the late traveller. He wore a kind of dark-grey travelling cloak with a capacious hood at the back. On his head was what was in essence a wide sombrero, but in light grey. He had silver grey curling hair, worn rather long, and a beautiful silver grey moustache curling up at the ends. The effect was that of a handsome stage bandit. Victoria, who disliked theatrical men who posed, looked at him with disapproval.

The air officials were, she noted with displeasure, all over him.

'Yes, Sir Rupert.' 'Of course, Sir Rupert.' 'The plane is leaving immediately, Sir Rupert.'

With a swirl of his voluminous cloak, Sir Rupert passed out through the door leading to the aerodrome. The door swung to behind him with vehemence.

'Sir Rupert,' murmured Mrs Clipp. 'Now who would he be, I wonder?'

Victoria shook her head, though she had a vague feeling that the face and general appearance were not unknown to her.

'Somebody important in your Government,' suggested Mrs Clipp.

'I shouldn't think so,' said Victoria.

The few members of the Government she had ever seen had impressed her as men anxious to apologize for being alive. Only on platforms did they spring into pompous and didactic life.

'Now then, please,' said the smart nursery governess air hostess. 'Take your seats in the plane. This way. As quickly as you can, please.'

Her attitude implied that a lot of dawdling children had been keeping the patient grown-ups waiting.

Everybody filed out on to the aerodrome.

The great plane was waiting, its engine ticking over like the satisfied purring of a gigantic lion.

Victoria and a steward helped Mrs Clipp on board and settled her in her seat. Victoria sat next to her on the aisle. Not until Mrs Clipp was comfortably ensconced, and Victoria had fastened her safety-belt, did the girl have leisure to observe that in front of them was sitting the great man.

The doors closed. A few seconds later the plane began to move slowly along the ground.

'We're really going,' thought Victoria in ecstasy. 'Oh, isn't it frightening? Suppose it never gets up off the ground? Really, I don't see how it *can*!'

During what seemed an age the plane taxied along the aerodrome, then it turned slowly round and stopped. The engines rose to a ferocious roar. Chewing-gum, barley sugar and cotton wool were handed round.

Louder and louder, fiercer and fiercer. Then, once more,

the aeroplane moved forward. Mincingly at first, then faster—faster still—they were rushing along the ground.

'It will never go up,' thought Victoria, 'we'll be killed.'

Faster—more smoothly—no jars—no bumps—they were off the ground skimming along, up, round, back over the car park and the main road, up, higher—a silly little train puffing below—dolls' houses—toy cars on roads . . . Higher still—and suddenly the earth below lost interest, was no longer human or alive—just a large flat map with lines and circles and dots.

Inside the plane people undid their safety-belts, lit cigarettes, opened magazines. Victoria was in a new world—a world so many feet long, and a very few feet wide, inhabited by twenty to thirty people. Nothing else existed.

She peered out of the small window again. Below her were clouds, a fluffy pavement of clouds. The plane was in the sun. Below the clouds somewhere was the world she had known heretofore.

Victoria pulled herself together. Mrs Hamilton Clipp was talking. Victoria removed cotton wool from her ears and bent attentively towards her.

In the seat in front of her, Sir Rupert rose, tossed his wide-brimmed grey felt hat to the rack, drew up his hood over his head and relaxed into his seat.

'Pompous ass,' thought Victoria, unreasonably prejudiced.

Mrs Clipp was established with a magazine open in front of her. At intervals she nudged Victoria, when on trying to turn the page with one hand, the magazine slipped.

Victoria looked round her. She decided that air travel was

really rather boring. She opened a magazine, found herself faced with an advertisement that said, 'Do you want to increase your efficiency as a shorthand typist?' shuddered, shut the magazine, leant back, and began to think of Edward.

They came down at Castel Benito Aerodrome in a storm of rain. Victoria was by now feeling slightly sick, and it took all her energies to accomplish her duties *vis-à-vis* her employer. They were driven through scurrying rain to the rest-house. The magnificent Sir Rupert, Victoria noted, had been met by an officer in uniform with red tabs, and hurried off in a staff car to some dwelling of the mighty in Tripolitania.

They were allotted rooms. Victoria helped Mrs Clipp with her toilet and left her to rest on her bed in a dressing-gown until it was time for the evening meal. Victoria retired to her own room, lay down and closed her eyes, grateful to be spared the sight of the heaving and sinking floor.

She awakened an hour later in good health and spirits and went to help Mrs Clipp. Presently a rather more peremptory air hostess instructed them that cars were ready to convey them to the evening meal. After dinner Mrs Clipp got into conversation with some of her fellow travellers. The man in the loud check coat seemed to have taken a fancy to Victoria and told her at some length all about the manufacture of lead pencils.

Later they were conveyed back to their sleeping quarters and told curtly that they must be ready to depart at 5.30 a.m. the following morning.

'We haven't seen much of Tripolitania, have we?' said Victoria rather sadly. 'Is air travel always like this?'

'Why, yes, I'd say so. It's just positively sadistic the way they get you up in the mornings. After that, often they keep you hanging round the aerodrome for an hour or two. Why, in Rome, I remember they called us at 3.30. Breakfast in the restaurant at 4 o'clock. And then actually at the Airport we didn't leave until eight. Still the great thing is they get you to your destination right away with no fooling about on the way.'

Victoria sighed. She could have done with a good deal of fooling about. She wanted to see the world.

'And what do you know, my dear,' continued Mrs Clipp excitedly, 'you know that interesting looking man? The Britisher? The one that there's all the fuss about. I've found out who he is. That's Sir Rupert Crofton Lee, the great traveller. You've heard of him, of course.'

Yes, Victoria remembered now. She had seen several pictures in the press about six months ago. Sir Rupert was a great authority upon the interior of China. He was one of the few people who had been to Tibet and visited Lhasa. He had travelled through the unknown parts of Kurdistan and Asia Minor. His books had had a wide sale, for they had been racily and wittily written. If Sir Rupert was just noticeably a self-advertiser, it was with good reason. He made no claims that were not fully justified. The cloak with the hood and the wide-brimmed hat were, Victoria remembered now, a deliberate fashion of his own choosing.

'Isn't that thrilling now?' demanded Mrs Clipp with all a lion-hunter's enthusiasm as Victoria adjusted the bedclothes over her recumbent form.

Victoria agreed that it was very thrilling, but she said to herself that she preferred Sir Rupert's books to his personality. He was, she considered, what children call 'a show-off'!

A start was made in good order the next morning. The weather had cleared and the sun was shining. Victoria still felt disappointed to have seen so little of Tripolitania. Still, the plane was due to arrive at Cairo by lunch-time and the departure to Baghdad did not take place until the following morning, so she would at least be able to see a little of Egypt in the afternoon.

They were flying over the sea, but clouds soon blocked out the blue water below them and Victoria settled back in her seat with a yawn. In front of her Sir Rupert was already asleep. The hood had fallen back from his head, which was hanging forwards, nodding at intervals. Victoria observed with a faint malicious pleasure that he had a small boil starting on the back of his neck. Why she should have been pleased at this fact was hard to say—perhaps it made the great man seem more human and vulnerable. He was as other men after all—prone to the small annoyances of the flesh. It may be said that Sir Rupert had kept up his Olympian manner and had taken no notice whatever of his fellow travellers.

'Who does he think he *is*, I wonder?' thought Victoria to herself. The answer was obvious. He was Sir Rupert Crofton Lee, a celebrity, and she was Victoria Jones, an indifferent shorthand typist, and of no account whatever.

On arrival at Cairo, Victoria and Mrs Hamilton Clipp had lunch together. The latter then announced that she was going to nap until six o'clock, and suggested that Victoria might like to go and see the Pyramids.

'I've arranged for a car for you, Miss Jones, because I know that owing to your Treasury regulations you won't be able to cash any money here.'

Victoria who had in any case no money to cash, was duly grateful, and said so with some effusion.

'Why, that's nothing at all. You've been very very kind to me. And travelling with dollars everything is easy for us. Mrs Kitchin—the lady with the two cute children—is very anxious to go also, so I suggested you'd join up with her—if that suits you?'

So long as she saw the world, anything suited Victoria.

'That's fine, then you'd better get off right now.'

The afternoon at the Pyramids was duly enjoyable. Victoria, though reasonably fond of children, might have enjoyed it more without Mrs Kitchin's offspring. Children when sight-seeing is in progress are apt to be somewhat of a handicap. The youngest child became so fretful that the two women returned earlier from the expedition than they had meant to do.

Victoria threw herself on her bed with a yawn. She wished very much that she could stay a week in Cairo—perhaps go up the Nile. 'And what would you use for money, my girl?' she asked herself witheringly. It was already a miracle that she was being transported to Baghdad free of charge.

And what, inquired a cold inward voice, are you going to do once you are landed in Baghdad with only a few pounds in your pocket?

Victoria waved that query aside. Edward must find her a job. Or failing that, she would find herself a job. Why worry?

Her eyes, dazzled with strong sunlight, closed gently.

A knock on the door, as she thought, roused her. She called 'Come in,' then as there was no response, she got off the bed, crossed to the door and opened it.

But the knock had not been at her door, but at the next door down the passage. Another of the inevitable air hostesses, dark haired and trim in her uniform, was knocking at Sir Rupert Crofton Lee's door. He opened it just as Victoria looked out.

'What's the matter now?'

He sounded annoyed and sleepy.

'I'm so sorry to disturb you, Sir Rupert,' cooed the air hostess, 'but would you mind coming to the BOAC office? It's just three doors down the passage here. Just a small detail about the flight to Baghdad tomorrow.'

'Oh, very well.'

Victoria withdrew into her room. She was less sleepy now. She glanced at her watch. Only half-past four. An hour and a half until Mrs Clipp would be requiring her. She decided to go out and walk about Heliopolis. Walking, at least, required no money.

She powdered her nose and resumed her shoes. They felt rather full of feet. The visit to the Pyramids had been hard on feet.

She came out of her room and walked along the corridor towards the main hall of the hotel. Three doors down she passed the BOAC office. It had a card announcing the fact nailed to the door. Just as she passed it, the door opened and Sir Rupert came out. He was walking fast and he overtook her in a couple of strides. He went on ahead of her, his cloak swinging, and Victoria fancied that he was annoyed about something.

Mrs Clipp was in a somewhat petulant mood when Victoria reported for duty at six o'clock.

'I'm worried about the excess on my baggage, Miss Jones. I took it that I'd paid for that right through, but it seems that it's only paid until Cairo. We go on tomorrow by Iraqi Airways. My ticket is a through ticket, but not the excess baggage. Perhaps you'd go and find out if that is really so? Because maybe I ought to change another traveller's cheque.'

Victoria agreed to make inquiries. She could not find the BOAC office at first, and finally located it in the far corridor—the other side of the hall—quite a big office. The other, she supposed, had been a small office only used during the afternoon siesta hours. Mrs Clipp's fears about the excess baggage were found to be justified, which annoyed that lady very much.

CHAPTER 8

On the fifth floor of a block of offices in the City of London are situated the offices of the Valhalla Gramophone Co. The man who sat behind the desk in that office was reading a book on economics. The telephone rang and he picked up the receiver. He said in a quiet unemotional voice:

'Valhalla Gramophone Co.'

'Sanders here.'

'Sanders of the River? What river?'

'River Tigris. Reporting as to A. S. We've lost her.'

There was a moment's silence. Then the quiet voice spoke again, with a steely note in it.

'Did I hear what you said correctly?'

'We've lost Anna Scheele.'

'No names. This is a very serious error on your part. How did it come about?'

'She went into that nursing home. I told you before. Her sister was having an operation.'

'Well?'

'The operation went off all right. We expected A. S. to return to the Savoy. She had kept on her suite. She didn't return. Watch had been kept on the nursing home and we were quite sure she hadn't left it. We assumed she was still there.'

'And she isn't?'

'We've just found out. She left there, *in an ambulance,* the day after the operation.'

'She deliberately fooled you?'

'Looks like it. I'd swear she didn't know she was being followed. We took every precaution. There were three of us and—'

'Never mind the excuses. Where did the ambulance take her?'

'To University College Hospital.'

'What have you learnt from the hospital?'

'That a patient was brought in accompanied by a hospital nurse. The hospital nurse must have been Anna Scheele. They've no idea where she went after she brought the patient in.'

'And the patient?'

'The patient knows nothing. She was under morphia.'

'So Anna Scheele walked out of University College Hospital dressed as a nurse and may now be anywhere?'

'Yes. If she goes back to the Savoy—'

The other interrupted.

'She won't go back to the Savoy.'

'Shall we check up on other hotels?'

'Yes, but I doubt if you'll get any result. That's what she'd expect you to do.'

'What instructions otherwise?'

'Check on the ports—Dover, Folkestone, etc. Check with

air lines. In particular check all bookings to Baghdad by plane for the next fortnight. The passage won't be booked in her own name. Check up on all passengers of suitable age.'

'Her baggage is still at the Savoy. Perhaps she'll claim it.'

'She won't do anything of the sort. *You* may be a fool—she isn't! Does the sister know anything?'

'We're in contact with her special nurse at the home. Apparently the sister thinks A. S. is in Paris doing business for Morganthal and staying at the Ritz Hotel. She believed A. S. is flying home to the States on 23rd.'

'In other words A. S. has told her nothing. She wouldn't. Check up on those air passages. It's the only hope. She's got to get to Baghdad—and air is the only way she can do it in time, and, Sanders—'

'Yes?'

'*No more failures*. This is your last chance.'

CHAPTER 9

Young Mr Shrivenham of the British Embassy shifted from one foot to the other and gazed upwards as the plane zoomed over Baghdad aerodrome. There was a considerable dust-storm in progress. Palm trees, houses, human beings were all shrouded in a thick brown haze. It had come on quite suddenly.

Lionel Shrivenham observed in a tone of deep distress:

'Ten to one they can't come down here.'

'What will they do?' asked his friend Harold.

'Go on to Basrah, I imagine. It's clear there, I hear.'

'You're meeting some kind of a VIP, aren't you?'

Young Mr Shrivenham groaned again.

'Just my luck. The new Ambassador has been delayed coming out. Lansdowne, the Counsellor, is in England. Rice, the Oriental Counsellor, is ill in bed with gastric flu, dangerously high temperature. Best is in Tehran, and here am I, left with the whole bag of tricks. No end of a flap about this fellow. I don't know why. Even the hush-hush boys are in a flap. He's one of these world travellers, always off somewhere inaccessible on a camel. Don't see why he's so

81

important, but apparently he's absolutely the cat's whiskers, and I'm to conform to his slightest wish. If he gets carried on to Basrah he'll probably be wild. Don't know what arrangements I'd better lay on. Train up tonight? Or get the RAF to fly him up tomorrow?'

Mr Shrivenham sighed again, as his sense of injury and responsibility deepened. Since his arrival three months ago in Baghdad he had been consistently unlucky. One more raspberry, he felt, would finally blight what might have been a promising career.

The plane swooped overhead once more.

'Evidently thinks he can't make it,' said Shrivenham, then added excitedly: 'Hallo—I believe he's coming down.'

A few moments later and the plane had taxied sedately to its place and Shrivenham stood ready to greet the VIP.

His unprofessional eye noted 'rather a pretty girl' before he sprang forward to greet the buccaneer-like figure in the swirling cloak.

'Practically fancy dress,' he thought to himself disapprovingly as he said aloud:

'Sir Rupert Crofton Lee? I'm Shrivenham of the Embassy.'

Sir Rupert, he thought, was slightly curt in manner—perhaps understandable after the strain of circling round the city uncertain whether a landing could be effected or not.

'Nasty day,' continued Shrivenham. 'Had a lot of this sort of thing this year. Ah, you've got the bags. Then, if you'll follow me, sir, it's all laid on . . .'

As they left the aerodrome in the car, Shrivenham said:

'I thought for a bit that you were going to be carried on

to some other airport, sir. Didn't look as though the pilot could make a landing. Came up suddenly, this dust-storm.'

Sir Rupert blew out his cheeks importantly as he remarked:

'That would have been disastrous—quite disastrous. Had my schedule been jeopardized, young man, I can tell you the results would have been grave and far-reaching in the extreme.'

'Lot of cock,' thought Shrivenham disrespectfully. 'These VIP's think their potty affairs are what makes the world go round.'

Aloud he said respectfully:

'I expect that's so, sir.'

'Have you any idea when the Ambassador will reach Baghdad?'

'Nothing definite as yet, sir.'

'I shall be sorry to miss him. Haven't seen him since—let me see, yes, India in 1938.'

Shrivenham preserved a respectful silence.

'Let me see, Rice is here, isn't he?'

'Yes, sir, he's Oriental Counsellor.'

'Capable fellow. Knows a lot. I'll be glad to meet him again.'

Shrivenham coughed.

'As a matter of fact, sir, Rice is on the sick list. They've taken him to hospital for observation. Violent type of gastroenteritis. Something a bit worse than the usual Baghdad tummy, apparently.'

'What's that?' Sir Rupert turned his head sharply. 'Bad gastroenteritis—hm. Came on suddenly, did it?'

'Day before yesterday, sir.'

Sir Rupert was frowning. The rather affected grandiloquence of manner had dropped from him. He was a simpler man—and somewhat of a worried one.

'I wonder,' he said. 'Yes, I wonder.'

Shrivenham looked politely inquiring.

'I'm wondering,' said Sir Rupert, 'if it might be a case of Scheele's Green . . .'

Baffled, Shrivenham remained silent.

They were just approaching the Feisal Bridge, and the car swung off to the left towards the British Embassy.

Suddenly Sir Rupert leaned forward.

'Just stop a minute, will you?' he said sharply. 'Yes, right-hand side. Where all those pots are.'

The car glided in to the right-hand kerb and stopped.

It was a small native shop piled high with crude white clay pots and water-jars.

A short stocky European who had been standing talking to the proprietor moved away towards the bridge as the car drew up. Shrivenham thought it was Crosbie of the I and P whom he had met once or twice.

Sir Rupert sprang from the car and strode up to the small booth. Picking up one of the pots, he started a rapid conversation in Arabic with the proprietor. The flow of speech was too fast for Shrivenham whose Arabic was as yet slow and painstaking and distinctly limited in vocabulary.

The proprietor was beaming, his hands flew wide, he gesticulated, he explained at length. Sir Rupert handled different pots, apparently asking questions about them.

Finally he selected a narrow-mouthed water-jar, tossed the man some coins and went back to the car.

'Interesting technique,' said Sir Rupert. 'Been making them like this for thousands of years, same shape as in one of the hill districts in Armenia.'

His finger slipped down through the narrow aperture, twisting round and round.

'It's very crude stuff,' said Shrivenham unimpressed.

'Oh, no artistic merit! But interesting historically. See these indications of lugs here? You pick up many a historical tip from observation of the simple things in daily use. I've got a collection of them.'

The car turned in through the gates of the British Embassy.

Sir Rupert demanded to be taken straight to his room. Shrivenham was amused to note that, his lecture on the clay pot ended, Sir Rupert had left it nonchalantly in the car. Shrivenham made a point of carrying it upstairs and placing it meticulously upon Sir Rupert's bedside table.

'Your pot, sir.'

'Eh? Oh, thank you, my boy.'

Sir Rupert appeared distrait. Shrivenham left him after repeating that luncheon would be ready shortly and drinks awaited his choice.

When the young man had left the room, Sir Rupert went to the window and unfolded the small slip of paper that had been tucked into the mouth of the pot. He smoothed it out. There were two lines of writing on it. He read them over carefully, then set light to the paper with a match.

Then he summoned a servant.

'Yes, sir? I unpack for you, sir?'

'Not yet. I want to see Mr Shrivenham—up here.'

Shrivenham arrived with a slightly apprehensive expression.

'Anything I can do, sir? Anything wrong?'

'Mr Shrivenham, a drastic change has occurred in my plans. I can count upon your discretion, of course?'

'Oh, absolutely, sir.'

'It is some time since I was in Baghdad, actually I have not been here since the war. The hotels lie mainly on the other bank, do they not?'

'Yes, sir. In Rashid Street.'

'Backing on the Tigris?'

'Yes. The Babylonian Palace is the biggest of them. That's the more or less official hotel.'

'What do you know about a hotel called the Tio?'

'Oh, a lot of people go there. Food's rather good and it's run by a terrific character called Marcus Tio. He's quite an institution in Baghdad.'

'I want you to book me a room there, Mr Shrivenham.'

'You mean—you're not going to stay at the Embassy?' Shrivenham looked nervously apprehensive. 'But—but—it's all laid on, sir.'

'What is laid on can be laid off,' barked Sir Rupert.

'Oh, of course, sir. I didn't mean—'

Shrivenham broke off. He had a feeling that in the future someone was going to blame him.

'I have certain somewhat delicate negotiations to carry out. I learn that they cannot be carried out from the Embassy. I want you to book me a room tonight at the Tio Hotel and I wish to leave the Embassy in a reasonably unobtrusive manner. That is to say I do not want to drive up to the Tio in an Embassy car. I also require a seat booked on the plane leaving for Cairo the day after tomorrow.'

Shrivenham looked more dismayed still.

'But I understood you were staying five days—'

'That is no longer the case. It is imperative that I reach Cairo as soon as my business here is terminated. It would not be safe for me to remain longer.'

'Safe?'

A sudden grim smile transformed Sir Rupert's face. The manner which Shrivenham had been likening to that of a Prussian drill sergeant was laid aside. The man's charm became suddenly apparent.

'Safety hasn't usually been one of my preoccupations, I agree,' he said. 'But in this case it isn't only my own safety I have to consider—my safety includes the safety of a lot of other people as well. So make those arrangements for me. If the air passage is difficult, apply for priority. Until I leave here tonight, I shall remain in my room.' He added, as Shrivenham's mouth opened in surprise, 'Officially, I'm sick. Touch of malaria.' The other nodded. 'So I shan't need food.'

'But surely we can send you up—'

'Twenty-four hours' fast is nothing to me. I've gone hungry longer than that on some of my journeys. You just do as I tell you.'

Downstairs Shrivenham was greeted by his colleagues and groaned in answer to their inquiries.

'Cloak and dagger stuff in a big way,' he said. 'Can't

quite make his grandiloquence Sir Rupert Crofton Lee out. Whether it's genuine or play-acting. The swirling cloak and bandit's hat and all the rest of it. Fellow who'd read one of his books told me that although he's a bit of a self-advertiser, he really *has* done all these things and been to these places—but I don't know . . . Wish Thomas Rice was up and about to cope. That reminds me, what's Scheele's Green?'

'Scheele's Green?' said his friend, frowning. 'Something to do with wallpaper, isn't it? Poisonous. It's a form of arsenic, I think.'

'Cripes!' said Shrivenham, staring. 'I thought it was a disease. Something like amoebic dysentery.'

'Oh, no, it's something in the chemical line. What wives do their husbands in with, or vice versa.'

Shrivenham had relapsed into startled silence. Certain disagreeable facts were becoming clear to him. Crofton Lee had suggested, in effect, that Thomas Rice, Oriental Counsellor to the Embassy, was suffering, not from gastro-enteritis, but from arsenical poisoning. Added to that Sir Rupert had suggested that his own life was in danger, and his decision not to eat food and drink prepared in the kitchens of the British Embassy shook Shrivenham's decorous British soul to the core. He couldn't imagine what to make of it all.

CHAPTER 10

Victoria, breathing in hot choking yellow dust, was unfavourably impressed by Baghdad. From the airport to the Tio Hotel, her ears had been assailed by continuous and incessant noise. Horns of cars blaring with maddening persistence, voices shouting, whistles blowing, then more deafening senseless blaring of motor horns. Added to the loud incessant noises of the street was a small thin trickle of continuous sound which was Mrs Hamilton Clipp talking.

Victoria arrived at the Tio Hotel in a dazed condition.

A small alleyway led back from the fanfare of Rashid Street towards the Tigris. A short flight of steps to go up and there at the entrance of the hotel they were greeted by a very stout young man with a beaming smile who, metaphorically at least, gathered them to his heart. This, Victoria gathered, was Marcus—or more correctly Mr Tio, the owner of the Tio Hotel.

His words of welcome were interrupted by shouted orders to various underlings regarding the disposal of their baggage.

'And here you are, once more, Mrs Clipp—but your

arm—why is it in that funny stuff?—(You fools, do not carry that with the strap! Imbeciles! Don't trail that coat!)—But, my dear—what a day to arrive—never, I thought, would the plane land. It went round and round and round. Marcus, I said to myself—it is not you that will travel by planes—all this hurry, what does it matter?—And you have brought a young lady with you—it is nice always to see a new young lady in Baghdad—why did not Mr Harrison come down to meet you—I expected him yesterday—but, my dear, you must have a drink at once.'

Now, somewhat dazed, Victoria, her head reeling slightly under the effect of a double whisky authoritatively pressed upon her by Marcus, was standing in a high whitewashed room containing a large brass bedstead, a very sophisticated dressing-table of newest French design, an aged Victorian wardrobe, and two vivid plush chairs. Her modest baggage reposed at her feet and a very old man with a yellow face and white whiskers had grinned and nodded at her as he placed towels in the bathroom and asked her if she would like the water made hot for a bath.

'How long would it take?'

'Twenty minutes, half an hour. I go and do it now.'

With a fatherly smile he withdrew. Victoria sat down on the bed and passed an experimental hand over her hair. It felt clogged with dust and her face was sore and gritty. She looked at herself in the glass. The dust had changed her hair from black to a strange reddish brown. She pulled aside a corner of the curtain and looked out on to a wide balcony which gave on the river. But there was nothing to be seen of the Tigris but a thick yellow haze. A prey to deep depression, Victoria said to herself: 'What a hateful place.'

Then rousing herself, she stepped across the landing and tapped on Mrs Clipp's door. Prolonged and active ministrations would be required of her here before she could attend to her own cleansing and rehabilitation.

After a bath, lunch and a prolonged nap, Victoria stepped out from her bedroom on to the balcony and gazed with approval across the Tigris. The dust-storm had subsided. Instead of a yellow haze, a pale clear light was appearing. Across the river was a delicate silhouette of palm trees and irregularly placed houses.

Voices came up to Victoria from the garden below. She stepped to the edge of the balcony and looked over.

Mrs Hamilton Clipp, that indefatigable talker and friendly soul, had struck up an acquaintanceship with an Englishwoman—one of those weather-beaten Englishwomen of indeterminate age who can always be found in any foreign city.

'—and whatever I'd have done without her, I really don't know,' Mrs Clipp was saying. 'She's just the sweetest girl you can imagine. And very well connected. A niece of the Bishop of Llangow.'

'Bishop of who?'

'Why, Llangow, I think it was.'

'Nonsense, there's no such person,' said the other.

Victoria frowned. She recognized the type of County

Englishwoman who is unlikely to be taken in by the mention of spurious Bishops.

'Why, then, perhaps I got the name wrong,' Mrs Clipp said doubtfully.

'But,' she resumed, 'she certainly is a very charming and competent girl.'

The other said 'Ha!' in a non-committal manner.

Victoria resolved to give this lady as wide a berth as possible. Something told her that inventing stories to satisfy that kind of woman was no easy job.

Victoria went back into her room, sat on the bed, and gave herself up to speculation on her present position.

She was staying at the Tio Hotel, which was, she was fairly sure, not at all inexpensive. She had four pounds seventeen shillings in her possession. She had eaten a hearty lunch for which she had not yet paid and for which Mrs Clipp was under no obligation to pay. Travelling expenses to Baghdad were what Mrs Clipp had offered. The bargain was completed. Victoria had got to Baghdad. Mrs Hamilton Clipp had received the skilled attention of a Bishop's niece, an ex-hospital nurse, and competent secretary. All that was over, to the mutual satisfaction of both parties. Mrs Hamilton Clipp would depart on the evening train to Kirkuk—and that was that. Victoria toyed hopefully with the idea that Mrs Clipp might press upon her a parting present in the form of hard cash, but abandoned it reluctantly as unlikely. Mrs Clipp could have no idea that Victoria was in really dire financial straits.

What then must Victoria do? The answer came immediately. Find Edward, of course.

With a sense of annoyance she realized that she was

quite unaware of Edward's last name. Edward—Baghdad. Very much, Victoria reflected, like the Saracen maid who arrived in England knowing only the name of her lover 'Gilbert' and 'England'. A romantic story—but certainly inconvenient. True that in England at the time of the Crusades, nobody, Victoria thought, had had any surname at all. On the other hand England was larger than Baghdad. Still, England was sparsely populated then.

Victoria wrenched her thoughts away from these interesting speculations and returned to hard facts. She must find Edward immediately and Edward must find her a job. Also immediately.

She did not know Edward's last name, but he had come to Baghdad as the secretary of a Dr Rathbone and presumably Dr Rathbone was a man of importance.

Victoria powdered her nose and patted her hair and started down the stairs in search of information.

The beaming Marcus, passing through the hall of his establishment, hailed her with delight.

'Ah, it is Miss Jones, you will come with me and have a drink, will you not, my dear? I like very much English ladies. All the English ladies in Baghdad, they are my friends. Every one is very happy in my hotel. Come, we will go into the bar.'

Victoria, not at all averse to free hospitality, consented gladly.

Sitting on a stool and drinking gin, she began her search for information.

'Do you know a Dr Rathbone who has just come to Baghdad?' she asked.

'I know everyone in Baghdad,' said Marcus Tio joyfully. 'And everybody knows Marcus. That is true, what I am telling you. Oh! I have many many friends.'

'I'm sure you have,' said Victoria. 'Do you know Dr Rathbone?'

'Last week I have the Air Marshal commanding all Middle East passing through. He says to me, "Marcus, you villain, I haven't seen you since '46. You haven't grown any thinner." Oh he is very nice man. I like him very much.'

'What about Dr Rathbone? Is he a nice man?'

'I like, you know, people who can enjoy themselves. I do not like sour faces. I like people to be gay and young and charming—like you. He says to me, that Air Marshal, "Marcus, you like too much the women." But I say to him: "No, my trouble is I like too much Marcus . . ."' Marcus roared with laughter, breaking off to call out, 'Jesus—Jesus!'

Victoria looked startled, but it appeared that Jesus was the barman's Christian name. Victoria felt again that the East was an odd place.

'Another gin and orange, and whisky,' Marcus commanded.

'I don't think I—'

'Yes, yes, you will—they are very very weak.'

'About Dr Rathbone,' persisted Victoria.

'That Mrs Hamilton Clipp—what an odd name—with whom you arrive, she is American—is she not? I like also American people but I like English best. American peoples, they look always very worried. But sometimes, yes, they are good sports. Mr Summers—you know him?—he drink so much when he come to Baghdad, he go to sleep for three days and not wake up. It is too much that. It is not nice.'

'Please, do help me,' said Victoria.

Marcus looked surprised.

'But of course I help you. I always help my friends. You tell me what you want—and at once it shall be done. Special steak—or turkey cooked very nice with rice and raisins and herbs—or little baby chickens.'

'I don't want baby chickens,' said Victoria. 'At least not now,' she added prudently. 'I want to find this Dr Rathbone. Dr *Rathbone*. He's just arrived in Baghdad. With a—with a—secretary.'

'I do not know,' said Marcus. 'He does not stay at the Tio.'

The implication was clearly that any one who did not stay at the Tio did not exist for Marcus.

'But there are other hotels,' persisted Victoria, 'or perhaps he has a house?'

'Oh yes, there are other hotels. Babylonian Palace, Sennacherib, Zobeide Hotel. They are good hotels, yes, but they are not like the Tio.'

'I'm sure they're not,' Victoria assured him. 'But you don't know if Dr Rathbone is staying at one of them? There is some kind of society he runs—something to do with culture—and books.'

Marcus became quite serious at the mention of culture.

'It is what we need,' he said. 'There must be much culture. Art and music, it is very nice, very nice indeed. I like violin sonatas myself if it is not very long.'

Whilst thoroughly agreeing with him, especially in regard to the end of the speech, Victoria realized that she was not getting any nearer to her objective. Conversation with Marcus was, she thought, most entertaining, and Marcus was a charming person in his childlike enthusiasm for life, but conversation with him reminded her of Alice in Wonderland's endeavours to find a path that led to the hill. Every topic found them returning to the point of departure—Marcus!

She refused another drink and rose sadly to her feet. She felt slightly giddy. The cocktails had been anything but weak. She went out from the bar on to the terrace outside and stood by the railing looking across the river, when somebody spoke from behind her.

'Excuse me, but you'd better go and put a coat on. Dare say it seems like summer to you coming out from England, but it gets very cold about sundown.'

It was the Englishwoman who had been talking to Mrs Clipp earlier. She had the hoarse voice of one who is in the habit of training and calling to sporting dogs. She wore a fur coat, had a rug over her knees and was sipping a whisky and soda.

'Oh thank you,' said Victoria and was about to escape hurriedly when her intentions were defeated.

'I must introduce myself. I'm Mrs Cardew Trench.' (The implication was clearly: one of *the* Cardew Trenches.) 'I believe you arrived with Mrs—what's her name—Hamilton Clipp.'

'Yes,' said Victoria, 'I did.'

'She told me you were the niece of the Bishop of Llangow.'

Victoria rallied.

'Did she really?' she inquired with the correct trace of light amusement.

'Got it wrong, I suppose?'

Victoria smiled.

'Americans are bound to get some of our names wrong. It does sound a little like Llangow. My uncle,' said Victoria improvising rapidly, 'is the Bishop of Languao.'

'Languao?'

'Yes—in the Pacific Archipelago. He's a Colonial Bishop, of course.'

'Oh, a Colonial Bishop,' said Mrs Cardew Trench, her voice falling at least three semitones.

As Victoria had anticipated: Mrs Cardew Trench was magnificently unaware of Colonial Bishops.

'That explains it,' she added.

Victoria thought with pride that it explained it very well for a spur of the moment plunge!

'And what are *you* doing out here?' asked Mrs Cardew Trench with that inexorable geniality that conceals natural curiosity of disposition.

'Looking for a young man I talked to for a few moments in a public square in London,' was hardly an answer that Victoria could give. She said, remembering the newspaper paragraph she had read, and her statement to Mrs Clipp:

'I'm joining my uncle, Dr Pauncefoot Jones.'

'Oh, so *that's* who you are.' Mrs Cardew Trench was clearly delighted at having 'placed' Victoria. 'He's a charming little man, though a bit absent-minded—still I suppose that's only to be expected. Heard him lecture last year in London—excellent delivery—couldn't understand a word of what it was all about, though. Yes, he passed through Baghdad about a fortnight ago. I think he mentioned some girls were coming out later in the season.'

Hurriedly, having established her status, Victoria chipped in with a question.

'Do you know if Dr Rathbone is out here?' she asked.

'Just come out,' said Mrs Cardew Trench. 'I believe they've asked him to give a lecture at the Institute next Thursday. On "World Relationships and Brotherhood"—or something like that. All nonsense if you ask me. The more you try to get people together, the more suspicious they get of each other. All this poetry and music and translating Shakespeare and Wordsworth into Arabic and Chinese and Hindustani. "A primrose by the river's brim," etc . . . what's the good of that to people who've never seen a primrose?'

'Where is he staying, do you know?'

'At the Babylonian Palace Hotel, I believe. But his headquarters are up near the Museum. The Olive Branch—ridiculous name. Full of young women in slacks with unwashed necks and spectacles.'

'I know his secretary slightly,' said Victoria.

'Oh yes, whatshisname Edward Thingummy—nice boy—too good for that long-haired racket—did well in the war, I hear. Still a job's a job, I suppose. Nice-looking boy—those earnest young women are quite fluttered by him, I fancy.'

A pang of devastating jealousy pierced Victoria.

'The Olive Branch,' she said. 'Where did you say it was?'

'Up past the turning to the second bridge. One of the turnings off Rashid Street—tucked away rather. Not far from the Copper Bazaar.

'And how's Mrs Pauncefoot Jones?' continued Mrs Cardew Trench. 'Coming out soon? I hear she's been in poor health?'

But having got the information she wanted, Victoria was taking no more risks in invention. She glanced at her wrist-watch and uttered an exclamation.

'Oh dear—I promised to wake Mrs Clipp at half-past six and help her to prepare for the journey. I must fly.'

The excuse was true enough, though Victoria had substituted half-past six for seven o'clock. She hurried upstairs quite exhilarated. Tomorrow she would get in touch with Edward at the Olive Branch. Earnest young women with unwashed necks, indeed! They sounded *most* unattractive . . . Still, Victoria reflected uneasily that men are less critical of dingy necks than middle-aged hygienic Englishwomen are—especially if the owners of the said necks were gazing with large eyes of admiration and adoration at the male subject in question.

The evening passed rapidly. Victoria had an early meal in the dining-room with Mrs Hamilton Clipp, the latter talking nineteen to the dozen on every subject under the sun. She urged Victoria to come and pay a visit later—and Victoria noted down the address carefully, because, after

all, one never knew . . . She accompanied Mrs Clipp to
Baghdad North Station, saw her safely ensconced in her
compartment and was introduced to an acquaintance also
travelling to Kirkuk who would assist Mrs Clipp with her
toilet on the following morning.

The engine uttered loud melancholy screams like a soul
in distress, Mrs Clipp thrust a thick envelope into Victoria's
hand, said: 'Just a little remembrance, Miss Jones, of our
very pleasant companionship which I hope you will accept
with my *most* grateful thanks.'

Victoria said: 'But it's really *too* kind of you, Mrs Clipp,'
in a delighted voice, the engine gave a fourth and final
supreme banshee wail of anguish and the train pulled slowly
out of the station.

Victoria took a taxi from the station back to the hotel
since she had not the faintest idea how to get back to it
any other way and there did not seem any one about whom
she could ask.

On her return to the Tio, she ran up to her room and
eagerly opened the envelope. Inside were a couple of pairs
of nylon stockings.

Victoria at any other moment would have been
enchanted—nylon stockings having been usually beyond
the reach of her purse. At the moment, however, hard cash
was what she had been hoping for. Mrs Clipp, however
had been far too delicate to think of giving her a five-dinar
note. Victoria wished heartily that she had not been quite
so delicate.

However, tomorrow there would be Edward. Victoria
undressed, got into bed and in five minutes was fast asleep,

dreaming that she was waiting at an aerodrome for Edward, but that he was held back from joining her by a spectacled girl who clasped him firmly round the neck while the aeroplane began slowly to move away . . .

CHAPTER 11

Victoria awoke to a morning of vivid sunshine. Having dressed, she went out on to the wide balcony outside her window. Sitting in a chair a little way along with his back to her was a man with curling grey hair growing down on to a muscular red brown neck. When the man turned his head sideways Victoria recognized, with a distinct feeling of surprise, Sir Rupert Crofton Lee. *Why* she should be so surprised she could hardly have said. Perhaps because she had assumed as a matter of course that a VIP such as Sir Rupert would have been staying at the Embassy and not at a hotel. Nevertheless there he was, staring at the Tigris with a kind of concentrated intensity. She noticed, even, that he had a pair of field-glasses slung over the side of his chair. Possibly, she thought, he studied birds.

A young man whom Victoria had at one time thought attractive had been a bird enthusiast, and she had accompanied him on several week-end tramps, to be made to stand as though paralysed in wet woods and icy winds, for what seemed like hours, to be at last told in tones of ecstasy to look through the glasses at some drab-looking bird on a remote twig which in appearance as far as Victoria could see, compared unfavourably in bird appeal with a common robin or chaffinch.

Victoria made her way downstairs, encountering Marcus Tio on the terrace between the two buildings of the hotel.

'I see you've got Sir Rupert Crofton Lee staying here,' she said.

'Oh yes,' said Marcus, beaming, 'he is a nice man—a very nice man.'

'Do you know him well?'

'No, this is the first time I see him. Mr Shrivenham of the British Embassy bring him here last night. Mr Shrivenham, he is very nice man, too. I know *him very* well.'

Proceeding in to breakfast Victoria wondered if there was any one whom Marcus would not consider a very nice man. He appeared to exercise a wide charity.

After breakfast, Victoria started forth in search of the Olive Branch.

A London-bred Cockney, she had no idea of the difficulties involved in finding any particular place in a city such as Baghdad until she had started on her quest.

Coming across Marcus again on her way out, she asked him to direct her to the Museum.

'It is a very nice museum,' said Marcus, beaming. 'Yes. Full of interesting, very very old things. Not that I have been there myself. But I have friends, archaeological friends, who stay here always when they come through Baghdad. Mr Baker—Mr Richard Baker, you know him? And Professor Kalzman? And Dr Pauncefoot Jones—and Mr and Mrs McIntyre—they all come to the Tio. They are my friends. And they tell me about what is in the Museum. Very very interesting.'

'Where is it, and how do I get there?'

'You go straight along Rashid Street—a long way—past the turn to the Feisal Bridge and past Bank Street—you know Bank Street?'

'I don't know anything,' said Victoria.

'And then there is another street—also going down to a bridge and it is along there on the right. You ask for Mr Betoun Evans, he is English Adviser there—very nice man. And his wife, she is very nice, too, she came here as Transport Sergeant during the war. Oh, she is very very nice.'

'I don't really want to go actually to the Museum,' said Victoria. 'I want to find a place—a society—a kind of club called the Olive Branch.'

'If you want olives,' said Marcus, 'I give you beautiful olives—very fine quality. They keep them especially for me—for the Tio Hotel. You see, I send you some to your table tonight.'

'That's very kind of you,' said Victoria and escaped towards Rashid Street.

'To the left,' Marcus shouted after her, 'not to the right. But it is a long way to the Museum. You had better take a taxi.'

'Would a taxi know where the Olive Branch was?'

'No, they do not know where *anything* is! You say to the driver left, right, stop, straight on—just where you want to go.'

'In that case, I might as well walk,' said Victoria.

She reached Rashid Street and turned to the left.

Baghdad was entirely unlike her idea of it. A crowded main thoroughfare thronged with people, cars hooting violently, people shouting, European goods for sale in the shop windows, hearty spitting all round her with prodigious throat-clearing as a preliminary. No mysterious Eastern figures, most of the people wore tattered or shabby Western clothes, old army and air force tunics, the occasional shuffling black-robed and veiled figures were almost inconspicuous amongst the hybrid European styles of dress. Whining beggars came up to her—women with dirty babies in their arms. The pavement under her feet was uneven with occasional gaping holes.

She pursued her way feeling suddenly strange and lost and far from home. Here was no glamour of travel, only confusion.

She came at last to the Feisal Bridge, passed it and went on. In spite of herself she was intrigued by the curious mixture of things in the shop windows. Here were babies' shoes and woollies, toothpaste and cosmetics, electric torches and china cups and saucers—all shown together. Slowly a kind of fascination came over her, the fascination of assorted merchandise coming from all over the world to meet the strange and varied wants of a mixed population.

She found the Museum, but not the Olive Branch. To one accustomed to finding her way about London it seemed incredible that here was no one she could *ask*. She knew no Arabic. Those shopkeepers who spoke to her in English as she passed, pressing their wares, presented blank faces when she asked for direction to the Olive Branch.

If one could only 'ask a policeman,' but gazing at the policemen actively waving their arms, and blowing their whistles, she realized that here that would be no solution.

She went into a bookshop with English books in the window, but a mention of the Olive Branch drew only a courteous shrug and shake of the head. Regrettably they had no idea at all.

And then, as she walked along the street, a prodigious hammering and clanging came to her ears and peering down a long dim alley, she remembered that Mrs Cardew Trench had said that the Olive Branch was near the Copper Bazaar. Here, at least, was the Copper Bazaar.

Victoria plunged in, and for the next three-quarters of an hour she forgot the Olive Branch completely. The Copper Bazaar fascinated her. The blow-lamps, the melting metal, the whole business of craftsmanship came like a revelation to the little Cockney used only to finished products stacked up for sale. She wandered at random through the souk, passed out of the Copper Bazaar, came to the gay striped horse blankets, and the cotton quilted bedcovers. Here European merchandise took on a totally different guise, in the arched cool darkness it had the exotic quality of something come from overseas, something strange and rare. Bales of cheap printed cottons in gay colours made a feast for the eyes.

Occasionally with a shout of *Balek, Balek*, a donkey or laden mule pushed past her, or men bearing great loads balanced on their backs. Little boys rushed up to her with trays slung round their necks.

'See, lady, elastic, *good* elastic, English elastic. Comb, English comb?'

The wares were thrust at her, close to her nose, with vehement urgings to buy. Victoria walked in a happy dream. This was really seeing the world. At every turn of the vast arched cool world of alleyways you came to something totally unexpected—an alley of tailors, sitting stitching, with smart pictures of European men's tailoring; a line of watches and cheap jewellery. Bales of velvets and rich metal embroidered brocades, then a chance turn and you were walking down an alley of cheap and shoddy second-hand European clothes, quaint pathetic little faded jumpers and long straggly vests.

Then every now and then there were glimpses into vast quiet courtyards open to the sky.

She came to a vast vista of men's trouserings, with cross-legged dignified merchants in turbans sitting in the middle of their little square recesses.

'*Balek!*'

A heavily-laden donkey coming up behind her made Victoria turn aside into a narrow alleyway open to the sky that turned and twisted through tall houses. Walking along it she came, quite by chance, to the object of her search. Through an opening she looked into a small square court-yard and at the farther side of it an open doorway with THE OLIVE BRANCH on a huge sign and a rather impossible-looking plaster bird holding an unrecognizable twig in its beak.

Joyously Victoria sped across the courtyard and in at the open door. She found herself in a dimly lit room with tables covered with books and periodicals and more books ranged round on shelves. It looked a little like a bookshop except that there were little groups of chairs arranged together here and there.

Out of the dimness a young woman came up to Victoria and said in careful English:

'What can I do for you, yes, please?'

Victoria looked at her. She wore corduroy trousers and an orange flannel shirt and had black dank hair cut in a kind of depressed bob. So far she would have looked more suited to Bloomsbury, but her face was not Bloomsbury. It was a melancholy Levantine face with great sad dark eyes and a heavy nose.

'This is—is this—is—is Dr Rathbone here?'

Maddening still not to know Edward's surname! Even Mrs Cardew Trench had called him Edward Thingummy.

'Yes. Dr Rathbone. The Olive Branch. You wish to join us? Yes? That will be very nice.'

'Well, perhaps. I'd—can I see Dr Rathbone, please?'

The young woman smiled in a tired way.

'We do not disturb. I have a form. I tell you all about everything. Then you sign your name. It is two dinars, please.'

'I'm not sure yet that I want to join,' said Victoria, alarmed at the mention of two dinars. 'I'd like to see Dr Rathbone—or his secretary. His secretary would do.'

'I explain. I explain to you everything. We all are friends here, friends together, friends for the future—reading very fine educational books—reciting poems each to other.'

'Dr Rathbone's secretary,' said Victoria loudly and clearly. 'He particularly told me to ask for him.'

A kind of mulish sullenness came into the young woman's face.

'Not today,' she said. 'I explain—'

'Why not today? Isn't he here? Isn't Dr Rathbone here?'

'Yais, Dr Rathbone is here. He is upstairs. We do not disturb.'

A kind of Anglo-Saxon intolerance of foreigners swept over Victoria. Regrettably, instead of the Olive Branch creating friendly international feelings, it seemed to be having the opposite effect as far as she was concerned.

'I have just arrived from England,' she said—and her accents were almost those of Mrs Cardew Trench herself—'and I have a very important message for Dr Rathbone which I must deliver to him personally. Please take me to him *at once*! I am sorry to disturb him, but I have got to see him.

'*At once!* ' she added, to clinch matters.

Before an imperious Briton who means to get his or her own way, barriers nearly always fall. The young woman turned at once and led the way to the back of the room and up a staircase and along a gallery overlooking the courtyard. Here she stopped before a door and knocked. A man's voice said, 'Come in.'

Victoria's guide opened the door and motioned to Victoria to pass in.

'It is a lady from England for you.'

Victoria walked in.

From behind a large desk covered with papers, a man got up to greet her.

He was an imposing-looking elderly man of about sixty with a high domed forehead and white hair. Benevolence, kindliness and charm were the most apparent qualities of his personality. A producer of plays would have cast him without hesitation for the role of the great philanthropist.

He greeted Victoria with a warm smile and an outstretched hand.

'So you've just come out from England,' he said. 'First visit East, eh?'

'Yes.'

'I wonder what you think of it all . . . You must tell me sometime. Now let me see, have I met you before or not? I'm so short-sighted and you didn't give your name.'

'You don't know me,' said Victoria, 'but I'm a friend of Edward's.'

'A friend of Edward's,' said Dr Rathbone. 'Why, that's splendid. Does Edward know you're in Baghdad?'

'Not yet,' said Victoria.

'Well, that will be a pleasant surprise for him when he gets back.'

'Back?' said Victoria, her voice falling.

'Yes, Edward's at Basrah at the moment. I had to send him down there to see about some crates of books that have come out for us. There have been most vexatious delays in the Customs—we simply have not been able to get them cleared. The personal touch is the only thing, and Edward's good at that sort of thing. He knows just when to charm and when to bully, and he won't rest till he's got the thing through. He's a sticker. A fine quality in a young man. I think a lot of Edward.'

His eyes twinkled.

'But I don't suppose I need to sing Edward's praises to you, young lady?'

'When—when will Edward be back from Basrah?' asked Victoria faintly.

'Well—now that I couldn't say, he won't come back till he's finished the job—and you can't hurry things too much in this country. Tell me where you are staying and I'll make sure he gets in touch with you as soon as he gets back.'

'I was wondering—' Victoria spoke desperately, aware of her financial plight. 'I was wondering if—if I could do some work here?'

'Now that I do appreciate,' said Dr Rathbone warmly. 'Yes, of course you can. We need all the workers, all the help we can get. And especially English girls. Our work is going splendidly—quite splendidly—but there's lots more to be done. Still, people are keen. I've got thirty voluntary helpers already—*thirty*—all of 'em as keen as mustard! If you're really in earnest, you can be *most* valuable.'

The word voluntary struck unpleasantly on Victoria's ear.

'I really wanted a paid position,' she said.

'Oh dear!' Dr Rathbone's face fell. 'That's rather more difficult. Our paid staff is very small—and for the moment, with the voluntary help, it's quite adequate.'

'I can't afford not to take a job,' explained Victoria. 'I'm a competent shorthand typist,' she added without a blush.

'I'm sure you're competent, my dear young lady, you radiate competence, if I may say so. But with us it's a question of £.s.d. But even if you take a job elsewhere, I hope you'll help us in your spare time. Most of our workers have their own regular jobs. I'm sure you'll find helping us really inspiring. There must be an end of all the savagery

111

in the world, the wars, the misunderstandings, the suspicions. A common meeting ground, that's what we all need. Drama, art, poetry—the great things of the spirit—no room there for petty jealousies or hatreds.'

'N-no,' said Victoria doubtfully, recalling friends of hers who were actresses and artists and whose lives seemed to be obsessed by jealousy of the most trivial kind, and by hatreds of a peculiarly virulent intensity.

'I've had *A Midsummer Night's Dream* translated into forty different languages,' said Dr Rathbone. 'Forty different sets of young people all reacting to the same wonderful piece of literature. *Young* people—that's the secret. I've no use for anybody but the young. Once the mind and spirit are muscle-bound, it's too late. No, it's the young who must get together. Take that girl downstairs, Catherine, the one who showed you up here. She's a Syrian from Damascus. You and she are probably about the same age. Normally you'd never come together, you'd have nothing in common. But at the Olive Branch you and she and many many others, Russians, Jewesses, Iraqis, Turkish girls, Armenians, Egyptians, Persians, all meet and like each other and read the same books and discuss pictures and music (we have excellent lecturers who come out) all of you finding out and being excited by encountering a different point of view—why, that's what the world is meant to be.'

Victoria could not help thinking that Dr Rathbone was slightly over-optimistic in assuming that all those divergent elements who were coming together would necessarily like each other. She and Catherine, for instance, had not liked each other at all. And Victoria strongly suspected that the more they saw of each other the greater their dislike would grow.

'Edward's splendid,' said Dr Rathbone. 'Gets on with everybody. Better perhaps, with the girls than with the young men. The men students out here are apt to be difficult at first—suspicious—almost hostile. But the girls adore Edward, they'll do anything for him. He and Catherine get on particularly well.'

'Indeed,' said Victoria coldly. Her dislike of Catherine grew even more intense.

'Well,' said Dr Rathbone, smiling, 'come and help us if you can.'

It was a dismissal. He pressed her hand warmly. Victoria went out of the room and down the stairs. Catherine was standing near the door talking to a girl who had just come in with a small suitcase in her hand. She was a good-looking dark girl, and just for a moment Victoria fancied that she had seen her before somewhere. But the girl looked at her without any sign of recognition. The two young women had been talking eagerly together in some language Victoria did not know. They stopped when she appeared and remained silent, staring at her. She walked past them to the door, forcing herself to say 'Goodbye' politely to Catherine as she went out.

She found her way out from the winding alley into Rashid Street and made her way slowly back to the hotel, her eyes unseeing of the throngs around her. She tried to keep her mind from dwelling on her own predicament (penniless in Baghdad) by fixing her mind on Dr Rathbone and the general set-up of the Olive Branch. Edward had

had an idea in London that there was something 'fishy' about his job. What was fishy? Dr Rathbone? Or the Olive Branch itself?

Victoria could hardly believe that there was anything fishy about Dr Rathbone. He appeared to her to be one of those misguided enthusiasts who insist on seeing the world in their own idealistic manner, regardless of realities.

What had Edward *meant* by fishy? He'd been very vague. Perhaps he didn't really know himself.

Could Dr Rathbone be some kind of colossal fraud?

Victoria, fresh from the soothing charm of his manner, shook her head. His manner had certainly changed, ever so slightly, at the idea of paying her a salary. He clearly preferred people to work for nothing.

But that, thought Victoria, was a sign of common sense.

Mr Greenholtz, for instance, would have felt just the same.

CHAPTER 12

Victoria arrived back at the Tio, rather footsore, to be hailed enthusiastically by Marcus who was sitting out on the grass terrace overlooking the river and talking to a thin rather shabby middle-aged man.

'Come and have a drink with us, Miss Jones. Martini—sidecar? This is Mr Dakin. Miss Jones from England. Now then, my dear, what will you have?'

Victoria said she would have a sidecar 'and some of those lovely nuts?' she suggested hopefully, remembering that nuts were nutritious.

'You like nuts. Jesus!' He gave the order in rapid Arabic. Mr Dakin said in a sad voice that he would have a lemonade.

'Ah,' cried Marcus, 'but that is ridiculous. Ah, here is Mrs Cardew Trench. You know Mr Dakin? What will you have?'

'Gin and lime,' said Mrs Cardew Trench, nodding to Dakin in an off-hand manner. 'You look hot,' she added to Victoria.

'I've been walking round seeing the sights.'

115

When the drinks came, Victoria ate a large plateful of pistachio nuts and also some potato chips.

Presently, a short thick-set man came up the steps and the hospitable Marcus hailed him in his turn. He was introduced to Victoria as Captain Crosbie, and by the way his slightly protuberant eyes goggled at her, Victoria gathered that he was susceptible to feminine charm.

'Just come out?' he asked her.

'Yesterday.'

'Thought I hadn't seen you around.'

'She is very nice and beautiful, is she not?' said Marcus joyfully. 'Oh yes, it is very nice to have Miss Victoria. I will give a party for her—a very nice party.'

'With baby chickens?' said Victoria hopefully.

'Yes, yes—and foie gras—Strasburg foie gras—and perhaps caviare—and then we have a dish with fish—very nice—a fish from the Tigris, but all with sauce and mushrooms. And then there is a turkey stuffed in the way we have it at my home—with rice and raisins and spice—and all cooked *so*! Oh it is very good—but you must eat very much of it—not just a tiny spoonful. Or if you like it better you shall have a steak—a really big steak and *tender*—I see to it. We will have a long dinner that goes on for hours. It will be very nice. I do not eat myself—I only drink.'

'That will be lovely,' said Victoria in a faint voice. The description of these viands made her feel quite giddy with hunger. She wondered if Marcus really meant to give this party and if so, how soon it could possibly happen.

'Thought you'd gone to Basrah,' said Mrs Cardew Trench to Crosbie.

'Got back yesterday,' said Crosbie.

He looked up at the balcony.

'Who's the bandit?' he asked. 'Feller in fancy dress in the big hat.'

'That, my dear, is Sir Rupert Crofton Lee,' said Marcus. 'Mr Shrivenham brought him here from the Embassy last night. He is a very nice man, very distinguished traveller. He rides on camels over the Sahara, and climbs up mountains. It is very uncomfortable and dangerous, that kind of life. I should not like it myself.'

'Oh he's that chap, is he?' said Crosbie. 'I've read his book.'

'I came over on the plane with him,' said Victoria.

Both men, or so it seemed to her, looked at her with interest.

'He's frightfully stuck up and pleased with himself,' said Victoria with disparagement.

'Knew his aunt in Simla,' said Mrs Cardew Trench. 'The whole family is like that. Clever as they make them, but can't help boasting of it.'

'He's been sitting out there doing nothing all the morning,' said Victoria with slight disapproval.

'It is his stomach,' explained Marcus. 'Today he cannot eat anything. It is sad.'

'I can't think,' said Mrs Cardew Trench, 'why you're the size you are, Marcus, when you never eat anything.'

'It is the drink,' said Marcus. He sighed deeply. 'I drink far too much. Tonight my sister and her husband come. I

117

will drink and drink almost until morning.' He sighed again, then uttered his usual sudden roar. 'Jesus! Jesus! Bring the same again.'

'Not for me,' said Victoria hastily, and Mr Dakin refused also, finishing up his lemonade, and ambling gently away while Crosbie went up to his room.

Mrs Cardew Trench flicked Dakin's glass with her finger-nail. 'Lemonade as usual?' she said. 'Bad sign, that.'

Victoria asked why it was a bad sign.

'When a man only drinks when he's alone.'

'Yes, my dear,' said Marcus. 'That is so.'

'Does he really drink, then?' asked Victoria.

'That's why he's never got on,' said Mrs Cardew Trench. 'Just manages to keep his job and that's all.'

'But he is a very nice man,' said the charitable Marcus.

'Pah,' said Mrs Cardew Trench. 'He's a wet fish. Potters and dilly-dallies about—no stamina—no grip on life. Just one more Englishman who's come out East and gone to seed.'

Thanking Marcus for the drink and again refusing a second, Victoria went up to her room, removed her shoes, and lay down on her bed to do some serious thinking. The three pounds odd to which her capital had dwindled was, she fancied, already due to Marcus for board and lodging. Owing to his generous disposition, and if she could sustain life mainly on alcoholic liquor assisted by nuts, olives and chip potatoes, she might solve the purely alimentary problem of the next few days. How long would it be before Marcus presented her with her bill, and how long would he allow it to run unpaid? She had no idea.

He was not really, she thought, careless in business matters. She ought, of course, to find somewhere cheaper to live. But how would she find out where to go? She ought to find herself a job—quickly. But where did one apply for jobs? What kind of a job? Whom could she ask about looking for one? How terribly handicapping to one's style it was to be dumped down practically penniless in a foreign city where one didn't know the ropes. With just a little knowledge of the terrain, Victoria felt confident (as always) that she could hold her own. When would Edward get back from Basrah? Perhaps (horror) Edward would have forgotten all about her. Why on earth had she come rushing out to Baghdad in this asinine way? Who and what was Edward after all? Just another young man with an engaging grin and an attractive way of saying things. And what—what—*what* was his surname? If she knew that, she might wire him—no good, she didn't even know where he was staying. She didn't know anything— that was the trouble—that was what was cramping her style.

And there was no one to whom she could go for advice. Not Marcus who was kind but never listened. Not Mrs Cardew Trench (who had had suspicions from the first). Not Mrs Hamilton Clipp who had vanished to Kirkuk. Not Dr Rathbone.

She must get some money—or get a job—*any* job. Look after children, stick stamps on in an office, serve in a restaurant . . . Otherwise they would send her to a Consul and she would be repatriated to England and never see Edward again . . .

At this point, worn out with emotion, Victoria fell asleep.

She awoke some hours later and deciding that she might as well be hanged for a sheep as a lamb, went down to the restaurant and worked her way solidly through the entire menu—a generous one. When she had finished, she felt slightly like a boa constrictor, but definitely heartened.

'It's no good worrying any more,' thought Victoria. 'I'll leave it all till tomorrow. Something may turn up, or I may think of something, or Edward may come back.'

Before going to bed she strolled out on to the terrace by the river. Since in the feelings of those living in Baghdad it was arctic winter nobody else was out there except one of the waiters, who was leaning over a railing staring down into the water, and he sprang away guiltily when Victoria appeared and hurried back into the hotel by the service door.

Victoria, to whom, coming from England, it appeared to be an ordinary summer night with a slight nip in the air, was enchanted by the Tigris seen in the moonlight with the farther bank looking mysterious and Eastern with its fringes of palms.

'Well, anyway, I've got here,' said Victoria, cheering up a good deal, 'and I'll manage somehow. Something is bound to turn up.'

With this Micawber-like pronouncement, she went up to bed, and the waiter slipped quietly out again and resumed his task of attaching a knotted rope so that it hung down to the river's edge.

Presently another figure came out of the shadows and joined him. Mr Dakin said in a low voice:

'All in order?'

'Yes, sir, nothing suspicious to report.'

Having completed the task to his satisfaction, Mr Dakin retreated into the shadows, exchanged his waiters' white coat for his own nondescript blue pin-stripe and ambled gently along the terrace until he stood outlined against the water's edge just where the steps led up from the street below.

'Getting pretty chilly in the evenings now,' said Crosbie, strolling out from the bar and down to join him. 'Suppose you don't feel it so much, coming from Tehran.'

They stood there for a moment or two smoking. Unless they raised their voices, nobody could overhear them. Crosbie said quietly:

'Who's the girl?'

'Niece apparently of the archaeologist, Pauncefoot Jones.'

'Oh well—that should be all right. But coming on the same plane as Crofton Lee—'

'It's certainly as well,' said Dakin, 'to take nothing for granted.'

The men smoked in silence for a few moments.

Crosbie said: 'You really think it's advisable to shift the thing from the Embassy to here?'

'I think so, yes.'

'In spite of the whole thing being taped down to the smallest detail.'

'It was taped down to the smallest detail in Basrah—and that went wrong.'

'Oh, I know. Salah Hassan was poisoned, by the way.'

'Yes—he would be. Were there any signs of an approach to the Consulate?'

'I suspect there may have been. Bit of a shindy there, Chap drew a revolver.' He paused and added, 'Richard Baker grabbed him and disarmed him.'

'Richard Baker,' said Dakin thoughtfully.

'Know him? He's—'

'Yes, I know him.'

There was a pause and then Dakin said:

'Improvisation. That's what I'm banking on. If we have, as you say, got everything taped—and our plans are known, then it's easy for the other side to have got us taped, too. I very much doubt if Carmichael would even so much as get near the Embassy—and even if he reached it—' He shook his head.

'Here, only you and I and Crofton Lee are wise to what's going on.'

'They'll know Crofton Lee moved here from the Embassy.'

'Oh of course. That was inevitable. But don't you see, Crosbie, that whatever show they put up against our improvisation has got to be improvised, too. It's got to be hastily thought of and hastily arranged. It's got to come, so to speak, from the *outside*. There's no question here of someone established in the Tio six months ago waiting. The Tio's never been in the picture until now. There's never been any idea or suggestion of using the Tio as the rendezvous.'

He looked at his watch. 'I'll go up now and see Crofton Lee.'

Dakin's raised hand had no need to tap on Sir Rupert's door. It opened silently to let him in.

The traveller had only one small reading-lamp alight and had placed his chair beside it. As he sat down again, he gently slipped a small automatic pistol on to the table within reach of his hand.

He said: 'What about it, Dakin? Do you think he'll come?'

'I think so, yes, Sir Rupert.' Then he said, 'You've never met him, have you?'

The other shook his head.

'No. I'm looking forward to meeting him tonight. That young man, Dakin, must have got guts.'

'Oh yes,' said Mr Dakin in his flat voice. 'He's got guts.'

He sounded a little surprised at the fact needing to be stated.

'I don't mean only courage,' said the other. 'Lots of courage in the war—magnificent. I mean—'

'Imagination?' suggested Dakin.

'Yes. To have the guts to believe something that isn't in the least degree probable. To risk your life finding out that a ridiculous story isn't ridiculous at all. That takes something that the modern young man usually hasn't got. I hope he'll come.'

'I think he'll come,' said Mr Dakin.

Sir Rupert glanced at him sharply.

'You've got it all sewn up?'

'Crosbie's on the balcony, and I shall be watching the stairs. When Carmichael reaches you, tap on the wall and I'll come in.'

Crofton Lee nodded.

Dakin went softly out of the room. He went to the left and on to the balcony and walked to the extreme corner. Here, too, a knotted rope dropped over the edge and came to earth in the shade of a eucalyptus tree and some judas bushes.

Mr Dakin went back past Crofton Lee's door and into his own room beyond. His room had a second door in it leading on to the passage behind the rooms and it opened within a few feet of the head of the stairs. With this door unobtrusively ajar, Mr Dakin settled down to his vigil.

It was about four hours later that a *gufa*, that primitive craft of the Tigris, dropped gently downstream and came to shore on the mudflat beneath the Tio Hotel. A few moments later a slim figure swarmed up the rope and crouched amongst the judas trees.

CHAPTER 13

It had been Victoria's intention to go to bed and to sleep and to leave all problems until the morning, but having already slept most of the afternoon, she found herself devastatingly wide-awake.

In the end she switched on the light, finished a magazine story she had been reading in the plane, darned her stockings, tried on her new nylons, wrote out several different advertisements requiring employment (she could ask tomorrow where these should be inserted), wrote three or four tentative letters to Mrs Hamilton Clipp, each setting out a different and more ingenious set of unforeseen circumstances which had resulted in her being 'stranded' in Baghdad, sketched out one or two telegrams appealing for help to her sole surviving relative, a very old, crusty, and unpleasant gentleman in the North of England who had never helped anybody in his life; tried out a new style of hair-do, and finally with a sudden yawn decided that at last she really was desperately sleepy and ready for bed and repose.

It was at this moment that without any warning her

bedroom door swung open, a man slipped in, turned the key in the lock behind him and said to her urgently:

'For God's sake hide me somewhere—quickly . . .'

Victoria's reactions were never slow. In a twinkling of an eye she had noted the laboured breathing, the fading voice, the way the man held an old red knitted scarf bunched on his breast with a desperate clutching hand. And she rose immediately in response to the adventure.

The room did not lend itself to many hiding-places. There was the wardrobe, a chest of drawers, a table and the rather pretentious dressing-table. The bed was a large one—almost a double bed and memories of childish hide-and-seek made Victoria's reaction prompt.

'Quick,' she said. She swept off pillows, and raised sheet and blanket. The man lay across the top of the bed. Victoria pulled sheet and blanket over him, dumped the pillows on top and sat down herself on the side of the bed.

Almost immediately there came a low insistent knocking on the door.

Victoria called out, 'Who is it?' in a faint, alarmed voice.

'Please,' said a man's voice outside. 'Open, please. It is the police.'

Victoria crossed the room, pulling her dressing-gown round her. As she did so, she noticed the man's red knitted scarf was lying on the floor and she caught it up and swept it into a drawer, then she turned the key and opened the door of her room a small way, peering out with an expression of alarm.

A dark-haired young man in a mauve pin-stripe suit was

126

standing outside and behind him was a man in police officer's uniform.

'What's the matter?' Victoria asked, letting a quaver creep into her voice.

The young man smiled brilliantly and spoke in very passable English.

'I am so sorry, miss, to disturb you at this hour,' he said, 'but we have a criminal escaped. He has run into this hotel. We must look in every room. He is a very dangerous man.'

'Oh dear!' Victoria fell back, opening the door wide. '*Do* come in, please, and look. How very frightening. Look in the bathroom, please. Oh! and the wardrobe—and, I wonder, *would* you mind looking *under* the bed? He might have been there all evening.'

The search was very rapid.

'No, he is not here.'

'You're sure he's not under the bed? No, how silly of me. He couldn't be in here at all. I locked the door when I went to bed.'

'Thank you, miss, and good evening.'

The young man bowed and withdrew with his uniformed assistant.

Victoria, following him to the door, said:

'I'd better lock it again, hadn't I? To be safe.'

'Yes, that will be best, certainly. Thank you.'

Victoria relocked the door and stood by it for some few minutes. She heard the police officers knock in the same way on the door the other side of the passage, heard the door open, an exchange of remarks and the indignant hoarse voice of Mrs Cardew Trench, and then the door closing. It reopened a few minutes later, the sound of their footsteps moved down the passage. The next knock came from much farther away.

Victoria turned and walked across the room to the bed. It was borne in upon her that she had probably been excessively foolish. Led away by the romantic spirit, and by the sound of her own language, she had impulsively lent aid to what was probably an extremely dangerous criminal. A disposition to be on the side of the hunted against the hunter sometimes brings unpleasant consequences. Oh well, thought Victoria, I'm in for it now, anyway!

Standing beside the bed she said curtly:

'Get up.'

There was no movement, and Victoria said sharply, though without raising her voice:

'They've gone. You can get up now.'

But still there was no sign of movement from under the slightly raised hump of pillows. Impatiently, Victoria threw them all off.

The young man lay just as she had left him. But now his face was a queer greyish colour and his eyes were closed.

Then, with a sharp catch in her breath, Victoria noticed something else—a bright red stain seeping through on to the blanket.

'Oh, *no*,' said Victoria, almost as though pleading with someone. 'Oh, no—*no!*'

And as though in recognition of that plea the wounded man opened his eyes. He stared at her, stared as though from very far away at some object he was not quite certain of seeing.

His lips parted—the sound was so faint that Victoria scarcely heard.

She bent down.

'What?'

She heard this time. With difficulty, great difficulty, the young man said two words. Whether she heard them correctly or not Victoria did not know. They seemed to her quite nonsensical and without meaning. What he said was, '*Lucifer—Basrah . . .*'

The eyelids drooped and flickered over the wide anxious eyes. He said one word more—a name. Then his head jerked back a little and he lay still.

Victoria stood quite still, her heart beating violently. She was filled now with an intense pity and anger. What to do next she had no idea. She must call someone—get someone to come. She was alone here with a dead man and sooner or later the police would want an explanation.

Whilst her brain worked rapidly on the situation, a small sound made her turn her head. The key had fallen out of her bedroom door, and whilst she stared at it, she heard the sound of the lock turning. The door opened and Mr Dakin came in, carefully closing the door behind him.

He walked across to her saying quietly:

'Nice work, my dear. You think quickly. How is he?'

With a catch in her voice Victoria said:

'I think he's—he's *dead*.'

She saw the other's face alter, caught just a flash of intense anger, then his face was just as she had seen it the day before—only now it seemed to her that the indecision and flabbiness of the man had vanished, giving place to something quite different.

He bent down—and gently loosened the ragged tunic.

'Very neatly stabbed through the heart,' said Dakin as he straightened up. 'He was a brave lad—and a clever one.'

Victoria found her voice.

'The police came. They said he was a criminal. *Was* he a criminal?'

'No. He wasn't a criminal.'

'Were they—were they the police?'

'I don't know,' said Dakin. 'They may have been. It's all the same.'

Then he asked her:

'Did he say anything—before he died?'

'Yes.'

'What was it?'

'He said Lucifer—and then Basrah. And then after a pause he said a name—a French name it sounded like—but I mayn't have got it right.'

'What did it sound like to you?'

'I think it was Lefarge.'

'Lefarge,' said Dakin thoughtfully.

'What does it all mean?' said Victoria, and added with some dismay: 'And what am I to do?'

'We must get you out of it as far as we can,' said Dakin. 'As for what it's all about, I'll come back and talk to you later. The first thing to do is to get hold of Marcus. It's his hotel and Marcus has a great deal of sense, though one doesn't always realize it in talking to him. I'll get hold of him. He won't have gone to bed. It's only half-past one.

130

He seldom goes to bed before two o'clock. Just attend to your appearance before I bring him in. Marcus is very susceptible to beauty in distress.'

He left the room. As though in a dream she moved over to the dressing-table, combed back her hair, made up her face to a becoming pallor and collapsed on to a chair as she heard footsteps approaching. Dakin came in without knocking. Behind him came the bulk of Marcus Tio.

This time Marcus was serious. There was not the usual smile on his face.

'Now, Marcus,' said Mr Dakin, 'you must do what you can about this. It's been a terrible shock to this poor girl. The fellow burst in, collapsed—she's got a very kind heart and she hid him from the police. And now he's dead. She oughtn't to have done it, perhaps, but girls are soft-hearted.'

'Of course she did not like the police,' said Marcus. 'Nobody likes the police. *I* do not like the police. But I have to stand well with them because of my hotel. You want me to square them with money?'

'We just want to get the body away quietly.'

'That is very nice, my dear. And I, too, I do not want a body in my hotel. But it is, as you say, not so easy to do?'

'I think it could be managed,' said Dakin. 'You've got a doctor in your family, haven't you?'

'Yes, Paul, my sister's husband, is a doctor. He is a very nice boy. But I do not want him to get into trouble.'

'He won't,' said Dakin. 'Listen, Marcus. We move the body from Miss Jones' room across into my room. That lets *her* out of it. Then I use your telephone. In ten minutes' time a young man reels into the hotel from the street. He

131

is very drunk, he clutches at his side. He demands me at the top of his voice. He staggers into my room and collapses. I come out and call you and ask for a doctor. You produce your brother-in-law. He sends for an ambulance and he goes in it with this drunken friend of mine. Before they get to the hospital my friend is dead. He has been stabbed. That is all right for you. He has been stabbed in the street before coming into your hotel.'

'My brother-in-law takes away the body—and the young man who plays the part of the drunkard, he goes away quietly in the morning perhaps?'

'That's the idea.'

'And there is no body found in my hotel? And Miss Jones she does not get any worry or annoyance? I think, my dear, that that is all a very good idea.'

'Good, then if you'll make sure the coast is clear, I'll get the body across to my room. Those servants of yours potter round the corridors half the night. Go along to your room and raise a shindy. Get them all running to fetch you things.'

Marcus nodded and left the room.

'You're a strong girl,' said Dakin. 'Can you manage to help me to carry him across the corridor to my room?'

Victoria nodded. Between them they lifted the limp body, carried it across the deserted corridor (in the distance Marcus' voice could be heard upraised in furious anger) and laid it on Dakin's bed.

Dakin said:

'Got a pair of scissors? Then cut off the top of your underblanket where it's stained. I don't think the stain's gone through to the mattress. The tunic soaked up most of it. I'll come along to you in about an hour. Here, wait a minute, take a pull from this flask of mine.'

Victoria obeyed.

'Good girl,' said Dakin. 'Now go back to your room. Turn out the light. As I said, I'll be along in about an hour.'

'And you'll tell me what it all means?'

He gave her a long rather peculiar stare but did not answer her question.

CHAPTER 14

Victoria lay in bed with her light out, listening through the darkness. She heard sounds of loud drunken altercation. Heard a voice declaring: 'Felt I got to look you up, ole man. Had a row with a fellow outside.' She heard bells ring. Heard other voices. Heard a good deal of commotion. Then came a stretch of comparative silence—except for the far-off playing of Arab music on a gramophone in somebody's room. When it seemed to her as though hours had passed, she heard the gentle opening of her door and sat up in bed and switched on the bedside lamp.

'That's right,' said Dakin approvingly.

He brought a chair up to the bedside and sat down in it. He sat there staring at her in the considering manner of a physician making a diagnosis.

'Tell me what it's all about?' demanded Victoria.

'Suppose,' said Dakin, 'that you tell me all about yourself first. What are you doing here? Why did you come to Baghdad?'

Whether it was the events of the night, or whether it was something in Dakin's personality (Victoria thought

134

afterwards that it was the latter), Victoria for once did not launch out on an inspired and meretricious account of her presence in Baghdad. Quite simply and straightforwardly she told him everything. Her meeting with Edward, her determination to get to Baghdad, the miracle of Mrs Hamilton Clipp, and her own financial destitution.

'I see,' said Dakin when she had finished.

He was silent for a moment before he spoke.

'Perhaps I'd like to keep you out of this. I'm not sure. But the point is, you *can't* be kept out of it! You're in it, whether I like it or not. And as you're in it, you might as well work for *me*.'

'You've got a job for me?' Victoria sat up in bed, her cheeks bright with anticipation.

'Perhaps. But not the kind of job you're thinking of. This is a serious job, Victoria. And it's dangerous.'

'Oh, that's all right,' said Victoria cheerfully. She added doubtfully, 'It's not *dishonest*, is it? Because though I know I tell an awful lot of lies, I wouldn't really like to do anything that was dishonest.'

Dakin smiled a little.

'Strangely enough, your capacity to think up a convincing lie quickly is one of your qualifications for the job. No, it's not dishonest. On the contrary, you are enlisted in the cause of law and order. I'm going to put you in the picture— only in a general kind of way, but so that you can understand fully what it is you are doing and exactly what the dangers are. You seem to be a sensible young woman and I don't suppose you've thought much about world politics which is just as well, because as Hamlet very wisely remarked,

"There is nothing either good or bad, but thinking makes it so".'

'I know everybody says there's going to be another war sooner or later,' said Victoria.

'Exactly,' said Mr Dakin. 'Why does everybody say so, Victoria?'

She frowned. 'Why, because Russia—the Communists—America—' she stopped.

'You see,' said Dakin. 'Those aren't your own opinions or words. They're picked up from newspapers and casual talk, and the wireless. There are two divergent points of view dominating different parts of the world, that is true enough. And they are represented loosely in the public mind as "Russia and the Communists" and "America". Now the only hope for the future, Victoria, lies in peace, in production, in constructive activities and not destructive ones. Therefore everything depends on those who hold those two divergent viewpoints, either agreeing to differ and each contenting themselves with their respective spheres of activity, or else finding a mutual basis for agreement, or at least toleration. Instead of that, the opposite is happening, a wedge is being driven in the whole time to force two mutually suspicious groups farther and farther apart. Certain things led one or two people to believe that this activity comes from a third party or group working under cover and so far absolutely unsuspected by the world at large. Whenever there is a chance of agreement being reached or any sign of dispersal of suspicion, some incident occurs to plunge one side back in distrust, or the other side into definite hysterical fear. These things are *not* accidents, Victoria, they are deliberately produced for a calculated effect.'

'But why do you think so and who's doing it?'

'One of the reasons we think so is because of money. The money, you see, is coming from the wrong sources. Money, Victoria, is always the great clue to what is happening in the world. As a physician feels your pulse, to get a clue to your state of health, so money is the life-blood that feeds any great movement or cause. Without it, the movement can't make headway. Now here, there are very large sums of money involved and although very cleverly and artfully camouflaged, there is definitely something wrong about where the money comes from and where it is going. A great many unofficial strikes, various threats to Governments in Europe who show signs of recovery, are staged and brought into being by Communists, earnest workers for their cause—but the funds for these measures do *not* come from Communist sources, and traced back, they come from very strange and unlikely quarters. In the same way an increasing wave of fear of Communism, of almost hysterical panic, is arising in America and in other countries, and here, too, the funds are not coming from the appropriate quarter—it is not Capitalist money, though it naturally passes through Capitalist hands. A third point, enormous sums of money seem to be going completely out of circulation. As much as though—to put it simply—you spent your salary every week on things—bracelets or tables or chairs—and those things then disappeared or passed out of ordinary circulation and sight. All over the world a great demand for diamonds and other precious stones has arisen.

They change hands a dozen or more times until finally they disappear and cannot be traced.

'This, of course, is only a vague sketch. The upshot is that somewhere a third group of people whose aim is as yet obscure, as fomenting strife and misunderstanding and are engaging in cleverly camouflaged money and jewel transactions for their own ends. We have reason to believe that in every country there are agents of this group, some established there many years ago. Some are in very high and respectable positions, others are playing humble parts, but all are working with one unknown end in view. In substance, it is exactly like the Fifth Column activities at the beginning of the last war, only this time it is on a worldwide scale.'

'But who are these people?' Victoria demanded.

'They are not, we think, of any special nationality. What they want is, I fear, the betterment of the world! The delusion that by force you can impose the Millennium on the human race is one of the most dangerous delusions in existence. Those who are out only to line their own pockets can do little harm—mere greed defeats its own ends. But the belief in a superstratum of human beings—in Supermen to rule the rest of the decadent world—that, Victoria, is the most evil of all beliefs. For when you say, "I am not as other men"—you have lost the two most valuable qualities we have ever tried to attain: humility and brotherhood.'

He coughed. 'Well, I mustn't preach a sermon. Let me just explain to you what we do know. There are various centres of activity. One in the Argentine, one in Canada—certainly one or more in the United States of America, and

I should imagine, though we can't tell, one in Russia. And now we come to a very interesting phenomenon.

'In the past two years, twenty-eight promising young scientists of various nationalities have quietly faded out of their background. The same thing has happened with constructional engineers, with aviators, with electricians and many other skilled trades. These disappearances have this in common: those concerned are all young, ambitious, and all without close ties. Besides those we know of, there must be many many more, and we are beginning to guess at something of what they are accomplishing.'

Victoria listened, her brows drawn together.

'You might say it was impossible in these days for anything to go on in any country unbeknownst to the rest of the world. I do not, of course, mean undercover activities; those may go on anywhere. But anything on a large scale of up-to-date production. And yet there are still obscure parts of the world, remote from trade routes, cut off by mountains and deserts, in the midst of peoples who still have the power to bar out strangers and which are never known or visited except by a solitary and exceptional traveller. Things could go on there the news of which would never penetrate to the outside world, or only as a dim and ridiculous rumour.

'I won't particularize the spot. It can be reached from China—and nobody knows what goes on in the interior of China. It can be reached from the Himalayas, but the journey there, save to the initiated, is hard and long to travel. Machinery and personnel dispatched from all over the globe reaches it after being diverted from its ostensible destination. The mechanics of it all need not be gone into.

'But one man got interested in following up a certain trail. He was an unusual man, a man who has friends and contacts throughout the East. He was born in Kashgar and he knows a score of local dialects and languages. He suspected and he followed up the trail. What he heard was so incredible that when he got back to civilization and reported it he was not believed. He admitted that he had had fever and he was treated as a man who had had delirium.

'Only two people believed his story. One was myself. I never object to believing impossible things—they're so often true. The other—' he hesitated.

'Yes?' said Victoria.

'The other was Sir Rupert Crofton Lee, a great traveller, and a man who had himself travelled through these remote regions and who knew something about their possibilities.

'The upshot of it all was that Carmichael, that's my man, decided to go and find out for himself. It was a desperate and hazardous journey, but he was as well equipped as any man to carry it through. That was nine months back. We heard nothing until a few weeks ago and then news came through. He was alive and he'd got what he went to get. Definite proof.

'But the other side were on to him. It was vital to them that he should never get back with his proofs. And we've had ample evidence of how the whole system is penetrated and infiltrated with their agents. Even in my own department there are leaks. And some of those leaks, Heaven help us, are at a very high level.

'Every frontier has been watched for him. Innocent lives have been sacrificed in mistake for his—they don't set much store by human life. But somehow or other he got through unscathed—until tonight.'

'Then that was who—*he* was?'

'Yes, my dear. A very brave and indomitable young man.'

'But what about the proofs? Did they get those?'

A very slow smile showed on Dakin's tired face.

'I don't think they did. No, knowing Carmichael, I'm pretty sure they didn't. But he died without being able to tell us where those proofs are and how to get hold of them. I think he probably tried to say something when he was dying that should give us the clue.' He repeated slowly, 'Lucifer—Basrah—Lefarge. He'd been in Basrah—tried to report at the Consulate and narrowly missed being shot. It's possible that he left the proofs somewhere in Basrah. What I want you to do, Victoria, is to go there and try to find out.'

'Me?'

'Yes. You've no experience. You don't know what you're looking for. But you heard Carmichael's last words and they may suggest something to you when you get there. Who knows—you may have beginner's luck?'

'I'd love to go to Basrah,' said Victoria eagerly.

Dakin smiled.

'Suits you because your young man is there, eh? That's all right. Good camouflage, too. Nothing like a genuine love affair for camouflage. You go to Basrah, keep your eyes and ears open and look about you. I can't give you any instructions for how to set about things—in fact I'd much rather not. You seem a young woman with plenty of ingenuity of your own. What the words Lucifer and

Lefarge mean, assuming that you heard correctly, I don't know. I'm inclined to agree with you that Lefarge must be a name. Look out for that name.'

'How do I get to Basrah?' said Victoria in a businesslike way. 'And what do I use for money?'

Dakin took out his pocket-book and handed her a wad of paper money.

'That's what you use for money. As for how you get to Basrah, fall into conversation with that old trout Mrs Cardew Trench tomorrow morning, say you're anxious to visit Basrah before you go off to this Dig you're pretending to work at. Ask her about a hotel. She'll tell you at once you must stay at the Consulate and will send a telegram to Mrs Clayton. You'll probably find your Edward there. The Claytons keep open house—everyone who passes through stays with them. Beyond that, I can't give you any tips except one. If—er—anything unpleasant happens, if you're asked what you know and who put you up to what you're doing—don't try and be heroic. Spill the beans at once.'

'Thank you very much,' said Victoria gratefully. 'I'm an awful coward about pain, and if anyone were to torture me I'm afraid I shouldn't hold out.'

'They won't bother to torture you,' said Mr Dakin. 'Unless some sadistic element enters in. Torture's very old-fashioned. A little prick with a needle and you answer every question truthfully without realizing you're doing it. We live in a scientific age. That's why I didn't want you to get grand ideas of secrecy. You won't be telling them anything they don't know already. They'll be wise to me after this evening—bound to be. And to Rupert Crofton Lee.'

'What about Edward? Do I tell him?'

'That I must leave to you. Theoretically, you're to hold your tongue about what you're doing to everybody. Practically!' His eyebrows went up quizzically. 'You can put him in danger, too. There's that aspect of it. Still, I gather he had a good record in the Air Force. I don't suppose danger will worry him. Two heads are often better than one. So he thinks there's something fishy about this "Olive Branch" he's working for? That's interesting—very interesting.'

'Why?'

'Because we think so, too,' said Dakin.

Then he added:

'Just two parting tips. First, if you don't mind my saying so, don't tell too many different kinds of lies. It's harder to remember and live up to. I know you're a bit of a virtuoso, but keep it simple, is my advice.'

'I'll remember,' said Victoria with becoming humility. 'And what's the other tip?'

'Just keep your ears strained for any mention of a young woman called Anna Scheele.'

'Who is she?'

'We don't know much about her. We could do with knowing a little more.'

CHAPTER 15

'Of course you must stay at the Consulate,' said Mrs Cardew Trench. 'Nonsense, my dear—you can't stay at the Airport Hotel. The Claytons will be delighted. I've known them for years. We'll send a wire and you can go down on tonight's train. They know Dr Pauncefoot Jones quite well.'

Victoria had the grace to blush. The Bishop of Llangow, alias the Bishop of Languao was one thing, a real flesh and blood Dr Pauncefoot Jones was quite another.

'I suppose,' thought Victoria guiltily, 'I could be sent to prison for that—false pretences or something.'

Then she cheered herself up by reflecting that it was only if you attempted to obtain money by false statements that the rigours of the law were set in motion. Whether this was really so or not, Victoria did not know, being as ignorant of the law as most average people, but it had a cheering sound.

The train journey had all the fascination of novelty—to Victoria's idea the train was hardly an express—but she had begun to feel conscious of her Western impatience.

A Consular car met her at the station and she was driven

to the Consulate. The car drove in through big gates into a delightful garden and drew up before a flight of steps leading up to a balcony surrounding the house. Mrs Clayton, a smiling energetic woman, came through the swinging wire mesh door to meet her.

'We're so pleased to see you,' she said. 'Basrah's really delightful this time of year and you oughtn't to leave Iraq without seeing it. Luckily there's no one much here just at the moment—sometimes we just don't know where to turn so as to fit people in, but there's no one here now except Dr Rathbone's young man who's quite charming. You've just missed Richard Baker, by the way. He left before I got Mrs Cardew Trench's telegram.'

Victoria had no idea who Richard Baker was—but it seemed fortunate he had left when he did.

'He had been down to Kuwait for a couple of days,' continued Mrs Clayton. 'Now, that's a place you ought to see—before it's spoilt. I dare say it soon will be. Every place gets ruined sooner or later. What would you like first—a bath or some coffee?'

'A bath, please,' said Victoria gratefully.

'How's Mrs Cardew Trench? This is your room and the bathroom's along here. Is she an old friend of yours?'

'Oh no,' said Victoria truthfully. 'I've only just met her.'

'And I suppose she turned you inside out in the first quarter of an hour? She's a terrific gossip as I expect you've gathered. Got quite a mania for knowing all about everybody. But she's quite good company and a really first-class bridge player. Now are you sure you wouldn't like some coffee or something first?'

'No, really.'

'Good—then I'll see you later. Have you got everything you want?'

Mrs Clayton buzzed away like a cheerful bee, and Victoria took a bath, and attended to her face and her hair with the meticulous care of a young woman who is shortly going to be reunited to a young man who has taken her fancy.

If possible, Victoria hoped to meet Edward alone. She did not think that he would make any tactless remarks—fortunately he knew her as Jones and the additional Pauncefoot would probably cause him no surprise. The surprise would be that she was in Iraq at all, and for that Victoria hoped that she could catch him alone even for a bare second or two.

With this end in view, when she had put on a summer frock (for to her the climate of Basrah recalled a June day in London) she slipped out quietly through the wire door and took up her position on the balcony where she could intercept Edward when he arrived back from whatever he was doing—wrestling with the Customs officials, she presumed.

The first arrival was a tall thin man with a thoughtful face, and as he came up the steps Victoria slipped round the corner of the balcony. As she did so, she actually saw Edward entering through a garden door that gave on to the river bend.

Faithful to the tradition of Juliet, Victoria leaned over the balcony and gave a prolonged hiss.

Edward (who was looking, Victoria thought, more attractive than ever) turned his head sharply, looking about him.

'Hist! Up here,' called Victoria in a low voice.

Edward raised his head, and an expression of utter astonishment appeared on his face.

'Good Lord,' he exclaimed. 'It's Charing Cross!'

'Hush. Wait for me. I'm coming down.'

Victoria sped round the balcony, down the steps and along round the corner of the house to where Edward had remained obediently standing, the expression of bewilderment still on his face.

'I can't be drunk so early in the day,' said Edward. 'It *is* you?'

'Yes, it's me,' said Victoria happily and ungrammatically.

'But what are you doing here? How did you get here? I thought I was never going to see you again.'

'I thought so too.'

'It's really just like a miracle. How *did* you get here?'

'I flew.'

'Naturally you flew. You couldn't have got here in time, otherwise. But I mean what blessed and wonderful chance brought you to Basrah?'

'The train,' said Victoria.

'You're doing it on purpose, you little brute. God, I'm pleased to see you. But how did you get here—really?'

'I came out with a woman who'd broken her arm—a Mrs Clipp, an American. I was offered the job the day after I met you, and you'd talked about Baghdad, and I was a bit fed up with London, so I thought, well why not see the world?'

'You really are awfully sporting, Victoria. Where's this Clipp woman, here?'

'No, she's gone to a daughter near Kirkuk. It was only a journey-out job.'

'Then what are you doing now?'

'I'm still seeing the world,' said Victoria. 'But it has required a few subterfuges. That's why I wanted to get at you before we met in public, I mean, I don't want any tactless references to my being a shorthand typist out of a job when you last saw me.'

'As far as I'm concerned you're anything you say you are. I'm ready for briefing.'

'The idea is,' said Victoria, 'that I am Miss Pauncefoot Jones. My uncle is an eminent archaeologist who is excavating in some more or less inaccessible place out here, and I am joining him there shortly.'

'And none of that is true?'

'Naturally not. But it makes quite a good story.'

'Oh yes, excellent. But suppose you and old Pussyfoot Jones come face to face?'

'Pauncefoot. I don't think that is likely. As far as I can make out once archaeologists start to dig, they go on digging like mad, and don't stop.'

'Rather like terriers. I say, there's a lot in what you say. Has he got a real niece?'

'How should I know?' said Victoria.

'Oh, then you're not impersonating anybody in particular. That makes it easier.'

'Yes, after all, a man can have lots of nieces. Or, at a pinch, I could say I'm only a cousin but that I always call him uncle.'

'You think of everything,' said Edward admiringly. 'You

really are an amazing girl, Victoria. I've never met anyone like you. I thought I wouldn't see you again for years, and when I did see you, you'd have forgotten all about me. And now here you are.'

The admiring and humble glance which Edward cast on her caused Victoria intense satisfaction. If she had been a cat she would have purred.

'But you'll want a job, won't you?' said Edward. 'I mean, you haven't come into a fortune or anything?'

'Far from it! Yes,' said Victoria slowly, 'I shall want a job. I went into your Olive Branch place, as a matter of fact, and saw Dr Rathbone and asked him for a job, but he wasn't very responsive—not to a salaried job, that is.'

'The old beggar's fairly tight with his money,' said Edward. 'His idea is that everybody comes and works for the love of the thing.'

'Do you think he's a phoney, Edward?'

'N-o. I don't know exactly what I do think. I don't see how he can be anything but on the square—he doesn't make any money out of the show. So far as I can see all that terrific enthusiasm *must* be genuine. And yet, you know, I don't really feel he's a fool.'

'We'd better go in,' said Victoria. 'We can talk later.'

'I'd no idea you and Edward knew each other,' exclaimed Mrs Clayton.

'Oh we're old friends,' laughed Victoria. 'Only, as a matter of fact, we'd lost sight of each other. I'd no idea Edward was in this country.'

Mr Clayton, who was the quiet thoughtful-looking man Victoria had seen coming up the steps, asked:

'How did you get on this morning, Edward? Any progress?'

'It seems very uphill work, sir. The cases of books are there, all present and correct, but the formalities needed to clear them seem unending.'

Clayton smiled.

'You're new to the delaying tactics of the East.'

'The particular official who's wanted, always seems to be away that day,' complained Edward. 'Everyone is very pleasant and willing—only nothing seems to happen.'

Everyone laughed and Mrs Clayton said consolingly:

'You'll get them through in the end. Very wise of Dr Rathbone to send someone down personally. Otherwise they'd probably stay here for months.'

'Since Palestine, they are very suspicious about bombs. Also subversive literature. They suspect everything.'

'Dr Rathbone isn't shipping bombs out here disguised as books, I hope,' said Mrs Clayton, laughing.

Victoria thought she caught a sudden flicker in Edward's eye, as though Mrs Clayton's remark had opened up a new line of thought.

Clayton said, with a hint of reproof: 'Dr Rathbone's a very learned and well-known man, my dear. He's a Fellow of various important societies and is known and respected all over Europe.'

'That would make it all the easier for him to smuggle in bombs,' Mrs Clayton pointed with irrepressible spirits.

Victoria could see that Gerald Clayton did not quite like this light-hearted suggestion.

He frowned at his wife.

Business being at a standstill during the midday hours, Edward and Victoria went out together after lunch to stroll about and see the sights. Victoria was delighted with the river, the Shatt el Arab, with its bordering of date palm groves. She adored the Venetian look of the high-prowed Arab boats tied up in the canal in the town. Then they wandered into the souk and looked at Kuwait bride-chests studded with patterned brass and other attractive merchandise.

It was not until they turned towards the Consulate and Edward was preparing himself to assail the Customs department once more that Victoria said suddenly:

'Edward, what's your name?'

Edward stared at her.

'What on earth do you mean, Victoria?'

'Your last name. Don't you realize that I don't know it?'

'Don't you? No, I suppose you don't. It's Goring.'

'Edward Goring. You've no idea what a fool I felt going into that Olive Branch place and wanting to ask for you and not knowing anything but Edward.'

'Was there a dark girl there? Rather long bobbed hair?'

'Yes.'

'That's Catherine. She's awfully nice. If you'd said Edward she'd have known at once.'

'I dare say she would,' said Victoria with reserve.

'She's a frightfully nice girl. Didn't you think so?'

'Oh quite . . .'

151

'Not actually good-looking—in fact nothing much to look at, but she's frightfully sympathetic.'

'Is she?' Victoria's voice was now quite glacial—but Edward apparently noticed nothing.

'I don't really know what I should have done without her. She put me in the picture and helped me out when I might have made a fool of myself. I'm sure you and she will be great friends.'

'I don't suppose we shall have the opportunity.'

'Oh yes, you will. I'm going to get you a job in the show.'

'How are you going to manage that?'

'I don't know but I shall manage it somehow. Tell old Rattlebones what a wonderful typist et cetera you are.'

'He'll soon find out that I'm not,' said Victoria.

'Anyway, I shall get you into the Olive Branch somehow. I'm not going to have you beetling round on your own. Next thing I know, you'd be heading for Burma or darkest Africa. No, young Victoria, I'm going to have you right under my eyes. I'm not going to take any chances on your running out on me. I don't trust you an inch. You're too fond of seeing the world.'

'You sweet idiot,' thought Victoria, 'don't you know wild horses wouldn't drive me away from Baghdad!'

Aloud she said: 'Well, it *would* be quite fun to have a job at the Olive Branch.'

'I wouldn't describe it as fun. It's all terribly earnest. As well as being absolutely goofy.'

'And you still think there's something wrong about it?'

'Oh, that was only a wild idea of mine.'

'No,' said Victoria thoughtfully, 'I don't think it was only a wild idea. I think it's true.'

Edward turned on her sharply.

'What makes you say that?'

'Something I heard—from a friend of mine.'

'Who was it?'

'Just a friend.'

'Girls like you have too many friends,' grumbled Edward. 'You are a devil, Victoria. I love you madly and you don't care a bit.'

'Oh yes, I do,' said Victoria. 'Just a little bit.'

Then, concealing her delighted satisfaction, she asked:

'Edward, is there anyone called Lefarge connected with the Olive Branch or with anything else?'

'Lefarge?' Edward looked puzzled. 'No, I don't think so, Who is he?'

Victoria pursued her inquiries.

'Or any one called Anna Scheele?'

This time Edward's reaction was very different. He turned on her abruptly, caught her by the arm and said:

'What do you know about Anna Scheele?'

'Ow! Edward, let go! I don't know anything about her. I just wanted to know if you did.'

'Where did you hear about her? Mrs Clipp?'

'No—not Mrs Clipp—at least I don't think so, but actually she talked so fast and so unendingly about everyone and everything that I probably wouldn't remember if she mentioned her.'

'But what made you think this Anna Scheele had anything to do with the Olive Branch?'

'Has she?'

Edward said slowly, 'I don't know . . . It's all so—so vague.'

They were standing outside the garden door to the Consulate. Edward glanced at his watch. 'I must go and do my stuff,' he said. 'Wish I knew some Arabic. But we've got to get together, Victoria. There's a lot I want to know.'

'There's a lot I want to tell you,' said Victoria.

Some tender heroine of a more sentimental age might have sought to keep her man out of danger. Not so, Victoria. Men, in Victoria's opinion, were born to danger as the sparks fly upwards. Edward wouldn't thank her for keeping him out of things. And, on reflection, she was quite certain that Mr Dakin hadn't intended her to keep him out of things.

At sunset that evening Edward and Victoria walked together in the Consulate garden. In deference to Mrs Clayton's insistence that the weather was wintry Victoria wore a woollen coat over her summer frock. The sunset was magnificent but neither of the young people noticed it. They were discussing more important things.

'It began quite simply,' said Victoria, 'with a man coming into my room at the Tio Hotel and getting stabbed.'

It was not, perhaps, most people's idea of a simple beginning. Edward stared at her and said: 'Getting *what*?'

'Stabbed,' said Victoria. 'At least I think it was stabbed, but it might have been shot only I don't think so because then I would have heard the noise of the shot. Anyway,' she added, 'he was dead.'

'How could he come into your room if he was dead?'

'Oh Edward, don't be stupid.'

Alternately baldly and vaguely, Victoria told her story. For some mysterious reason Victoria could never tell of truthful occurrences in a dramatic fashion. Her narrative was halting and incomplete and she told it with the air of one offering a palpable fabrication.

When she had come to the end, Edward looked at her doubtfully and said, 'You do feel all right, Victoria, don't you? I mean you haven't had a touch of the sun or—a dream, or anything?'

'Of course not.'

'Because, I mean, it seems such an absolutely impossible thing to have happened.'

'Well, it did happen,' said Victoria touchily.

'And all that melodramatic stuff about world forces and mysterious secret installations in the heart of Tibet or Baluchistan. I mean, all that simply *couldn't* be true. Things like that don't *happen*.'

'That's what people always say before they've happened.'

'Honest to God, Charing Cross—are you making all this up?'

'No!' cried Victoria, exasperated.

'And you've come down here looking for someone called Lefarge and someone called Anna Scheele—'

'Whom you've heard of yourself,' Victoria put in. 'You had heard of *her* hadn't you?'

'I'd heard the name—yes.'

'How? Where? At the Olive Branch?'

Edward was silent for some moments, then said:

'I don't know if it means anything. It was just—odd—'

'Go on. Tell me.'

'You see, Victoria. I'm so different from you. I'm not as sharp as you are. I just feel, in a queer kind of way, that things are wrong somehow—I don't know *why* I think so. You spot things as you go along and deduce things from them. I'm not clever enough for that. I just feel vaguely that things are—well—wrong—but I don't know why.'

'I feel like that sometimes, too,' said Victoria. 'Like Sir Rupert on the balcony of the Tio.'

'Who's Sir Rupert?'

'Sir Rupert Crofton Lee. He was on the plane coming out. Very haughty and showing-off. A VIP. *You* know. And when I saw him sitting out on the balcony at the Tio in the sun, I had that queer feeling you've just said of *something* being wrong, but not knowing what it was.'

'Rathbone asked him to lecture to the Olive Branch, I believe, but he couldn't make it. Flew back to Cairo or Damascus or somewhere yesterday morning, I believe.'

'Well, go on about Anna Scheele.'

'Oh, Anna Scheele. It was nothing really. It was just one of the girls.'

'Catherine?' said Victoria instantly.

'I believe it *was* Catherine now I think of it.'

'Of course it was Catherine. That's why you don't want to tell me about it.'

'Nonsense, that's quite absurd.'

'Well, what *was* it?'

'Catherine said to one of the other girls, "When Anna Scheele comes, we can go forward. Then we take our orders from her—and her alone".'

'That's frightfully important, Edward.'

'Remember, I'm not even sure that that was the name,' Edward warned her.

'Didn't you think it queer at the time?'

'No, of course I didn't. I thought it was just some female who was coming out to boss things. A kind of Queen Bee. Are you sure you're not imagining all this, Victoria?'

Immediately he quailed before the glance his young friend gave him.

'All right, all right,' he said hastily. 'Only you'll admit the whole story does sound queer. So like a thriller—a young man coming in and gasping out one word that doesn't mean anything—and then dying. It just doesn't seem *real*.'

'You didn't see the blood,' said Victoria and shivered slightly.

'It must have given you a terrible shock,' said Edward sympathetically.

'It did,' said Victoria. 'And then on top of it, *you* come along and ask me if I'm making it all up.'

'I'm sorry. But you *are* rather good at making things up. The Bishop of Llangow and all that!'

'Oh, that was just girlish *joie de vivre*,' said Victoria. 'This is serious, Edward, really serious.'

'This man, Dakin—is that his name?—impressed you as knowing what he was talking about?'

'Yes, he was very convincing. But, look here, Edward, how do you know—'

A hail from the balcony interrupted her.

'Come in—you two—drinks waiting.'

'Coming,' called Victoria.

Mrs Clayton, watching them coming towards the steps, said to her husband:

'There's something in the wind there! Nice couple of children—probably haven't got a bean between them. Shall I tell you what *I* think, Gerald?'

'Certainly, dear. I'm always interested to hear your ideas.'

'I think that girl has come out here to join her uncle on his Dig simply and solely because of that young man.'

'I hardly think so, Rosa. They were quite astonished to see each other.'

'Pooh!' said Mrs Clayton. '*That's* nothing. *He* was astonished, I dare say.'

Gerald Clayton shook his head at her and smiled.

'She's not an archaeological type,' said Mrs Clayton. 'They're usually earnest girls with spectacles—and very often damp hands.'

'My dear, you can't generalize in that way.'

'And intellectual and all that. This girl is an amiable nitwit with a lot of common sense. *Quite* different. He's a nice boy. A pity he's tied up with all this silly Olive Branch stuff—but I suppose jobs are hard to get. They should find jobs for these boys.'

'It's not so easy, dear, they do try. But you see, they've no training, no experience and usually not much habit of concentration.'

158

Victoria went to bed that night in a turmoil of mixed feelings.

The object of her quest was attained. Edward was found! She shuddered from the inevitable reaction. Do what she might a feeling of anticlimax persisted.

It was partly Edward's disbelief that made everything that had happened seem stagy and unreal. She, Victoria Jones, a little London typist, had arrived in Baghdad, had seen a man murdered almost before her eyes, had become a secret agent or something equally melodramatic, and had finally met the man she loved in a tropical garden with palms waving overhead, and in all probability not far from the spot where the original Garden of Eden was said to be situated.

A fragment of a nursery rhyme floated through her head.

How many miles to Babylon?
Threescore and ten,
Can I get there by candlelight?
Yes, and back again.

But she wasn't back again—she was still in Babylon.

Perhaps she would never get back—she and Edward in Babylon.

Something she had meant to ask Edward—there in the garden. Garden of Eden—she and Edward—Ask Edward—but Mrs Clayton had called—and it had gone out of her head—But she must remember—because it was important—It didn't make sense—Palms—garden—Edward—Saracen Maiden—Anna Scheele—Rupert Crofton Lee—All wrong somehow—And if only she could remember—

A woman coming towards her along a hotel corridor—
a woman in a tailored suit—it was herself—but when the
woman got near she saw the face was Catherine's. Edward
and Catherine—absurd! 'Come with me,' she said to
Edward, 'we will find M. Lefarge—' And suddenly there
he was, wearing lemon yellow kid gloves and a little pointed
black beard.

Edward had gone now and she was alone. She must get
back from Babylon before the candles went out.

And we are for the dark.

Who said that? Violence, terror—evil—blood on a ragged
khaki tunic. She was running—running—down a hotel
corridor. And they were coming after her.

Victoria woke up with a gasp.

'Coffee?' said Mrs Clayton. 'How do you like your eggs?
Scrambled?'

'Lovely.'

'You look rather washed out. Not feeling ill?'

'No, I didn't sleep very well last night. I don't know
why. It's a very comfortable bed.'

'Turn the wireless on, will you, Gerald? It's time for the
news.'

Edward came in just as the pips were sounding.

*'In the House of Commons last night, the Prime Minister
gave fresh details of the cuts in dollar imports.*

*'A report from Cairo announces that the body of Sir
Rupert Crofton Lee has been taken from the Nile.*

(Victoria put down her coffee-cup sharply, and Mrs Clayton uttered an ejaculation.) *Sir Rupert left his hotel after arriving by plane from Baghdad, and did not return to it that night. He had been missing for twenty-four hours when his body was recovered. Death was due to a stab wound in the heart and not to drowning. Sir Rupert was a renowned traveller, was famous for his travels through China and Baluchistan and was the author of several books.'*

'Murdered!' exclaimed Mrs Clayton. 'I think Cairo is worse than any place now. Did you know anything about all this, Gerry?'

'I knew he was missing,' said Mr Clayton. 'It appears he got a note, brought by hand, and left the hotel in a great hurry on foot without saying where he was going.'

'You see,' said Victoria to Edward after breakfast when they were alone together. 'It *is* all true. First this man Carmichael and now Sir Rupert Crofton Lee. I feel sorry now I called him a show-off. It seems unkind. All the people who know or guess about this queer business are being got out of the way. Edward, do you think it will be *me* next?'

'For Heaven's sake don't look so pleased by the idea, Victoria! Your sense of drama is much too strong. I don't see why any one should eliminate you because you don't really *know* anything—but do, please, do, be awfully careful.'

'We'll *both* be careful. I've dragged you into it.'

'Oh, that's all right. Relieves the monotony.'

161

'Yes, but take care of yourself.' She gave a sudden shiver.

'It's rather awful—he was so very much alive—Crofton Lee, I mean—and now he's dead too. It's frightening, really frightening.'

CHAPTER 16

'Find your young man?' asked Mr Dakin.

Victoria nodded.

'Find anything else?'

Rather mournfully, Victoria shook her head.

'Well, cheer up,' said Mr Dakin. 'Remember, in this game, results are few and far between. You might have picked up *something* there—one never knows, but I wasn't in any way counting on it.'

'Can I still go on trying?' asked Victoria.

'Do you want to?'

'Yes, I do. Edward thinks he can get me a job at the Olive Branch. If I keep my ears and eyes open, I might find out something, mightn't I? They know something about Anna Scheele there.'

'Now that's very interesting, Victoria. How did you learn that?'

Victoria repeated what Edward had told her—about Catherine's remark that when 'Anna Scheele came' they would take their orders from her.

'Very interesting,' said Mr Dakin.

'Who *is* Anna Scheele?' asked Victoria. 'I mean, you must know *something* about her—or is she just a name?'

'She's more than a name. She's confidential secretary to an American banker—head of an international banking firm. She left New York and came to London about ten days ago. Since then she's disappeared.'

'Disappeared? She's not *dead*?'

'If so, her dead body hasn't been found.'

'But she *may* be dead?'

'Oh yes, she may be dead.'

'Was she—coming to Baghdad?'

'I've no idea. It would seem from the remarks of this young woman Catherine, that she was. Or shall we say— *is*—since as yet there's no reason to believe she isn't still alive.'

'Perhaps I can find out more at the Olive Branch.'

'Perhaps you can—but I must warn you once more to be very careful, Victoria. The organization you are up against is quite ruthless. I would much rather not have your dead body found floating down the Tigris.'

Victoria gave a little shiver and murmured:

'Like Sir Rupert Crofton Lee. You know that morning he was at the hotel here there was something odd about him—something that surprised me. I wish I could remember what it was . . .'

'In what way—odd?'

'Well—different.' Then in response to the inquiring look, she shook her head vexedly. 'It will come back to me, perhaps. Anyway, I don't suppose it really matters.'

'Anything might matter.'

'If Edward gets me a job, he thinks I ought to get a room like the other girls in a sort of boarding-house or paying guest-place, not stay on here.'

'It would create less surmise. Baghdad hotels are very expensive. Your young man seems to have his head screwed on the right way.'

'Do you want to see him?'

Dakin shook his head emphatically.

'No, tell him to keep right away from me. You, unfortunately, owing to the circumstances on the night of Carmichael's death, are bound to be suspect. But Edward is not linked with that occurrence or with me in any way—and that's valuable.'

'I've been meaning to ask you,' said Victoria. 'Who actually did stab Carmichael? Was it someone who followed him here?'

'No,' said Dakin slowly. 'That couldn't have been so.'

'Couldn't?'

'He came in a *gufa*—one of those native boats—and he wasn't followed. We know that because I had someone watching the river.'

'Then it was someone—in the hotel?'

'Yes, Victoria. And what is more someone in one particular wing of the hotel—for I myself was watching the stairs and no one came up them.'

He watched her rather puzzled face and said quietly:

'That doesn't really give us very many names. You and I and Mrs Cardew Trench, and Marcus and his sisters. A couple of elderly servants who have been here for years. A man called Harrison from Kirkuk against whom nothing is known. A nurse who works at the Jewish Hospital . . . It might be any of them—yet all of them are unlikely for one very good reason.'

'What is that?'

'Carmichael was on his guard. He knew that the peak moment of his mission was approaching. He was a man with a very keen instinct for danger. How did that instinct let him down?'

'Those police that came—' began Victoria.

'Ah, they came *after*—up from the street. They'd had a signal, I suppose. But they didn't do the stabbing. That must have been done by someone Carmichael knew well, whom he trusted . . . or alternatively whom he judged negligible. If I only knew . . .'

Achievement brings with it its own anticlimax. To get to Baghdad, to find Edward, to penetrate the secrets of the Olive Branch: all this had appeared as an entrancing programme. Now, her objective attained, Victoria, in a rare moment of self-questioning, sometimes wondered what on earth she was doing! The rapture of reunion with Edward had come and gone. She loved Edward, Edward loved her. They were, on most days, working under the same roof—but thinking about it dispassionately, what on earth were they doing?

By some means or other, sheer force of determination, or ingenious persuasion, Edward had been instrumental in Victoria's being offered a meagrely-paid job at the Olive Branch. She spent most of her time in a small dark room with the electric light on, typing on a very faulty machine various notices and letters and manifestos of the milk-and water-programme of the Olive Branch activities. Edward had had a hunch there was something wrong about the Olive Branch. Mr Dakin had seemed to agree with that view. She, Victoria, was here to find out what she could, but as far as she could see, there was nothing to find out! The Olive Branch activities dripped with the honey of international peace. Various gatherings were held with orangeade to drink and depressing edibles to go with it, and at these Victoria was supposed to act as quasi-hostess; to mix, to introduce, to promote general good feeling amongst various foreign nationals, who were inclined to stare with animosity at one another and wolf refreshments hungrily.

As far as Victoria could see, there were no under-currents, no conspiracies, no inner rings. All was above board, mild as milk and water, and desperately dull. Various dark-skinned young men made tentative love to her, others lent her books to read which she skimmed through and found tedious. She had, by now, left the Tio Hotel and had taken up her quarters with some other young women workers of various nationalities in a house on the west bank of the river. Amongst these young women was Catherine, and it seemed to Victoria that Catherine watched her with a suspicious eye, but whether this was because Catherine suspected her of being a spy on the activities of the Olive Branch or whether it was the more delicate matter of Edward's affections, Victoria was unable to make up her mind. She rather fancied the latter. It was known that Edward had secured Victoria her job and several pairs of jealous dark eyes looked at her without undue affection.

The fact was, Victoria thought moodily, that Edward was far too attractive. All these girls had fallen for him, and Edward's engaging friendly manner to one and all did nothing to help. By agreement between them, Victoria and Edward were to show no signs of special intimacy. If they were to find out anything worth finding out, they must not be suspected of working together. Edward's manner to her was the same as to any of the other young women, with an added shade of coldness.

Though the Olive Branch itself seemed so innocuous Victoria had a distinct feeling that its head and founder was in a different category. Once or twice she was aware of Dr Rathbone's dark thoughtful gaze resting upon her and though she countered it with her most innocent and kitten-like expression, she felt a sudden throb of something like fear.

Once, when she had been summoned to his presence (for explanation of a typing error), the matter went farther than a glance.

'You are happy working with us, I hope?' he asked.

'Oh yes, indeed, sir,' said Victoria, and added: 'I'm sorry I make so many mistakes.'

'We don't mind mistakes. A soulless machine would be no use to us. We need youth, generosity of spirit, broadness of outlook.'

Victoria endeavoured to look eager and generous.

'You must *love* the work . . . love the object for which

you are working . . . look forward to the glorious future. Are you truly feeling all that, dear child?'

'It's all so new to me,' said Victoria. 'I don't feel I have taken it all in yet.'

'Get together—get together—young people everywhere must get together. That is the main thing. You enjoy your evenings of free discussion and comradeship?'

'Oh! yes,' said Victoria, who loathed them.

'Agreement, not dissension—brotherhood, not hatred. Slowly and surely it is growing—you do feel that, don't you?'

Victoria thought of the endless petty jealousies, the violent dislikes, the endless quarrels, hurt feelings, apologies demanded; and hardly knew what she was expected to say.

'Sometimes,' she said cautiously, 'people are difficult.'

'I know . . . I know . . .' Dr Rathbone sighed. His noble domed forehead furrowed itself in perplexity. 'What is this I hear of Michael Rakounian striking Isaac Nahoum and cutting his lip open?'

'They were just having a little argument,' said Victoria.

Dr Rathbone brooded mournfully.

'Patience and faith,' he murmured. 'Patience and faith.'

Victoria murmured a dutiful assent and turned to leave. Then, remembering she had left her typescript, she came back again. The glance she caught in Dr Rathbone's eye startled her a little. It was a keen suspicious glance, and she wondered uneasily just how closely she was being watched, and what Dr Rathbone really thought about her.

Her instructions from Mr Dakin were very precise. She was to obey certain rules for communicating with him if she had anything to report. He had given her an old faded pink handkerchief. If she had anything to report she was to walk, as she often did when the sun was setting along the river bank, near her hostel. There was a narrow path in front of the houses there for perhaps a quarter of a mile. In one place a big flight of steps led down to the water's edge and boats were constantly being tied up there. There was a rusty nail in one of the wooden posts at the top. Here she was to affix a small piece of the pink handkerchief if she wanted to get into communication with Dakin. So far, Victoria reflected bitterly, there had been no need for anything of the sort. She was merely doing an ill-paid job in a slovenly fashion. Edward she saw at rare intervals, since he was always being sent to far-off places by Dr Rathbone. At the moment, he had just come back from Persia. During his absence, she had had one short and somewhat unsatisfactory interview with Dakin. Her instructions had been to go to the Tio Hotel and ask if she had left a cardigan behind. The answer having been in the negative, Marcus appeared and immediately swept her out on to the river bank for a drink. During the process Dakin had shambled in from the street and had been hailed by Marcus to join them, and presently, as Dakin supped lemonade, Marcus had been called away and the two of them sat there on opposite sides of the small painted table.

Rather apprehensively Victoria confessed her utter lack of success, but Dakin was indulgently reassuring.

'My dear child, you don't even know what you are looking for or even if there is anything to find. Taken by and large what is your considered opinion of the Olive Branch?'

'It's a thoroughly dim show,' said Victoria slowly.

'Dim, yes. But not bogus?'

'I don't know,' said Victoria slowly. 'People are so sold on the idea of culture if you know what I mean?'

'You mean that where anything cultured is concerned, nobody examines *bona fides* in the way they would if it were a charitable or a financial proposition? That's true. And you'll find genuine enthusiasts there, I've no doubt. But is the organization being used?'

'I think there's a lot of Communist activity going on,' said Victoria doubtfully. 'Edward thinks so too—he's making me read Karl Marx and leave it about just to see what reactions there will be.'

Dakin nodded.

'Interesting. Any response so far?'

'No, not yet.'

'What about Rathbone? Is *he* genuine?'

'I think really that he is—' Victoria sounded doubtful.

'He's the one I worry about, you see,' said Dakin. 'Because he's a *big* noise. Suppose there *is* Communist plotting going on—students and young revolutionaries have very little chance of coming into contact with the President. Police measures will look after bombs thrown from the street. But Rathbone's different. He's one of the high-ups, a distinguished man with a fine record of public beneficence. He could come in close contact with the distinguished visitors. He probably will. I'd like to know about Rathbone.'

Yes, Victoria thought to herself, it all centred round Rathbone. On the first meeting in London, weeks ago, Edward's vague remarks about the 'fishiness' of the show had had their origin in his employer. And there must, Victoria decided suddenly, have been some incident, some word, that had awakened Edward's uneasiness. For that, in Victoria's belief, was how minds worked. Your vague doubt or distrust was never just a hunch—it was really always due to a cause. If Edward, now, could be made to think back, to remember; between them they might hit upon the fact or incident that had aroused his suspicions. In the same way, Victoria thought, she herself must try to think back to what it was that had so surprised her when she came out upon the balcony at the Tio and found Sir Rupert Crofton Lee sitting there in the sun. It was true that she had expected him to be at the Embassy and not at the Tio Hotel but that was not enough to account for the strong feeling she had had that his sitting there was quite impossible! She would go over and over the events of that morning, and Edward must be urged to go over and over his early association with Dr Rathbone. She would tell him so when next she got him alone. But to get Edward alone was not easy. To begin with he had been away in Persia and now that he was back, private communications at the Olive Branch were out of the question where the slogan of the last war ('*Les oreilles enemies vous écoutent*') might have been written up all over the walls. In the Armenian household where she was a paying guest, privacy was equally impossible. Really, thought Victoria to herself, for all I see of Edward, I might as well have stayed in England!

That this was not quite true was proved very shortly afterwards.

Edward came to her with some sheets of manuscripts and said:

'Dr Rathbone would like this typed out at once, please, Victoria. Be especially careful of the *second page*, there are some rather tricky Arab names on it.'

Victoria, with a sigh, inserted a sheet of paper in her typewriter and started off in her usual dashing style. Dr Rathbone's handwriting was not particularly difficult to read and Victoria was just congratulating herself that she had made less mistakes than usual. She laid the top sheet aside and proceeded to the next—and at once realized the meaning of Edward's injunction to be careful of the second page. A tiny note in Edward's handwriting was pinned to the top of it.

Go for a walk along the Tigris bank past the Beit Melek Ali tomorrow morning about eleven.

The following day was Friday, the weekly holiday. Victoria's spirits rose mercurially. She would wear her jade-green pullover. She ought really to get her hair shampooed. The amenities of the house where she lived made it difficult to wash it herself. 'And it really needs it,' she murmured aloud.

'What did you say?' Catherine, at work on a pile of circulars and envelopes, raised her head suspiciously from the next table.

Victoria quickly crumpled up Edward's note in her hand as she said lightly:

'My hair wants washing. Most of these hairdressing places look so frightfully dirty, I don't know where to go.'

'Yes, they are dirty and expensive too. But I know a girl who washes hair very well and the towels are clean. I will take you there.'

'That's very kind of you, Catherine,' said Victoria.

'We will go tomorrow. It is holiday.'

'Not tomorrow,' said Victoria.

'Why not tomorrow?'

A suspicious stare was bent upon her. Victoria felt her usual annoyance and dislike of Catherine rising.

'I'd rather go for a walk—get some air. One is so cooped up here.'

'Where can you walk? There is nowhere to walk in Baghdad.'

'I shall find somewhere,' said Victoria.

'It would be better to go to the cinema. Or is there an interesting lecture?'

'No, I want to get out. In England we like going for walks.'

'Because you are English, you are so proud and stuck up. What does it mean to be English? Next to nothing. Here we spit upon the English.'

'If you start spitting on me you may get a surprise,' said Victoria, wondering as usual at the ease with which angry passions seemed to rise at the Olive Branch.

'What would you do?'

'Try and see.'

'Why do you read Karl Marx? You cannot understand it. You are much too stupid. Do you think they would ever accept you as a member of the Communist Party? You are not well enough educated politically.'

'Why shouldn't I read it? It was meant for people like me—workers.'

'You are not a worker. You are bourgeoise. You cannot even type properly. Look at the mistakes you make.'

'Some of the cleverest people can't spell,' said Victoria with dignity. 'And how can I work when you keep talking to me?'

She rattled off a line at break-neck speed—and was then somewhat chagrined to find that as a result of unwittingly depressing the shift key, she had written a line of exclamation marks, figures and brackets. Removing the sheet from the machine she replaced it with another and applied herself diligently until, her task finished, she took the result in to Dr Rathbone.

Glancing over it and murmuring, 'Shiraz is in *Iran* not Iraq—and anyway you don't spell Iraq with a k . . . *Wasit*—not Wuzle—er—thank you, Victoria.'

Then as she was leaving the room he called her back.

'Victoria, are you happy here?'

'Oh yes, Dr Rathbone.'

The dark eyes under the massive brows were very searching. She felt uneasiness rising.

'I'm afraid we do not pay you very much.'

'That doesn't matter,' said Victoria. 'I like to work.'

'Do you really?

'Oh yes,' said Victoria. 'One feels,' she added, 'that this sort of thing is really worthwhile.'

Her limpid gaze met the dark searching eyes and did not falter.

'And you manage—to live?'

'Oh yes—I've found quite a good cheap place—with some Armenians. I'm quite all right.'

'There is a shortage at present of shorthand typists in Baghdad,' said Dr Rathbone. 'I think, you know, that I could get you a better position than the one you have here.'

'But I don't want any other position.'

'You might be *wise* to take one.'

'Wise?' Victoria faltered a little.

'That is what I said. Just a word of warning—of advice.'

There was something faintly menacing now in his tone. Victoria opened her eyes still wider.

'I really don't understand, Dr Rathbone,' she said.

'Sometimes it is wiser not to mix oneself up in things one does not understand.'

She felt quite sure of the menace this time, but she continued to stare in kitten-eyed innocence.

'Why did you come and work here, Victoria? Because of Edward?'

Victoria flushed angrily.

'Of course not,' she said indignantly. She was much annoyed.

Dr Rathbone nodded his head.

'Edward has his way to make. It will be many many years before he is in a position to be of any use to you. I should give up thinking of Edward if I were you. And, as I say, there are good positions to be obtained at present, with a good salary and prospects—and which will bring you amongst your own kind.'

He was still watching her, Victoria thought, very closely. Was this a test? She said with an affectation of eagerness:

'But I really am very keen on the Olive Branch, Dr Rathbone.'

He shrugged his shoulders then and she left him, but she could feel his eyes in the centre of her spine as she left the room.

She was somewhat disturbed by the interview. Had something occurred to arouse his suspicions? Did he guess that she might be a spy placed in the Olive Branch to find out its secrets? His voice and manner had made her feel unpleasantly afraid. His suggestion that she had come there to be near Edward had made her angry at the time and she had vigorously denied it, but she realized now that it was infinitely safer that Dr Rathbone should suppose her to have come to the Olive Branch for Edward's sake than to have even an inkling that Mr Dakin had been instrumental in the matter. Anyway, owing to her idiotic blush, Rathbone probably *did* think that it was Edward—so that all had really turned out for the best.

Nevertheless she went to sleep that night with an unpleasant little clutch of fear at her heart.

CHAPTER 17

It proved fairly simple on the following morning for Victoria to go out by herself with few explanations. She had inquired about the Beit Melek Ali and had learnt it was a big house built right out on the river some way down the West Bank.

So far Victoria had had very little time to explore her surroundings and she was agreeably surprised when she came to the end of the narrow street and found herself actually on the river bank. She turned to her right and made her way slowly along the edge of the high bank. Sometimes the going was precarious—the bank had been eaten away and had not always been repaired or built up again. One house had steps in front of it which, if you took one more, would land you in the river on a dark night. Victoria looked down at the water below and edged her way round. Then, for a while, the way was wide and paved. The houses on her right hand had an agreeable air of secrecy. They offered no hint as to their occupancy. Occasionally the central door stood open and peering inside Victoria was fascinated by the contrasts. On one such occasion she looked into a courtyard with a fountain playing and cushioned seats and deck-chairs round it, with tall palms growing up and a garden beyond, that looked like the backcloth of a stage set. The next house, looking much the same outside, opened on a litter of confusion and dark passages, with five or six dirty children playing in rags. Then she came to palm gardens in thick groves. On her left she had passed uneven steps leading down to the river and an Arab boatman seated in a primitive rowing boat gesticulated and called, asking evidently if she wanted to be taken across to the other side. She must by now, Victoria judged, be just about opposite the Tio Hotel, though it was hard to distinguish differences in the architecture viewed from this side and the hotel buildings looked more or less alike. She came now to a road leading down through the palms and then to two tall houses with balconies. Beyond was a big house built right out on to the river with a garden and balustrade. The path on the bank passed on the inside of what must be the Beit Melek Ali or the House of King Ali.

In a few minutes more Victoria had passed its entrance and had come to a more squalid part. The river was hidden from her by palm plantations fenced off with rusty barbed wire. On the right were tumble-down houses inside rough mud-brick walls, and small shanties with children playing in the dirt and clouds of flies hanging over garbage heaps. A road led away from the river and a car was standing there—a somewhat battered and archaic car. By the car, Edward was standing.

'Good,' said Edward, 'you've got here. Get in.'

'Where are we going?' asked Victoria, entering the

179

battered automobile with delight. The driver, who appeared to be an animate bundle of rags, turned round and grinned happily at her.

'We're going to Babylon,' said Edward. 'It's about time we had a day out.'

The car started with a terrific jerk and bumped madly over the rude paving stones.

'To Babylon?' cried Victoria. 'How lovely it sounds. Really to Babylon?'

The car swerved to the left and they were bowling along upon a well-paved road of imposing width.

'Yes, but don't expect too much. Babylon—if you know what I mean—isn't quite what it was.'

Victoria hummed.

'How many miles to Babylon?
Threescore and ten,
Can I get there by candlelight?
Yes, and back again.

'I used to sing that when I was a small child. It always fascinated me. And now we're really going there!'

'And we'll get back by candlelight. Or we should do. Actually you never know in this country.'

'This car looks very much as though it might break down.'

'It probably will. There's sure to be simply everything wrong with it. But these Iraqis are frightfully good at tying it up with string and saying Inshallah and then it goes again.'

'It's always Inshallah, isn't it?'

'Yes, nothing like laying the responsibility upon the Almighty.'

'The road isn't very good, is it?' gasped Victoria, bouncing in her seat. The deceptively well-paved and wide road had not lived up to its promise. The road was still wide but was now corrugated with ruts.

'It gets worse later on,' shouted Edward.

They bounced and bumped happily. The dust rose in clouds round them. Large lorries covered with Arabs tore along in the middle of the track and were deaf to all intimations of the horn.

They passed walled-in gardens, and parties of women and children and donkeys and to Victoria it was all new and part of the enchantment of going to Babylon with Edward beside her.

They reached Babylon bruised and shaken in a couple of hours. The meaningless pile of ruined mud and burnt brick was somewhat of a disappointment to Victoria, who expected something in the way of columns and arches, looking like pictures she had seen of Baalbek.

But little by little her disappointment ebbed as they scrambled over mounds and lumps of burnt brick led by the guide. She listened with only half an ear to his profuse explanations, but as they went along the Processional Way to the Ishtar Gate, with the faint reliefs of unbelievable animals high on the walls, a sudden sense of the grandeur of the past came to her and a wish to know something about this vast proud city that now lay dead and abandoned. Presently, their duty to Antiquity accomplished, they sat down by the Babylonian Lion to eat the picnic lunch that Edward had brought with him. The guide moved away, smiling indulgently and telling them firmly that they must see the Museum later.

'Must we?' said Victoria dreamily. 'Things all labelled and put into cases don't seem a bit real somehow. I went to the British Museum once. It was awful, and dreadfully tiring on the feet.'

'The past is always boring,' said Edward. 'The future's much more important.'

'This isn't boring,' said Victoria, waving a sandwich towards the panorama of tumbling brick. 'There's a feeling of—of greatness here. What's the poem "*When you were a King in Babylon and I was a Christian Slave*"? Perhaps we were. You and I, I mean.'

'I don't think there were any Kings in Babylon by the time there were Christians,' said Edward. 'I think Babylon stopped functioning somewhere about five or six hundred BC. Some archaeologist or other is always turning up to give lectures about these things—but I really never grasp any of the dates—I mean not until proper Greek and Roman ones.'

'Would you have liked being a King in Babylon, Edward?'

Edward drew a deep breath.

'Yes, I should.'

'Then we'll say you were. You're in a new incarnation now.'

'They understood *how* to be Kings in those days!' said Edward. 'That's why they could rule the world and bring it into shape.'

'I don't know that I should have liked being a slave much,' said Victoria meditatively, 'Christian or otherwise.'

'Milton was quite right,' said Edward. '"Better to reign in Hell than serve in Heaven." I always admired Milton's Satan.'

'I never quite got around to Milton,' said Victoria apologetically. 'But I did go and see *Comus* at Sadler's Wells and it was lovely and Margot Fonteyn danced like a kind of frozen angel.'

'If you were a slave, Victoria,' said Edward, 'I should free you and take you into my harem—over there,' he added gesticulating vaguely at a pile of debris.

A glint came into Victoria's eye.

'Talking of harems—' she began.

'How are you getting on with Catherine?' asked Edward hastily.

'How did you know I was thinking about Catherine?'

'Well, you were, weren't you? Honestly, Viccy, I do want you to become friends with Catherine.'

'Don't call me Viccy.'

'All right, Charing Cross. I want you to become friends with Catherine.'

'How fatuous men are! Always wanting their girl friends to like each other.'

Edward sat up energetically. He had been reclining with his hands behind his head.

'You've got it all wrong, Charing Cross. Anyway, your references to harems are simply silly—'

'No, they're not. The way all those girls glower intensely at you and yearn at you! It makes me mad.'

'Splendid,' said Edward. 'I love you to be mad. But to return to Catherine. The reason I want you to be friends with Catherine is that I'm fairly sure she's the best way of approach to all the things we want to find out. She knows something.'

'You really think so?'

'Remember what I heard her say about Anna Scheele?'

'I'd forgotten that.'

'How have you been getting on with Karl Marx? Any results?'

'Nobody's made a bee-line at me and invited me into the fold. In fact, Catherine told me yesterday the party wouldn't accept me, because I'm not sufficiently politically educated. And to have to read all that dreary stuff—honestly, Edward, I haven't the brains for it.'

'You are not politically aware, are you?' Edward laughed. 'Poor Charing Cross. Well, well, Catherine may be frantic with brains and intensity and political awareness, my fancy is still a little Cockney typist who can't spell any words of three syllables.'

Victoria frowned suddenly. Edward's words brought back to her mind the curious interview she had had with Dr Rathbone. She told Edward about it. He seemed much more upset than she would have expected him to be.

'This is serious, Victoria, really serious. Try and tell me exactly what he said.'

Victoria tried her best to recall the exact words Rathbone had used.

'But I don't see,' she said, 'why it upsets you so.'

'Eh?' Edward seemed abstracted. 'You don't see—But

184

my dear girl, don't you realize that this shows that they've got wise to you. They're warning you off. I don't like it Victoria—I don't like it at all.'

He paused and then said gravely:

'Communists, you know, are very ruthless. It's part of their creed to stick at nothing. I don't want you knocked on the head and thrown into the Tigris, darling.'

How odd, thought Victoria, to be sitting amidst the ruins of Babylon debating whether or not she was likely in the near future to be knocked on the head and thrown into the Tigris. Half closing her eyes she thought dreamily, 'I shall wake up soon and find I'm in London dreaming a wonderful melodramatic dream about dangerous Babylon. Perhaps,' she thought, closing her eyes altogether, 'I am in London . . . and the alarm clock will go off very soon, and I shall get up and go to Mr Greenholtz's office—and there won't be any Edward . . .'

And at that last thought she opened her eyes again hastily to make sure that Edward was indeed really there (and what was it I was going to ask him at Basrah and they interrupted us and I forgot?) and it was not a dream. The sun was glaring down in a dazzling and most un-London-like way, and the ruins of Babylon were pale and shimmering with a background of dark palms and sitting up with his back a little towards her was Edward. How extraordinarily nicely his hair grew down with a little twirl into his neck—and what a nice neck—bronzed red brown from the sun—with no blemishes on it—so many men had necks with cysts or pimples where their collars had rubbed—a neck like Sir Rupert's for instance, with a boil just starting.

Suddenly with a stifled exclamation Victoria sat bolt upright and her daydreams were a thing of the past. She was wildly excited.

Edward turned an inquiring head.

'What's the matter, Charing Cross?'

'I've just remembered,' said Victoria, 'about Sir Rupert Crofton Lee.'

As Edward still turned a blank inquiring look upon her Victoria proceeded to elucidate her meaning which truth to tell, she did not do very clearly.

'It was a boil,' she said, 'on his neck.'

'A boil on his neck?' Edward was puzzled.

'Yes, in the aeroplane. He sat in front of me, you know, and that hood thing he wore fell back and I saw it—the boil.'

'Why shouldn't he have a boil? Painful, but lots of people get them.'

'Yes, yes, of course they do. But the point is that that morning on the balcony he *hadn't.*'

'Hadn't what?'

'Hadn't got a boil. Oh, Edward, do try and take it in. In the aeroplane he had a boil and on the balcony at the Tio he hadn't got a boil. His neck was quite smooth and unscarred—like yours now.'

'Well, I suppose it had gone away.'

'Oh no, Edward, it couldn't have. It was only a day later, and it was just coming up. It couldn't have gone away—not completely without a trace. So you see what it means—yes, it must mean—the man at the Tio wasn't Sir Rupert at all.'

She nodded her head with vehemence. Edward stared at her.

'You're crazy, Victoria. It must have been Sir Rupert. You didn't see any other difference in him.'

'But don't you see, Edward, I'd never really looked at him properly—only at his—well, you might call it general effect. The hat—and the cape—and the swashbuckling attitude. He'd be a very easy man to impersonate.'

'But they'd have known at the Embassy—'

'He didn't stay at the Embassy, did he? He came to the Tio. It was one of the minor secretaries or people who met him. The Ambassador's in England. Besides, he's travelled and been away from England so much.'

'But why—'

'Because of Carmichael, of course. Carmichael was coming to Baghdad to meet him—to tell him what he'd found out. Only they'd never met before. So Carmichael wouldn't know he wasn't the right man—and he wouldn't be on his guard. Of course—it was Rupert Crofton Lee (the false one) who stabbed Carmichael! Oh, Edward, it all fits in.'

'I don't believe a word of it. It's crazy. Don't forget Sir Rupert was killed afterwards in Cairo.'

'That's where it all happened. I know now. Oh Edward, how awful. I saw it happen.'

'You saw it happen—Victoria, are you quite mad?'

'No, I'm not in the least mad. Just listen, Edward. There was a knock on my door—in the hotel in Heliopolis—at least I thought it was on my door and I looked out, but it wasn't—it was one door down, Sir Rupert Crofton Lee's.

It was one of the stewardesses or air hostesses or whatever they call them. She asked him if he would mind coming to the BOAC office—just along the corridor. I came out of my room just afterwards. I passed a door which had a notice with BOAC on it, and the door opened and he came out. I thought then that he had had some news that made him walk quite differently. Do you see, Edward? It was a trap, the substitute was waiting, all ready, and as soon as he came in, they just conked him on the head and the other one came out and took up the part. I think they probably kept him somewhere in Cairo, perhaps in the hotel as an invalid, kept him drugged and then killed him just at the right moment when the wrong one had come back to Cairo.'

'It's a magnificent story,' said Edward. 'But you know, Victoria, quite frankly you are making the whole thing up. There's no corroboration of it.'

'There's the boil—'

'Oh, damn the boil!'

'And there are one or two other things.'

'What?'

'The BOAC notice on the door. It wasn't there later. I remembered being puzzled when I found the BOAC office was on the other side of the entrance hall. That's one thing. And there's another. That air stewardess, the one who knocked at his door. I've seen her since—here in Baghdad—and what's more, at the Olive Branch. The first day I went there. She came in and spoke to Catherine. I thought then I'd seen her before.'

After a moment's silence, Victoria said:

188

'So you must admit, Edward, that it isn't all my fancy.'
Edward said slowly:

'It all comes back to the Olive Branch—and to Catherine. Victoria, all ragging apart, you've got to get closer to Catherine. Flatter her, butter her up, talk Bolshie ideas to her. Somehow or other get sufficiently intimate with her to know who her friends are and where she goes and whom she's in touch with outside the Olive Branch.'

'It won't be easy,' said Victoria, 'but I'll try. What about Mr Dakin. Ought I to tell him about this?'

'Yes, of course. But wait a day or two. We may have more to go on,' Edward sighed. 'I shall take Catherine to Le Select to hear the cabaret one night.'

And this time Victoria felt no pang of jealousy. Edward had spoken with a grim determination that ruled out any anticipation of pleasure in the commission he had undertaken.

Exhilarated by her discoveries, Victoria found it no effort to greet Catherine the following day with an effusion of friendliness. It was so kind of Catherine she said, to have told her of a place to have her hair washed. It needed washing terribly badly. (This was undeniable, Victoria had returned from Babylon with her dark hair the colour of red rust from the clogging sand.)

'It is looking terrible, yes,' said Catherine, eyeing it with a certain malicious satisfaction. 'You went out then in that dust-storm yesterday afternoon?'

'I hired a car and went to see Babylon,' said Victoria.

'It was very interesting, but on the way back, the dust-storm got up and I was nearly choked and blinded.'

'It is interesting, Babylon,' said Catherine, 'but you should go with someone who understands it and can tell you about it properly. As for your hair, I will take you to this Armenian girl tonight. She will give you a cream shampoo. It is the best.'

'I don't know how you keep your hair looking so wonderful,' said Victoria, looking with what appeared to be admiring eyes at Catherine's heavy erections of greasy sausage-like curls.

A smile appeared on Catherine's usually sour face, and Victoria thought how right Edward had been about flattery.

When they left the Olive Branch that evening, the two girls were on the friendliest of terms. Catherine wove in and out of narrow passages and alleys and finally tapped on an unpromising door which gave no sign of hairdressing operations being conducted on the other side of it. They were, however, received by a plain but competent looking young woman who spoke careful slow English and who led Victoria to a spotlessly clean basin with shining taps and various bottles and lotions ranged round it. Catherine departed and Victoria surrendered her mop of hair into Miss Ankoumian's deft hands. Soon her hair was a mass of creamy lather.

'And now if you please . . .'

Victoria bent forward over the basin. Water streamed over her hair and gurgled down the waste-pipe.

Suddenly her nose was assailed by a sweet rather sickly smell that she associated vaguely with hospitals. A wet saturated pad was clasped firmly over her nose and mouth. She struggled wildly, twisting and turning, but an iron grip kept the pad in place. She began to suffocate, her head reeled dizzily, a roaring sound came in her ears . . .

And after that blackness, deep and profound.

CHAPTER 18

When Victoria regained consciousness, it was with a sense of an immense passage of time. Confused memories stirred in her—jolting in a car—high jabbering and quarrelling in Arabic—lights that flashed into her eyes—a horrible attack of nausea—then vaguely she remembered lying on a bed and someone lifting her arm—the sharp agonizing prick of a needle—then more confused dreams and darkness and behind it a mounting sense of urgency . . .

Now at last, dimly, she was herself—Victoria Jones . . . And something had happened to Victoria Jones—a long time ago—months—perhaps years . . . after all, perhaps only days.

Babylon—sunshine—dust—hair—Catherine. Catherine, of course, smiling, her eyes sly under the sausage curls—Catherine had taken her to have her hair shampooed and then—what had happened? That horrible smell—she could still smell it—nauseating—chloroform, of course. They had chloroformed her and taken her—where?

Cautiously Victoria tried to sit up. She seemed to be lying on a bed—a very hard bed—her head ached and felt dizzy—she was still drowsy, horribly drowsy . . . that prick, the prick of a hypodermic, they had been drugging her . . . she was still half-drugged.

Well, anyway they hadn't killed her. (Why not?) So that was all right. The best thing, thought the still half-drugged Victoria, is to go to sleep. And promptly did so.

When next she awakened she felt much more clear-headed. It was daylight now and she could see more clearly where she was.

She was in a small but very high room, distempered a depressing pale bluish grey. The floor was of beaten earth. The only furniture in the room seemed to be the bed on which she was lying with a dirty rug thrown over her and a rickety table with a cracked enamel basin on it and a zinc bucket underneath it. There was a window with a kind of wooden lattice-work outside it. Victoria got gingerly off the bed, feeling distinctly head-achy and queer, and approached the window. She could see through the lattice-work quite plainly and what she saw was a garden with palm trees beyond it. The garden was quite a pleasant one by Eastern standards though it would have been looked down on by an English suburban householder. It had a lot of bright orange marigolds in it, and some dusty eucalyptus trees and some rather wispy tamarisks.

A small child with a face tattooed in blue, and a lot of bangles on, was tumbling about with a ball and singing in a high nasal whine rather like distant bagpipes.

Victoria next turned her attention to the door, which was large and massive. Without much hope she went to it and tried it. The door was locked. Victoria went back and sat on the side of the bed.

Where was she? Not in Baghdad, that was certain. And what was she going to do next?

It struck her after a minute or two that the last question did not really apply. What was more to the point was what was someone else going to do to her? With an uneasy feeling in the pit of the stomach she remembered Mr Dakin's admonition to tell all she knew. But perhaps they had already got all that out of her whilst she was under the drug.

Still—Victoria returned to this one point with determined cheerfulness—she was *alive*. If she could manage to keep alive until Edward found her—what would Edward do when he found she had vanished? Would he go to Mr Dakin? Would he play a lone hand? Would he put the fear of the Lord into Catherine and force her to tell? Would he suspect Catherine at all? The more Victoria tried to conjure up a reassuring picture of Edward in action, the more the image of Edward faded and became a kind of faceless abstraction. How clever was Edward? That was really what it amounted to. Edward was adorable. Edward had glamour. But had Edward got brains? Because clearly, in her present predicament, brains were going to be needed.

Mr Dakin, now, would have the necessary brains. But would he have the impetus? Or would he merely cross off her name from a mental ledger, scoring it through, and writing after it a neat RIP. After all, to Mr Dakin she was merely one of a crowd. They took their chance, and if luck failed, it was just too bad. No, she didn't see Mr Dakin staging a rescue. After all, he had warned her.

And Dr Rathbone had warned her. (Warned her or threatened her?) And on her refusing to be threatened there had not been much delay in carrying out the threat . . .

But I'm still alive, repeated Victoria, determined to look upon the bright side of things.

Footsteps approached outside and there was the grinding of an outsize key in a rusty lock. The door staggered on its hinges and flew open. In the aperture appeared an Arab. He carried an old tin tray on which were dishes.

He appeared to be in good spirits, grinned broadly, uttered some incomprehensible remarks in Arabic, finally deposited the tray, opened his mouth and pointed down his throat and departed relocking the door behind him.

Victoria approached the tray with interest. There was a large bowl of rice, something that looked like rolled-up cabbage leaves and a large flap of Arab bread. Also a jug of water and a glass.

Victoria started by drinking a large glass of water and then fell to on the rice, the bread, and the cabbage leaves which were full of rather peculiar tasting chopped meat. When she had finished everything on the tray she felt a good deal better.

She tried her best to think things out clearly. She had been chloroformed and kidnapped. How long ago? As to that, she had only the foggiest idea. From drowsy memories of sleeping and waking she judged that it was some days ago. She had been taken out of Baghdad—where? There again, she had no means of knowing. Owing to her ignorance of Arabic, it was not even possible to ask questions. She could not find out a place, or a name, or a date.

Agatha Christie

Several hours of acute boredom followed.

That evening her gaoler reappeared with another tray of food. With him this time came a couple of women. They were in rusty black with their faces hidden. They did not come into the room but stood just outside the door. One had a baby in her arms. They stood there and giggled. Through the thinness of the veil their eyes, she felt, were appraising her. It was exciting to them and highly humorous to have a European woman imprisoned here.

Victoria spoke to them in English and in French, but got only giggles in reply. It was queer, she thought, to be unable to communicate with her own sex. She said slowly and with difficulty one of the few phrases she had picked up:

'*El hamdu lillah.*'

Its utterance was rewarded by a delighted spate of Arabic. They nodded their heads vigorously. Victoria moved towards them, but quickly the Arab servant or whatever he was, stepped back and barred her way. He motioned the two women back and went out himself, closing and locking the door again. Before he did so, he uttered one word several times over.

'*Bukra—Bukra . . .*'

It was a word Victoria had heard before. It meant tomorrow.

Victoria sat down on her bed to think things over. Tomorrow? Tomorrow, someone was coming or something was going to happen. Tomorrow her imprisonment would end (or wouldn't it?)—or if it did end, she herself might end too! Taking all things together, Victoria didn't much care for the idea of tomorrow. She felt instinctively that it would be much better if by tomorrow she was somewhere else.

But was that possible? For the first time, she gave this problem full attention. She went first to the door and examined it. Certainly nothing doing there. This wasn't the kind of lock you picked with a hairpin—if indeed she would have been capable of picking *any* lock with a hairpin, which she very much doubted.

There remained the window. The window, she soon found, was a much more hopeful proposition. The wooden lattice-work that screened it was in the final stages of decrepitude. Granted she could break away sufficient of the rotten woodwork to force herself through, she could hardly do so without a good deal of noise which could not fail to attract attention. Moreover, since the room in which she was confined was on an upper floor, it meant either fashioning a rope of some kind or else jumping with every likelihood of a sprained ankle or other injury. In books, thought Victoria, you make a rope of strips of bedclothes. She looked doubtfully at the thick cotton quilt and ragged blanket. Neither of them seemed at all suitable to her purpose. She had nothing with which to cut the quilt in strips, and though she could probably tear the blanket, its condition of rottenness would preclude any possibility of trusting her weight to it.

'Damn,' said Victoria aloud.

She was more and more enamoured of the idea of escape. As far as she could judge, her gaolers were people of very simple mentality to whom the mere fact that she was locked in a room spelt finality. They would not be expecting her to escape for the simple reason that she was a prisoner and could not. Whoever had used the hypodermic on her and presumably brought her here was not now on the premises—of that she was sure. He or she or they were expected '*bukra.*' They had left her in some remote spot in the guardianship of simple folk who would obey instructions but who would not appreciate subtleties, and who were not, presumably, alive to the inventive faculties of a European young woman in imminent fear of extinction.

'I'm getting out of here somehow,' said Victoria to herself.

She approached the table and helped herself to the new supply of food. She might as well keep her strength up. There was rice again and some oranges, and some bits of meat in a bright orange sauce.

Victoria ate everything and then had a drink of water. As she replaced the jug on the table, the table tilted slightly and some of the water went on the floor. The floor in that particular spot at once became a small puddle of liquid mud. Looking at it, an idea stirred in Miss Victoria Jones' always fertile brain.

The question was, had the key been left in the lock on the outside of the door?

The sun was setting now. Very soon it would be dark. Victoria went over to the door, knelt down and peered into the immense keyhole. She could see no light. Now what she needed was something to prod with—a pencil or the end of a fountain pen. How tiresome that her handbag had been taken away. She looked round the room frowning.

The only article of cutlery on the table was a large spoon. That was no good for her immediate need, though it might come in handy later. Victoria sat down to puzzle and contrive. Presently she uttered an exclamation, took off her shoe and managed to pull out the inner leather sole. She rolled this up tightly. It was reasonably stiff. She went back to the door, squatted down and poked vigorously through the keyhole. Fortunately the immense key fitted loosely into the lock. After three or four minutes it responded to the efforts and fell out of the door on the outside. It made little noise falling on the earthen floor.

Now, Victoria thought, I must hurry, before the light goes altogether. She fetched the jug of water and poured a little carefully on a spot at the bottom of the door frame as near as possible to where she judged the key had fallen. Then, with the spoon and her fingers she scooped and scrabbled in the muddy patch that resulted. Little by little, with fresh applications of water from the jug, she scooped out a low trough under the door. Lying down she tried to peer through it but it wasn't easy to see anything. Rolling up her sleeves, she found she could get her hand and part of her arm under the door. She felt about with exploratory fingers and finally the tip of one finger touched something metallic. She had located the key, but she was unable to get her arm far enough to claw it nearer. Her next procedure was to detach the safety-pin which was holding up a torn shoulder strap. Bending it into a hook, she embedded it in a wedge of Arab bread and lay down again to fish. Just as she was ready to cry with vexation the hooked safety-pin caught in the key and she was able to draw it within reach of her fingers and then to pull it through the muddy trough to her side of the door.

Victoria sat back on her heels full of admiration for her own ingenuity. Grasping the key in her muddy hand, she got up and fitted it into the lock. She waited for a moment when there was a good chorus of pi-dogs barking in the near neighbourhood, and turned it. The door yielded to her push and swung open a little way. Victoria peered cautiously through the aperture. The door gave on to another small room with an open door at the end of it. Victoria waited a moment, then tiptoed out and across. This outside room had large gaping holes in the roof and one or two in the floor. The door at the end gave on the top of a flight of rough mud-brick stairs affixed to the side of the house, and which led down to the garden.

That was all Victoria wanted to see. She tiptoed back to her own place of imprisonment. There was little likelihood that anyone would come near her again tonight. She would wait until it was dark and the village or town more or less settled down to sleep and then she would go.

One other thing she noted. A torn shapeless bit of black material lay in a heap near the outside door. It was, she thought, an old *aba* and would come in useful to cover her Western clothes.

How long she waited Victoria did not know. It seemed to her interminable hours. Yet at last the various noises of local human kind died down. The far-off blaring of a gramophone or phonograph stopped its Arab songs, the raucous voices and the spitting ceased, and there was no more far-off women's high pitched squealing laughter; no children's crying.

At last she heard only a far-off howling noise which she took to be jackals, and the intermittent bursts of dog barking which she knew would continue through the night.

'Well, here goes!' said Victoria and stood up.

After a moment's cogitation she locked the door of her prison on the outside and left the key in the lock. Then she felt her way across the outer room, picked up the black heap of material and came out at the top of the mud stairs. There was a moon, but it was still low in the sky. It gave sufficient light for Victoria to see her way. She crept down the stairs, then paused about four steps from the bottom. She was level here with the mudwall that enclosed the garden. If she continued down the stairs she would have to pass along the side of the house. She could hear snoring from the downstairs rooms. If she went along the top of the wall it might be better. The wall was sufficiently thick to walk along.

She chose the latter course and went swiftly and somewhat precariously to where the wall turned at right angles. Here, outside, was what seemed to be a palm garden, and at one point the wall was crumbling away. Victoria found her way there, partly jumped and partly slithered down and a few moments later was threading her way through palm trees towards a gap in the far wall. She came out upon a narrow street of a primitive nature, too small for the passage of a car, but suitable for donkeys. It ran between mud-brick walls. Victoria sped along it as fast as she could.

Now dogs began to bark furiously. Two fawn-coloured

pi-dogs came snarlingly out of a doorway at her. Victoria picked up a handful of rubble and brick and shied a piece at them. They yelped and ran away. Victoria sped on. She rounded a corner and came into what was evidently the main street. Narrow and heavily rutted, it ran through a village of mud-brick houses, uniformly pale in the moonlight. Palms peeped over walls, dogs snarled and barked. Victoria took a deep breath and ran. Dogs continued to bark, but no human being took any interest in this possible night marauder. Soon she came out on a wide space with a muddy stream and a decrepit hump-backed bridge over it. Beyond, the road, or track, lay heading towards what seemed infinite space. Victoria continued to run until she was out of breath.

The village was well behind her now. The moon was high in the sky. To the left and the right and in front of her, was bare stony ground, uncultivated and without a sign of human habitation. It looked flat but was really faintly contoured. It had, as far as Victoria could see, no landmarks, and she had no idea in what direction the track led. She was not learned enough in the stars to know even towards what point of the compass she was heading. There was something subtly terrifying in this large empty waste, but it was impossible to turn back. She could only go on.

Pausing a few moments to get her breath back, and assuring herself by looking back over her shoulder, that her flight had not been discovered, she set forth, walking a steady three and a half miles an hour towards the unknown.

Dawn came at last to find Victoria weary, footsore, and

almost on the verge of hysteria. By noting the light in the sky she ascertained that she was heading roughly southwest, but since she did not know where she was, that knowledge was of little use to her.

A little to the side of the road ahead of her was a kind of small compact hill or knob. Victoria left the track and made her way to the knob, the sides of which were quite steep, and climbed up to the top of it.

Here she was able to take a survey of the country all around and her feeling of meaningless panic returned. For everywhere there was nothing . . . The scene was beautiful in the early morning light. The ground and horizon shimmered with faint pastel shades of apricot and cream and pink on which were patterns of shadows. It was beautiful but frightening. 'I know what it means now,' thought Victoria, 'when anyone says they are alone in the world . . .'

There was a little faint scrubby grass in dark patches here and there and some dry thorn. But otherwise there was no cultivation, and no signs of life. There was only Victoria Jones.

Of the village from which she had fled there were no signs either. The road along which she had come stretched back apparently into an infinity of waste. It seemed incredible to Victoria that she could have walked so far as to have lost the village altogether from view. For a moment she had a panic-stricken yearning to go back. Somehow or other to regain touch with human kind . . .

Then she took herself in hand. She had meant to escape, and had escaped but her troubles were not likely to be at an end simply because she had placed several miles between her and her gaolers. A car, however old and rickety, would make short work of those miles. As soon as her escape was discovered, someone would come in search of her. And how on earth was she going to take cover or hide. There simply wasn't anywhere to hide. She still carried the ragged black *aba* she had snatched up. Now tentatively she wrapped herself in its folds, pulling it down over her face. She had no idea what she looked like because she had no mirror with her. If she took off her European shoes and stockings and shuffled along with bare feet, she might possibly evade detection. A virtuously veiled Arab woman, however ragged and poor, had, she knew, all possible immunity. It would be the height of bad manners for any man to address her. But would that disguise fool Western eyes who might be out in a car looking for her? At any rate, it was the only chance.

She was much too tired to go on at present. She was terribly thirsty too, but it was impossible to do anything about that. The best thing, she decided, was to lie down on the side of this hillock. She could hear a car coming and if she kept herself flattened in to a little ravine which had eroded down the side of the hillock, she could get some idea of who was in the car.

She could take cover by moving round the back of the hillock so as to keep out of sight of the road.

On the other hand, what she badly needed was to get back to civilization, and the only means, as far as she could see, was to stop a car with Europeans in it and ask for a lift.

But she must be sure that the Europeans were the right

Europeans. And how on earth was she to make sure of that?

Worrying over this point, Victoria quite unexpectedly fell asleep, worn out by her long trudge and her general exhaustion.

When she awoke the sun was directly overhead. She felt hot and stiff and dizzy and her thirst was now a raging torment. Victoria gave a groan, but as the groan issued from her dry sore lips, she suddenly stiffened and listened. She heard faintly but distinctly the sound of a car. Very cautiously she raised her head. The car was not coming from the direction of the village but towards it. That meant that it was not in pursuit. It was as yet a small black dot far off on the track. Still lying as much concealed as she could, Victoria watched it come nearer. How she wished she had field-glasses with her.

It disappeared for a few minutes in a depression of landscape, then reappeared surmounting a rise not very far away. There was an Arab driver and beside him was a man in European dress.

'Now,' thought Victoria, 'I've got to decide.' Was this her chance? Should she run down to the road and hail the car to stop?

Just as she was getting ready to do so, a sudden qualm stopped her. Suppose, just suppose, that this was the Enemy?

After all, how could she tell? The track was certainly a very deserted one. No other car had passed. No lorry. Not even a train of donkeys. This car was making, perhaps for the village she had left last night . . .

What should she do? It was a horrible decision to have

to make at a moment's notice. If it was the Enemy, it was the end. But if it wasn't the Enemy, it might be her only hope of survival. Because if she went on wandering about, she would probably die of thirst and exposure. What should she do?

And as she crouched paralysed with indecision, the note of the approaching car changed. It slackened speed, then, swerving, it came off the road and across the stony ground towards the mound on which she squatted.

It had seen her! It was looking for her!

Victoria slithered down the gully and crawled round the back of the mound away from the approaching car. She heard it come to a stop and the bang of the door as someone got out.

Then somebody said something in Arabic. After that, nothing happened. Suddenly, without any warning, a man came into view. He was walking round the mound, about half-way up it. His eyes were bent on the ground and from time to time he stooped and picked something up. Whatever he was looking for, it did not seem to be a girl called Victoria Jones. Moreover, he was unmistakably an Englishman.

With an exclamation of relief Victoria struggled to her feet and came towards him. He lifted his head and stared in surprise.

'Oh please,' said Victoria. 'I'm so glad you've come.'

He still stared.

'Who on earth—' he began. 'Are you English? But—'

With a spurt of laughter, Victoria cast away the enveloping *aba*.

'Of course I'm English,' she said. 'And please, can you take me back to Baghdad?'

'I'm not going to Baghdad. I've just come from it. But what on earth are you doing all alone out here in the middle of the desert?'

'I was kidnapped,' said Victoria breathlessly. 'I went to have my hair shampooed and they gave me chloroform. And when I woke up I was in an Arab house in a village over there.'

She gesticulated towards the horizon:

'In Mandali?'

'I don't know its name. I escaped last night. I walked all through the night and then I hid behind this hill in case you were an Enemy.'

Her rescuer was staring at her with a very odd expression on his face. He was a man of about thirty-five, fair-haired, with a somewhat supercilious expression. His speech was academic and precise. He now put on a pair of pince-nez and stared at her through them with an expression of distaste. Victoria realized that this man did not believe a word of what she was saying.

She was immediately moved to furious indignation.

'It's perfectly true,' she said. 'Every word of it!'

The stranger looked more disbelieving than ever.

'Very remarkable,' he said in a cold tone.

Despair seized Victoria. How unfair it was that whilst she could always make a lie sound plausible, in recitals of stark truth she lacked the power to make herself believed. Actual facts she told badly and without conviction.

'And if you haven't got anything to drink with you, I

shall die of thirst,' she said. 'I'm going to die of thirst anyway, if you leave me here and go on without me.'

'Naturally I shouldn't dream of doing that,' said the stranger stiffly. 'It is most unsuitable for an Englishwoman to be wandering about alone in the wilds. Dear me, your lips are quite cracked . . . Abdul.'

'Sahib?'

The driver appeared round the side of the mound.

On receiving instructions in Arabic he ran off towards the car to return shortly with a large Thermos flask and a bakelite cup.

Victoria drank water avidly.

'Oo!' she said. 'That's better.'

'My name's Richard Baker,' said the Englishman.

Victoria responded.

'I'm Victoria Jones,' she said. And then, in an effort to recover lost ground and to replace the disbelief she saw by a respectful attention, she added:

'Pauncefoot Jones. I'm joining my uncle, Dr Pauncefoot Jones on his excavation.'

'What an extraordinary coincidence,' said Baker, staring at her surprisedly. 'I'm on my way to the Dig myself. It's only about fifteen miles from here. I'm just the right person to have rescued you, aren't I?'

To say that Victoria was taken aback is to put it mildly. She was completely flabbergasted. So much so that she was quite incapable of saying a word of any kind. Meekly and in silence she followed Richard to the car and got in.

'I suppose you're the anthropologist,' said Richard, as

he settled her in the back seat and removed various impedimenta. 'I heard you were coming out, but I didn't expect you so early in the season.'

He stood for a moment sorting through various potsherds which he removed from his pockets and which, Victoria now realized, were what he had been picking up from the surface of the mound.

'Likely looking little *Tell*,' he said, gesturing towards the mound. 'But nothing out of the way on it so far as I can see. Late Assyrian ware mostly—a little Parthian, some quite good ring bases of the Kassite period.' He smiled as he added, 'I'm glad to see that in spite of your troubles your archaeological instincts led you to examine a *Tell*.'

Victoria opened her mouth and then shut it again. The driver let in the clutch and they started off.

What, after all, could she say? True, she would be unmasked as soon as they reached the Expedition House— but it would be infinitely better to be unmasked there and confess penitence for her inventions, than it would be to confess to Mr Richard Baker in the middle of nowhere. The worst they could do to her would be to send her into Baghdad. And, anyway, thought Victoria, incorrigible as ever, perhaps before I get there I shall have thought of something. Her busy imagination got to work forthwith. A lapse of memory? She had travelled out with a girl who had asked her to—no, really, as far as she could see, she would have to make a complete breast of it. But she infinitely preferred making a clean breast of it to Dr Pauncefoot Jones whatever kind of man he was, than to Mr Richard

Baker, with his supercilious way of lifting his eyebrows and his obvious disbelief of the exact and true story she had told him.

'We don't go right into Mandali,' said Mr Baker, turning in the front seat. 'We branch off from the road into the desert about a mile farther on. A bit difficult to hit the exact spot sometimes with no particular landmarks.'

Presently he said something to Abdul and the car turned sharply off the track and made straight for the desert. With no particular landmarks to guide him, as far as Victoria could see, Richard Baker directed Abdul with gestures—the car now to the right—now to the left. Presently Richard gave an exclamation of satisfaction.

'On the right track now,' he said.

Victoria could not see any track at all. But presently she did catch sight every now and again of faintly marked tyre tracks.

Once they crossed a slightly more clearly marked track and when they did so, Richard made an exclamation and ordered Abdul to stop.

'Here's an interesting sight for you,' he said to Victoria. 'Since you're new to this country you won't have seen it before.'

Two men were advancing towards the car along the cross track. One man carried a short wooden bench on his back, the other a big wooden object about the size of an upright piano.

Richard hailed them, they greeted him with every sign of pleasure. Richard produced cigarettes and a cheerful party spirit seemed to be developing.

Then Richard turned to her.

'Fond of the cinema? Then you shall see a performance.'

He spoke to the two men and they smiled with pleasure. They set up the bench and motioned to Victoria and Richard to sit on it. Then they set up the round contrivance on a stand of some kind. It had two eye-holes in it and as she looked at it, Victoria cried:

'It's like things on piers. *What the butler saw.*'

'That's it,' said Richard. 'It's a primitive form of same.'

Victoria applied her eyes to the glass-fronted peephole, one man began slowly to turn a crank or handle, and the other began a monotonous kind of chant.

'What is he saying?' Victoria asked.

Richard translated as the sing-song chant continued:

'Draw near and prepare yourself for much wonder and delight. Prepare to behold the wonders of antiquity.'

A crudely coloured picture of Negroes reaping wheat swam into Victoria's gaze.

'Fellahin in America,' announced Richard, translating.

Then came:

'The wife of the great Shah of the Western world,' and the Empress Eugénie simpered and fingered a long ringlet. A picture of the King's Palace in Montenegro, another of the Great Exhibition.

An odd and varied collection of pictures followed each other, all completely unrelated and sometimes announced in the strangest terms.

The Prince Consort, Disraeli, Norwegian Fjords and Skaters in Switzerland completed this strange glimpse of olden far-off days.

The showman ended his exposition with the following words:

'And so we bring to you the wonders and marvels of antiquity in other lands and far-off places. Let your donation be generous to match the marvels you have seen, for all these things are true.'

It was over. Victoria beamed with delight. 'That really was *marvellous*!' she said. 'I wouldn't have believed it.'

The proprietors of the travelling cinema were smiling proudly. Victoria got up from the bench and Richard who was sitting on the other end of it was thrown to the ground in a somewhat undignified posture. Victoria apologized but was not ill pleased. Richard rewarded the cinema men and with courteous farewells and expressions of concern for each other's welfare, and invoking the blessing of God on each other, they parted company. Richard and Victoria got into the car again and the men trudged away into the desert.

'Where are they going?' asked Victoria.

'They travel all over the country. I met them first in Transjordan coming up the road from the Dead Sea to Amman. Actually they're bound now for Kerbela, going of course by unfrequented routes so as to give shows in remote villages.'

'Perhaps someone will give them a lift?'

Richard laughed.

'They probably wouldn't take it. I offered an old man a lift once who was walking from Basrah to Baghdad. I asked him how long he expected to be and he said a couple of months. I told him to get in and he would be there late that evening, but he thanked me and said no. Two months ahead would suit him just as well. Time doesn't mean anything out here. Once one gets that into one's head, one finds a curious satisfaction in it.'

'Yes. I can imagine that.'

'Arabs find our Western impatience for doing things quickly extraordinarily hard to understand, and our habit of coming straight to the point in conversation strikes them as extremely ill-mannered. You should always sit round and offer general observations for about an hour—or if you prefer it, you need not speak at all.'

'Rather odd if we did that in offices in London. One would waste a lot of time.'

'Yes, but we're back again at the question: What is time? And what is waste?'

Victoria meditated on these points. The car still appeared to be proceeding to nowhere with the utmost confidence.

'Where is this place?' she said at last.

'Tell Aswad? Well out in the middle of the desert. You'll see the Ziggurat very shortly now. In the meantime, look over to your left. There—where I'm pointing.'

'Are they clouds?' asked Victoria. 'They can't be *mountains*.'

'Yes, they are. The snow-capped mountains of Kurdistan. You can only see them when it's very clear.'

A dream-like feeling of contentment came over Victoria. If only she could drive on like this for ever. If only she wasn't such a miserable liar. She shrank like a child at the thought of the unpleasant denouement ahead of her. What would Dr Pauncefoot Jones be like? Tall, with a long grey beard,

and a fierce frown. Never mind, however annoyed Dr
Pauncefoot Jones might be, she had circumvented Catherine
and the Olive Branch and Dr Rathbone.

'There you are,' said Richard.

He pointed ahead. Victoria made out a kind of pimple
on the far horizon.

'It looks miles away.'

'Oh no, it's only a few miles now. You'll see.'

And indeed the pimple developed with astonishing
rapidity into first a blob and then a hill and finally into a
large and impressive *Tell*. On one side of it was a long
sprawling building of mud-brick.

'The Expedition House,' said Richard.

They drew up with a flourish amidst the barking of
dogs. White robed servants rushed out to greet them,
beaming with smiles.

After an interchange of greetings, Richard said:

'Apparently they weren't expecting you so soon. But
they'll get your bed made. And they'll take you in hot
water at once. I expect you'd like to have a wash and a
rest? Dr Pauncefoot Jones is up on the *Tell*. I'm going up
to him. Ibrahim will look after you.'

He strode away and Victoria followed the smiling
Ibrahim into the house. It seemed dark inside at first after
coming in out of the sun. They passed through a living-
room with some big tables and a few battered armchairs
and she was then led round a courtyard and into a small
room with one tiny window. It held a bed, a rough chest
of drawers and a table with a jug and basin on it and a
chair. Ibrahim smiled and nodded and brought her a large

jug of rather muddy-looking hot water and a rough towel. Then, with an apologetic smile, he returned with a small looking-glass which he carefully affixed upon a nail on the wall.

Victoria was thankful to have the chance of a wash. She was just beginning to realize how utterly weary and worn out she was and how very much encrusted with grime.

'I suppose I look simply frightful,' she said to herself and approached the looking-glass.

For some moments she stared at her reflection uncomprehendingly.

This wasn't her—this wasn't Victoria Jones.

And then she realized that, though her features were the small neat features of Victoria Jones, her hair was now platinum blonde!

CHAPTER 19

Richard found Dr Pauncefoot Jones in the excavations squatting by the side of his foreman and tapping gently with a small pick at a section of wall.

Dr Pauncefoot Jones greeted his colleague in a matter of fact manner.

'Hallo, Richard my boy, so you've turned up. I had an idea you were arriving on Tuesday. I don't know why.'

'This is Tuesday,' said Richard.

'Is it really now?' said Dr Pauncefoot Jones without interest. 'Just come down here and see what you think of this. Perfectly good walls coming out already and we're only down three feet. Seems to me there are a few traces of paint here. Come and see what you think. It looks very promising to me.'

Richard leapt down into the trench and the two archaeologists enjoyed themselves in a highly technical manner for about a quarter of an hour.

'By the way,' said Richard, 'I've brought a girl.'

'Oh have you? What sort of girl?'

'She says she's your niece.'

'My niece?' Dr Pauncefoot Jones brought his mind back with a struggle from his contemplation of mud-brick walls. 'I don't think I have a niece,' he said doubtfully, as though he might have had one and forgotten about her.

'She's coming out to work with you here, I gathered.'

'Oh.' Dr Pauncefoot Jones' face cleared. 'Of course. That will be Veronica.'

'Victoria, I think she said.'

'Yes, yes, Victoria. Emerson wrote to me about her from Cambridge. A very able girl, I understand. An anthropologist. Can't think why anyone wants to be an anthropologist, can you?'

'I heard you had some anthropologist girl coming out.'

'There's nothing in her line so far. Of course we're only just beginning. Actually I understood she wasn't coming out for another fortnight or so, but I didn't read her letter very carefully, and then I mislaid it, so I didn't really remember what she said. My wife arrives next week— or the week after—now what have I done with *her* letter?—and I rather thought Venetia was coming out with her—but of course I may have got it all wrong. Well, well, I dare say we can make her useful. There's a lot of pottery coming up.'

'There's nothing odd about her, is there?'

'Odd?' Dr Pauncefoot Jones peered at him. 'In what way?'

'Well, she hasn't had a nervous breakdown or anything?'

'Emerson did say, I remember, that she had been working very hard. Diploma or degree or something, but I don't think he said anything about a breakdown. Why?'

'Well, I picked up her up at the side of the road, wandering about all by herself. It was on that little *Tell* as a matter of fact that you come to about a mile before you turn off the road—'

'I remember,' said Dr Pauncefoot Jones. 'You know I once picked up a bit of Nuzu ware on that *Tell*. Extraordinary really, to find it so far south.'

Richard refused to be diverted to archaeological topics and went on firmly:

'She told me the most extraordinary story. Said she'd gone to have her hair shampooed, and they chloroformed her and kidnapped her and carried her off to Mandali and imprisoned her in a house and she'd escaped in the middle of the night—the most preposterous rigmarole you ever heard.'

Dr Pauncefoot Jones shook his head.

'Doesn't sound at all probable,' he said. 'Country's perfectly quiet and well policed. It's never been safer.'

'Exactly. She'd obviously made the whole thing up. That's why I asked if she'd had a breakdown. She must be one of those hysterical girls who say curates are in love with them, or that doctors assault them. She may give us a lot of trouble.'

'Oh, I expect she'll calm down,' said Dr Pauncefoot Jones optimistically. 'Where is she now?'

'I left her to have a wash and brush up.' He hesitated. 'She hasn't got any luggage of any kind with her.'

'Hasn't she? That really is awkward. You don't think she'll expect me to lend her pyjamas? I've only got two pairs and one of them is badly torn.'

'She'll have to do the best she can until the lorry goes in next week. I must say I wonder what she can have been up to—all alone and out in the blue.'

'Girls are amazing nowadays,' said Dr Pauncefoot Jones vaguely. 'Turn up all over the place. Great nuisance when you want to get on with things. This place is far enough out, you'd think, to be free of visitors, but you'd be surprised how cars and people turn up when you can least do with them. Dear me, the men have stopped work. It must be lunch-time. We'd better go back to the house.'

Victoria, waiting in some trepidation, found Dr Pauncefoot Jones wildly far from her imaginings. He was a small rotund man with a semi-bald head and a twinkling eye. To her utter amazement he came towards her with outstretched hands.

'Well, well, Venetia—I mean Victoria,' he said. 'This is quite a surprise. Got it into my head you weren't arriving until next month. But I'm delighted to see you. Delighted. How's Emerson? Not troubled too much by asthma, I hope?'

Victoria rallied her scattered senses and said cautiously that the asthma hadn't been too bad.

'Wraps his throat up too much,' said Dr Pauncefoot Jones. 'Great mistake. I told him so. All these academic fellows who stick around universities get far too absorbed in their health. Shouldn't think about it—that's the way to keep fit. Well, I hope you'll settle down—my wife will be out next week—or the week after—she's been seedy, you know. I really *must* find her letter. Richard tells me your luggage has gone astray. How are you going to manage? Can't very well send the lorry in before next week?'

'I expect I can manage until then,' said Victoria. 'In fact I shall have to.'

Dr Pauncefoot Jones chuckled.

'Richard and I can't lend you much. Toothbrush will be all right. There are a dozen of them in our stores—and cotton wool if that's any good to you and—let me see—talcum powder—and some spare socks and handerchiefs. Not much else, I'm afraid.'

'I shall be all right,' said Victoria and smiled happily.

'No signs of a cemetery for you,' Dr Pauncefoot Jones warned her. 'Some nice walls coming up—and quantities of potsherds from the far trenches. Might get some joins. We'll keep you busy somehow or other. I forget if you do photography?'

'I know something about it,' said Victoria cautiously, relieved by a mention of something that she did actually have a working knowledge of.

'Good, good. You can develop negatives? I'm old-fashioned—use plates still. The dark-room is rather primitive. You young people who are used to all the gadgets, often find these primitive conditions rather upsetting.'

'I shan't mind,' said Victoria.

From the Expedition's stores, she selected a toothbrush, toothpaste, a sponge and some talcum powder.

Her head was still in a whirl as she tried to understand exactly what her position was. Clearly she was being mistaken for a girl called Venetia Someone who was coming out to join the Expedition and who was an anthropologist. Victoria didn't even know what an anthropologist was. If there was a dictionary somewhere about, she must look it up. The other girl was presumably not arriving for at least another week. Very well then, for a week—or until such time as the car or lorry went into Baghdad, Victoria would be Venetia Thingummy, keeping her end up as best she could. She had no fears for Dr Pauncefoot Jones who seemed delightfully vague, but she was nervous of Richard Baker. She disliked the speculative way he looked at her, and she had an idea that unless she was careful he would soon see through her pretences. Fortunately she had been, for a brief period, a secretary typist at the Archaeological Institute in London, and she had a smattering of phrases and odds and ends that would be useful now. But she would have to be very careful not to make any real slip. Luckily, thought Victoria, men were always so superior about women that any slip she did make would be treated less as a suspicious circumstance than as a proof of how ridiculously addle-pated all women were!

This interval would give her a respite which, she felt, she badly needed. For, from the point of view of the Olive Branch, her complete disappearance would be very disconcerting. She had escaped from her prison, but what had happened to her afterwards would be very hard to trace. Richard's car had not passed through Mandali so that nobody could guess she was now at Tell Aswad. No, from their point of view, Victoria would seem to have vanished into thin air. They might conclude, very possibly they would conclude, that she was dead. That she had strayed into the desert and died of exhaustion.

Well, let them think so. Regrettably, of course, Edward would think so, too! Very well, Edward must lump it. In any case he would not have to lump it long. Just when he was torturing himself with remorse for having told her to cultivate Catherine's society—there she would be—suddenly restored to him—back from the dead—only a blonde instead of a brunette.

That brought her back to the mystery of why They (whoever they were) had dyed her hair. There must, Victoria thought, be some reason—but she could not for the life of her understand what the reason could be. As it was, she was soon going to look very peculiar when her hair started growing out black at the roots. A phony platinum blonde, with no face powder and no lipstick! Could any girl be more unfortunately placed? Never mind, thought Victoria, I'm alive, aren't I? And I don't see at all why I shouldn't enjoy myself a good deal—at any rate for a week. It was really great fun to be on an archaeological expedition and see what it was like. If only she could keep her end up and not give herself away.

She did not find her role altogether easy. References to people, to publications, to styles of architecture and categories of pottery had to be dealt with cautiously. Fortunately a good listener is always appreciated. Victoria was an excellent listener to the two men, and warily feeling her way, she began to pick up the jargon fairly easily.

Surreptitiously, she read furiously when she was alone in the house. There was a good library of archaeological publications. Victoria was quick to pick up a smattering of the subject. Unexpectedly, she found the life quite enchanting. Tea brought to her in the early morning, then out on the Dig. Helping Richard with camera work. Piecing together and sticking up pottery. Watching the men at work, appreciating the skill and delicacy of the pick men— enjoying the songs and laughter of the little boys who ran to empty their baskets of earth on the dump. She mastered the periods, realized the various levels where digging was going on, and familiarized herself with the work of the previous season. The only thing she dreaded was that burials might turn up. Nothing that she read gave her any idea of what would be expected of her as a working anthropologist! 'If we do get bones or a grave,' said Victoria to herself, 'I shall have to have a frightful cold—no, a severe bilious attack—and take to my bed.'

But no graves did appear. Instead, the walls of a palace were slowly excavated. Victoria was fascinated and had no occasion to show any aptitude or special skill.

Richard Baker still looked at her quizzically sometimes and she sensed his unspoken criticism, but his manner was pleasant and friendly, and he was genuinely amused by her enthusiasm.

'It's all new to you coming out from England,' he said one day. 'I remember how thrilled I was my first season.'

'How long ago was that?'

He smiled.

'Rather a long time. Fifteen—no, sixteen years ago.'

'You must know this country very well.'

'Oh, it's not only been here. Syria—and Persia as well.'

223

Agatha Christie

'You talk Arabic very well, don't you. If you were dressed as one could you pass as an Arab?'

He shook his head.

'Oh no—that takes some doing. I doubt if any Englishman has ever been able to pass as an Arab—for any length of time, that is.'

'Lawrence?'

'I don't think Lawrence ever passed as an Arab. No, the only man I know who is practically indistinguishable from the native product is a fellow who was actually born out in these parts. His father was Consul at Kashgar and other wild spots. He talked all kinds of outlandish dialects as a child and, I believe, kept them up later.'

'What happened to him?'

'I lost sight of him after we left school. We were at school together. Fakir, we used to call him, because he could sit perfectly still and go into a queer sort of trance. I don't know what he's doing now—though actually I could make a pretty good guess.'

'You never saw him after school?'

'Strangely enough, I ran into him only the other day—at Basrah, it was. Rather a queer business altogether.'

'Queer?'

'Yes. I didn't recognize him. He was got up as an Arab, *keffiyah* and striped robe and an old army coat. He had a string of those amber beads they carry sometimes and he was clicking it through his fingers in the orthodox way— only, you see, he was actually using army code. Morse. He was clicking out a message—to *me*!'

'What did it say?'

224

'My name—or nickname, rather—and his, and then a signal to stand by, expecting trouble.'

'And was there trouble?'

'Yes. As he got up and started out of the door, a quiet inconspicuous commercial traveller sort of fellow tugged out a revolver. I knocked his arm up—and Carmichael got away.'

'Carmichael?'

He switched his head round quickly at her tone.

'That was his real name. Why—do you know him?'

Victoria thought to herself—How odd it would sound if I said: 'He died in my bed.'

'Yes,' she said slowly. 'I knew him.'

'*Knew* him? Why—is he—'

Victoria nodded.

'Yes,' she said. 'He's dead.'

'When did he die?'

'In Baghdad. In the Tio Hotel.' She added quickly, 'It was—hushed up. Nobody knows.'

He nodded his head slowly.

'I see. It was that kind of business. But you—' He looked at her. 'How did you know?'

'I got mixed up in it—by accident.'

He gave her a long considering look.

Victoria asked suddenly:

'Your nickname at school wasn't Lucifer, was it?'

He looked surprised.

'Lucifer, no? I was called Owl—because I always had to wear shiny glasses.'

'You don't know any one who is called Lucifer—in Basrah?'

Richard shook his head.

'Lucifer, Son of the Morning—the fallen Angel.'

He added: 'Or an old-fashioned wax match. Its merit if I remember rightly, was that it didn't go out in a wind.'

He watched her closely as he spoke, but Victoria was frowning.

'I wish you'd tell me,' she said presently, 'exactly what happened at Basrah.'

'I have told you.'

'No. I mean where were you when all this occurred?'

'Oh I see. Actually it was in the waiting-room of the Consulate. I was waiting to see Clayton, the Consul.'

'And who else was there? This commercial traveller person and Carmichael? Any one else?'

'There were a couple of others, a thin dark Frenchman or Syrian, and an old man—a Persian, I should say.'

'And the commercial traveller got the revolver out and you stopped him, and Carmichael got out—how?'

'He turned first towards the Consul's office. It's at the other end of a passage with a garden—'

She interrupted.

'I know. I stayed there for a day or two. As a matter of fact, it was just after you left.'

'It was, was it?' Once again he watched her narrowly— but Victoria was unaware of it. She was seeing the long passage at the Consulate, but with the door open at the other end—opening on to green trees and sunlight.

'Well, as I was saying, Carmichael headed that way first. Then he wheeled round and dashed the other way into the street. That's the last I saw of him.'

'What about the commercial traveller?'

Richard shrugged his shoulders.

'I understand he told some garbled story about having been attacked and robbed by a man the night before and fancying he had recognized his assailant in the Arab in the Consulate. I didn't hear much more about it because I flew on to Kuwait.'

'Who was staying at the Consulate just then?' Victoria asked.

'A fellow called Crosbie—one of the oil people. Nobody else. Oh yes, I believe there was someone else down from Baghdad, but I didn't meet him. Can't remember his name.'

'Crosbie,' thought Victoria. She remembered Captain Crosbie, his short stocky figure, his staccato conversation. A very ordinary person. A decent soul without much *finesse* about him. And Crosbie had been back in Baghdad the night when Carmichael came to the Tio. Could it be because he had seen *Crosbie* at the other end of the passage, silhouetted against the sunlight, that Carmichael had turned so suddenly and made for the street instead of attempting to reach the Consul General's office?

She had been thinking this out in some absorption. She started rather guiltily when she looked up to find Richard Baker watching her with close attention.

'Why do you want to know all this?' he asked.

'I'm just interested.'

'Any more questions?'

Victoria asked:

'Do you know anybody called Lefarge?'

'No—I can't say I do. Man or woman?'

227

'I don't know.'

She was wondering about Crosbie. Crosbie? Lucifer? Did Lucifer equal Crosbie?

That evening, when Victoria had said good night to the two men and gone to bed, Richard said to Dr Pauncefoot Jones:

'I wonder if I might have a look at that letter from Emerson. I'd like to see just exactly what he said about this girl.'

'Of course, my dear fellow, of course. It's somewhere lying around. I made some notes on the back of it, I remember. He spoke very highly of Veronica, if I remember rightly—said she was terrifically keen. She seems to me a charming girl—quite charming. Very plucky the way she's made so little fuss about the loss of her luggage. Most girls would have insisted on being motored into Baghdad the very next day to buy a new outfit. She's what I call a sporting girl. By the way, how *was* it that she came to lose her luggage?'

'She was chloroformed, kidnapped, and imprisoned in a native house,' said Richard impassively.

'Dear, dear, yes so you told me. I remember now. All *most* improbable. Reminds me—now what does it remind me of ?—ah! yes, Elizabeth Canning, of course. You remember she turned up with a most impossible story after being missing a fortnight. Very interesting conflict of evidence—about some gypsies, if it's the right case I'm thinking of. And she was such a plain girl, it didn't seem likely there could be a man in the case. Now little Victoria—Veronica—I never *can* get her name right—she's a remarkably pretty little thing. Quite likely there *is* a man in her case.'

'She'd be better looking if she didn't dye her hair,' said Richard drily.

'Does she dye it? In-deed. How knowledgeable you are in these matters.'

'About Emerson's letter, sir—'

'Of course—of course—I've no idea where I put it. But look anywhere you choose—I'm anxious to find it anyway because of those notes I made on the back—and a sketch of that coiled wire bead.'

CHAPTER 20

On the following afternoon Dr Pauncefoot Jones uttered a disgusted exclamation as the sound of a car came faintly to his ears. Presently he located it, winding across the desert towards the *Tell*.

'Visitors,' he said with venom. 'At the worst possible moment, too. I want to superintend the cellulosing of that painted rosette on the north-east corner. Sure to be some idiots come out from Baghdad with a lot of social chatter and expecting to get shown all over the excavations.'

'This is where Victoria comes in useful,' said Richard. 'You hear, Victoria? It's up to you to do a personally conducted tour.'

'I shall probably say all the wrong things,' said Victoria. 'I'm really very inexperienced, you know.'

'I think you're doing very well indeed,' said Richard pleasantly. 'Those remarks you made this morning about plano convex bricks might have come straight out of Delongaz's book.'

Victoria changed colour slightly, and resolved to para-phrase her erudition more carefully. Sometimes the quizzical glance through the thick lenses made her uncomfortable.

'I'll do my best,' she said meekly.

'We push all the odd jobs on to you,' said Richard.

Victoria smiled.

Indeed her activities during the last five days surprised her not a little. She had developed plates with water filtered through cotton wool and by the light of a primitive dark lantern containing a candle which always went out at the most crucial moment. The dark-room table was a packing case and to work she had to crouch or kneel—the dark-room itself being as Richard remarked, a modern model of the famous medieval Little Ease. There would be more amenities in the season to come, Dr Pauncefoot Jones assured her—but at the moment every penny was needed to pay workmen and get results.

The baskets of broken potsherds had at first excited her astonished derision (though this she had been careful not to display). All these broken bits of coarse stuff—what was the good of them?

Then as she found joins, stuck them and propped them up in boxes of sand, she began to take an interest. She learned to recognize shapes and types. And she came finally to try and reconstruct in her own mind just how and for what these vessels had been used some three thousand odd years ago. In the small area where some poor quality private houses had been dug, she pictured the houses as they had orginally stood and the people who had lived in them with their wants and possessions and occupations, their hopes and their fears. Since Victoria had a lively imagination, a picture rose up easily enough in her mind. On a day when a small clay pot was found encased in a wall with a half-dozen gold earrings in it, she was enthralled. Probably the dowry of a daughter, Richard had said, smiling.

Dishes filled with grain, gold earrings saved up for a dowry, bone needles, querns and mortars, little figurines and amulets. All the everyday life and fears and hopes of a community of unimportant simple people.

'That's what I find so fascinating,' said Victoria to Richard. 'You see, I always used to think that archaeology was just Royal graves and palaces.

'Kings in Babylon,' she added, with a strange little smile. 'But what I like so much about all this is that it's the ordinary everyday people—people like me. My St Anthony who finds things for me when I lose them—and a lucky china pig I've got—and an awfully nice mixing bowl, blue inside and white out, that I used to make cakes in. It got broken and the new one I bought wasn't a bit the same. I can understand why these people mended up their favourite bowls or dishes so carefully with bitumen. Life's all the same really, isn't it—then or now?'

She was thinking of these things as she watched the visitors ascending the side of the *Tell*. Richard went to greet them, Victoria following behind him.

They were two Frenchmen, interested in archaeology, who were making a tour through Syria and Iraq. After civil greetings, Victoria took them round the excavations, reciting parrot wise what was going on, but being unable to resist, being Victoria, adding sundry embellishments of her own, just, as she put it to herself, to make it more exciting.

She noticed that the second man was a very bad colour, and that he dragged himself along without much interest. Presently he said, if Mademoiselle would excuse him, he would retire to the house. He had not felt well since early that morning—and the sun was making him worse.

He departed in the direction of the Expedition House, and the other, in suitably lowered tones explained that, unfortunately, it was his *estomac*. The Baghdad tummy they called it, did they not? He should not really have come out today.

The tour was completed, the Frenchman remained talking to Victoria, finally Fidos was called and Dr Pauncefoot Jones, with a determined air of hospitality suggested the guests should have tea before departing.

To this, however, the Frenchman demurred. They must not delay their departure until it was dark or they would never find the way. Richard Baker said immediately that this was quite right. The sick friend was retrieved from the house and the car rushed off at top speed.

'I suppose that's just the beginning,' grunted Dr Pauncefoot Jones. 'We shall have visitors every day now.'

He took a large flap of Arab bread and covered it thickly with apricot jam.

Richard went to his room after tea. He had letters to answer, and others to write in preparation for going into Baghdad on the following day.

Suddenly he frowned. Not a man of particular neatness to the outward view, he yet had a way of arranging his clothes and his papers that never varied. Now he saw at once that every drawer had been disturbed. It was not the servants, of that he was sure. It must be, then, that sick visitor who had made a pretext to go down to the house, had coolly ransacked through his belongings. Nothing was missing, he assured himself of that. His money was untouched. What, then, had they been looking for? His face grew grave as he considered the implications.

He went into the Antika Room and looked in the drawer which held the seals and seal impressions. He gave a grim smile—nothing had been touched or removed. He went into the living-room. Dr Pauncefoot Jones was out in the courtyard with the foreman. Only Victoria was there, curled up with a book.

Richard said, without preamble, 'Somebody's been searching my room.'

Victoria looked up, astonished.

'But why? And who?'

'It wasn't you?'

'Me?' Victoria was indignant. 'Of course not? Why should I want to pry among your things?'

He gave her a hard stare. Then he said:

'It must have been that damned stranger—the one who shammed sick and came down to the house.'

'Did he steal something?'

'No,' said Richard. 'Nothing was taken.'

'But why on earth should anyone—'

Richard cut in to say:

'I thought *you* might know that.'

'Me?'

'Well, by your own account, rather odd things have happened to *you*.'

'Oh that—yes.' Victoria looked rather startled. She said slowly: 'But I don't see why they should search *your* room. You've got nothing to do with—'

'With what?'

Victoria did not answer for a moment or two. She seemed lost in thought.

'I'm sorry,' she said at last. 'What did you say? I wasn't listening.'

Richard did not repeat his question. Instead he asked:

'What are you reading?'

'You don't have much choice of light fiction here. *Tale of Two Cities*, *Pride and Prejudice* and *The Mill on the Floss*. I'm reading the *Tale of Two Cities*.'

'Never read it before?'

'Never. I always thought Dickens would be stuffy.'

'What an idea!'

'I'm finding it most exciting.'

'Where have you got to?' He looked over her shoulder and read out: 'And the knitting women count One.'

'I think she's awfully frightening,' said Victoria.

'Madame Defarge? Yes, a good character. Though whether you could keep a register of names in knitting has always seemed to me rather doubtful. But then, of course, I'm not a knitter.'

'Oh I think you could,' said Victoria, considering the point. 'Plain and purl—and fancy stitches—and the wrong stitch at intervals and dropped stitches. Yes—it could be done—camouflaged, of course, so that it looked like someone who was rather bad at knitting and made mistakes . . .'

Suddenly, with a vividness like a flash of lightning, two things came together in her mind and affected her with the force of an explosion. A name—a visual memory. The man with the ragged hand-knitted red scarf clasped in his hands—the scarf she had hurriedly picked up later and flung into a drawer. And together with that name. *Defarge*—not Lefarge—*Defarge*, Madame Defarge.

She was recalled to herself by Richard saying to her courteously:

'Is anything the matter?'

'No—no, that is, I just thought of something.'

'I see.' Richard raised his eyebrows in his most supercilious way.

Tomorrow, thought Victoria, they would all go in to Baghdad. Tomorrow her respite would be over. For over a week she had had safety, peace, time to pull herself together. And she had enjoyed that time—enjoyed it enormously. Perhaps I'm a coward, thought Victoria, perhaps that's it. She had talked gaily about adventure, but she hadn't liked it very much when it really came. She hated that struggle against chloroform and the slow suffocation, and she had been frightened, horribly frightened, in that upper room when the ragged Arab had said *'Bukra.'*

And now she'd got to go back to it all. Because she was employed by Mr Dakin and paid by Mr Dakin and she had to earn her pay and show a brave front! She might even have to go back to the Olive Branch. She shivered a little when she remembered Dr Rathbone and that searching dark glance of his. He'd warned her . . .

But perhaps she wouldn't have to go back. Perhaps Mr

Dakin would say it was better not—now that they knew about her. But she would have to go back to her lodgings and get her things because thrust carelessly into her suitcase was the red knitted scarf . . . She had bundled everything into suitcases when she left for Basrah. Once she had put that scarf into Mr Dakin's hands, perhaps her task would be done. He would say to her perhaps, like on the pictures: 'Oh! Good show, Victoria.'

She looked up to find Richard Baker watching her.

'By the way,' he said, 'will you be able to get hold of your passport tomorrow?'

'My passport?'

Victoria considered the position. It was characteristic of her that she had not as yet defined her plan of action as regards the Expedition. Since the real Veronica (or Venetia) would shortly be arriving from England, a retreat in good order was necessary. But whether she would merely fade away, or confess her deception with suitable penitence, or indeed what she intended to do, had not yet presented itself as a problem to be solved. Victoria was always prone to adopt the Micawber-like attitude that Something would Turn Up.

'Well,' she said temporizing, 'I'm not sure.'

'It's needed, you see, for the police of this district,' explained Richard. 'They enter its number and your name and age and special distinguishing marks, etc., all the whole caboodle. As we haven't got the passport, I think we ought at any rate to send your name and description to them. By the way, what is your last name? I've always called you "Victoria".'

Victoria rallied gallantly.

'Come now,' she said. 'You know my last name as well as I do.'

'That's not quite true,' said Richard. His smile curved upwards with a hint of cruelty. 'I *do* know your last name. It's *you*, I think who don't know it.'

Through the glasses the eyes watched her.

'Of course I know my own name,' snapped Victoria.

'Then I'll challenge you to tell it to me—now.'

His voice was suddenly hard and curt.

'It's no good lying,' he said. 'The game's up. You've been very clever about it. You've read up your subject, you've brought out very telling bits of knowledge—but it's the kind of imposture you can't keep up all the time. I've laid traps for you and you've fallen into them. I've quoted bits of sheer rubbish to you and you've accepted them.' He paused. 'You're *not* Venetia Savile. Who are you?'

'I told you who I was the first time I met you,' said Victoria. 'I'm Victoria Jones.'

'Dr Pauncefoot Jones' niece?'

'I'm not his niece—but my name *is* Jones.'

'You told me a lot of other things.'

'Yes, I did. And they were all *true*! But I could see you didn't believe me. And that made me mad, because though I do tell lies sometimes—in fact quite often—what I'd just told you wasn't a lie. And so, just to make myself more convincing, I said my name was Pauncefoot Jones—I've said that before out here, and it's always gone down frightfully well. How could I tell you were actually coming to this place?'

'It must have been a slight shock to you,' said Richard grimly. 'You carried it off very well—cool as a cucumber.'

'Not inside,' said Victoria. 'I was absolutely *shaking*. But I felt that if I waited to explain until I got here—well at any rate I should be safe.'

'Safe?' he considered the word. 'Look here, Victoria, *was* that incredible rigmarole you told me about being chloroformed really true?'

'Of course it was true! Don't you see, if I wanted to make up a story I could make up a much better one than that, *and* tell it better!'

'Knowing you a little more closely now, I can see the force of that! But you must admit that, on first hearing, the story was wildly improbable.'

'But you are willing to think it's possible *now*. Why?' Richard said slowly.

'Because if, as you say, you were mixed up in Carmichael's death—well, then it might be true.'

'That's what it all began with,' said Victoria.

'You'd better tell me about it.'

Victoria stared at him very hard.

'I'm wondering,' she said, 'if I can trust you.'

'The boot is on the other leg! Do you realize that I've had grave suspicions that you'd planted yourself here under a false name in order to get information out of *me*? And perhaps that *is* what you are doing.'

'Meaning that you know something about Carmichael that They would like to know?'

'Who exactly are They?'

'I shall have to tell you all about it,' said Victoria. 'There isn't any other way—and if you are one of Them you know it already, so it doesn't matter.'

She told him of the night of Carmichael's death, of her interview with Mr Dakin, of her journey to Basrah, her employment in the Olive Branch, of Catherine's hostility, of Dr Rathbone and his warning and of the final denouement, including this time the enigma of the dyed hair. The only things she left out were the red scarf and Madame Defarge.

'Dr Rathbone?' Richard seized on that point. 'You think *he's* mixed up in this? Behind it? But my dear girl, he's a very important man. He's known all over the world. Subscriptions pour in from all over the globe for his schemes.'

'Wouldn't he have to be all those things?' asked Victoria.

'I've always regarded him as a pompous ass,' said Richard meditatively.

'And that's a very good camouflage, too.'

'Yes—yes, I suppose it is. Who was Lefarge that you asked me about?'

'Just another name,' said Victoria. 'There's Anna Scheele, too,' she said.

'Anna Scheele? No, I've never heard of her.'

'She's important,' said Victoria. 'But I don't know exactly how or why. It's all so mixed up.'

'Just tell me again,' said Richard. 'Who's the man who started you on to all this?'

'Edwar—oh, you mean Mr Dakin. He's in Oil, I think.'

'Is he a tired, stooping, rather vacant-looking chap?'

'Yes—but he's not really. Vacant, I mean.'

'Doesn't he drink?'

'People say so, but I don't think he does.'

Richard sat back and looked at her.

'Phillips Oppenheim, William Le Queux and several distinguished imitators since? Is this real? Are *you* real? And are you the persecuted heroine, or the wicked adventuress?'

Victoria said in a practical manner:

'The real point is, what are we going to say to Dr Pauncefoot Jones about me?'

'Nothing,' said Richard. 'It really won't be necessary.'

CHAPTER 21

They started in to Baghdad early. Victoria's spirits felt curiously low. She had almost a lump in her throat as she looked back on the Expedition House. However, the acute discomfort entailed in the mad bumping of the lorry effectively distracted her mind from anything but the torture of the moment. It seemed strange to be driving along a so-called road again, passing donkeys and meeting dusty lorries. It took nearly three hours to reach the outskirts of Baghdad. The lorry decanted them at the Tio Hotel and then went off with the cook and the driver to do all the necessary shopping. A large bundle of mail was awaiting Dr Pauncefoot Jones and Richard. Marcus appearing suddenly, massive and beaming, welcomed Victoria with his usual friendly radiance.

'Ah,' he said, 'it is a long time since I have seen you. You do not come to my hotel. Not for a week—two weeks. Why is that? You lunch here today, you have everything you want? The baby chickens? The big steak? Only not the turkey stuffed very special with flavouring and rice, because for that you must let me know the day before.'

It seemed clear that as far as the Tio Hotel was concerned, the kidnapping of Victoria had not been noticed. Possibly Edward, on the advice of Mr Dakin, had not been to the police.

'Is Mr Dakin in Baghdad, do you know, Marcus?' she asked.

'Mr Dakin—ah yes, very nice man—of course, he is friend of yours. He was here yesterday—no, day before. And Captain Crosbie, you know him? A friend of Mr Dakin's. He arrives today from Kermanshah.'

'You know where Mr Dakin's office is?'

'Sure I know. Everybody knows the Iraqi Iranian Oil Co.'

'Well, I want to go there now. In a taxi. But I want to be sure the taxi knows where to take me.'

'I tell him myself,' said Marcus obligingly.

He escorted her to the head of the alleyway and yelled in his usual violent fashion. A startled minion arrived at a run. Marcus commanded him to procure a taxi. Then Victoria was escorted to the taxi and Marcus addressed the driver. Then he stepped back and waved a hand.

'And I want a room,' said Victoria. 'Can I have one?'

'Yes, yes. I give you a beautiful room and I order you the big steak and tonight I have—very special—some caviare. And before that we have a little drink.'

'Lovely,' said Victoria. 'Oh Marcus, can you lend me some money?'

'Of course, my dear. Here you are. Take all you want.'

The taxi started off with a violent honk and Victoria fell back on the seat clutching an assortment of coins and notes.

Agatha Christie

Five minutes later Victoria entered the offices of the Iraqi Iranian Oil Co. and asked for Mr Dakin.

Mr Dakin looked up from his desk where he was writing when Victoria was shown in. He rose and shook hands with her in a formal manner.

'Miss—er—Miss Jones, isn't it? Bring coffee, Abdullah.'

As the sound-proof door closed behind the clerk, he said quietly:

'You shouldn't really come here, you know.'

'I had to this time,' said Victoria. 'There's something I've got to tell you at once—before anything more happens to me.'

'Happens to you? Has anything happened to you?'

'Don't you know?' asked Victoria. 'Hasn't Edward told you?'

'As far as I know, you are still working at the Olive Branch. Nobody has told me anything.'

'Catherine,' exclaimed Victoria.

'I beg your pardon.'

'The cat Catherine! I bet she's stuffed Edward up with some tale or other and the goop has believed her.'

'Well, let's hear about it,' said Mr Dakin. 'Er—if I may say so,' his eye went discreetly to Victoria's blonde head, 'I prefer you as a brunette.'

'That's only part of it,' said Victoria.

There was a tap at the door and the messenger entered with two little cups of sweet coffee. When he had gone, Dakin said:

'Now take your time and tell me all about it. We can't be overheard here.'

Victoria plunged into the story of her adventures. As always when she was talking to Dakin, she managed to be both coherent and concise. She finished her story with an account of the red scarf Carmichael had dropped and her association of it with Madame Defarge.

Then she looked anxiously at Dakin.

He had seemed to her when she came in, to be even more bowed and tired-looking. Now she saw a new glint come into his eye.

'I should read my Dickens more often,' he said.

'Then you do think I'm right? You think it *was* Defarge he said—and you think some message is knitted into the scarf?'

'I think,' said Dakin, 'that this is the first real break we've had—and we've got you to thank for it. But the important thing is the scarf. Where is it?'

'With all the rest of my things. I shoved it into a drawer that night—and when I packed I remember bundling everything in without sorting or anything.'

'And you've never happened to mention to anyone—to *anyone at all*—that that scarf belonged to Carmichael?'

'No, because I'd forgotten all about it. I bundled it into a suitcase with some other things when I went to Basrah and I've never even opened the case since.'

'Then it ought to be all right. Even if they've been through your things, they won't have attached any importance to an old dirty woollen scarf—unless they were tipped off to it, which as far as I can see, is impossible. All we've got to do now is to have all your things collected and sent to you at—have you got anywhere to stay, by the way?'

'I've booked a room at the Tio.'

Dakin nodded.

'Best place for you.'

'Have I—do you want me—to go back to the Olive Branch?'

Dakin looked at her keenly.

'Scared?'

Victoria stuck her chin out.

'No,' she said with defiance. 'I'll go if you like.'

'I don't think it's necessary—or even wise. However they learned it, I presume that someone there got wise to your activities. That being so, you wouldn't be able to find out anything more, so you'd better stay clear.'

He smiled.

'Otherwise you may be a redhead next time I see you.'

'That's what I want to know most of all,' cried Victoria. 'Why did they dye my hair? I've thought and I've thought and I can't see any point in it. Can you?'

'Only the somewhat unpleasant one that your dead body might be less easy to identify.'

'But if they wanted me to be a dead body, why didn't they kill me straight away?'

'That's a very interesting question, Victoria. It's the question I want answered most of all.'

'And you haven't any idea?'

'I haven't got a clue,' said Mr Dakin with a faint smile.

'Talking of clues,' said Victoria, 'do you remember my saying that there was something about Sir Rupert Crofton Lee that didn't seem right, that morning at the Tio?'

'Yes.'

'You didn't know him personally, did you?'

'I hadn't met him before, no.'

'I thought not. Because, you see, he *wasn't* Sir Rupert Crofton Lee.'

And she plunged once more into animated narrative, starting with the incipient boil on the back of Sir Rupert's neck.

'So that was how it was done,' said Dakin. 'I didn't see *how* Carmichael could have been sufficiently off his guard to be killed that night. He got safely to Crofton Lee—and Crofton Lee stabbed him, but he managed to get away and burst into your room before he collapsed. And he hung on to the scarf—literally like grim death.'

'Do you think it was because I was coming to tell you this that they kidnapped me? But nobody knew except Edward.'

'I think they felt they had to get you out of the picture quickly. You were tumbling to too much that was going on at the Olive Branch.'

'Dr Rathbone warned me,' said Victoria. 'It was—more of a threat than a warning. I think he realized that I wasn't what I pretended to be.'

'Rathbone,' said Dakin dryly, 'is no fool.'

'I'm glad I haven't got to go back there,' said Victoria. 'I pretended to be brave just now—but really I'm scared stiff. Only if I don't go to the Olive Branch, how can I get hold of Edward?'

Dakin smiled.

'If Mohammed won't come to the mountain, the mountain must come to Mohammed. Write him a note now. Just say you're at the Tio and ask him to get your clothes and luggage and bring them along there. I'm going to consult Dr Rathbone this morning about one of his Club soirées. It will be easy for me to slip a note to his secretary—so there will be no danger of your enemy Catherine causing it to go astray. As for you, go back to the Tio and stay there—and, Victoria—'

'Yes?'

'If you're in a jam—of any kind—do the best you can for yourself. As far as possible you'll be watched over, but your adversaries are rather formidable, and unfortunately you know rather a lot. Once your luggage is in the Tio Hotel your obligations to me are over. Understand that.'

'I'll go straight back to the Tio now,' said Victoria. 'At least I shall just buy some face powder and lipstick and vanishing cream on the way. After all—'

'After all,' said Mr Dakin, 'one cannot meet one's young man completely unarmoured.'

'It didn't matter so much with Richard Baker though I'd like him to know I can look quite nice if I try,' said Victoria. 'But *Edward* . . .'

CHAPTER 22

Her blonde hair carefully arranged, her nose powdered and her lips freshly painted, Victoria sat upon the balcony of the Tio, once more in the role of a modern Juliet, waiting for Romeo.

And in due course Romeo came. He appeared on the grass sward, looking this way and that.

'Edward,' said Victoria.

Edward looked up.

'Oh, there you are, Victoria!'

'Come up here.'

'Right.'

A moment later he came out upon the balcony which was deserted.

'It's more peaceful up here,' said Victoria. 'We'll go down and let Marcus give us drinks presently.'

Edward was staring at her in perplexity.

'I say, Victoria, haven't you done something to your hair?'

Victoria gave an exasperated sigh.

'If anybody mentions hair to me, I really think I shall bat them over the head.'

'I think I liked it better as it was,' said Edward.

'Tell Catherine so!'

'Catherine? What has she got to do with it?'

'Everything,' said Victoria. 'You told me to chum up with her, and I did, and I don't suppose you've any idea what it let me in for!'

'Where've you been all this time, Victoria? I've been getting quite worried.'

'Oh you have, have you? Where did you think I'd been?'

'Well, Catherine gave me your message. Said you'd told her to tell me that you'd gone off to Mosul suddenly. It was something very important and good news, and I'd hear from you in due course.'

'And you believed that?' said Victoria in an almost pitying voice.

'I thought you'd got on the track of something. Naturally, you couldn't say much to Catherine—'

'It didn't occur to you that Catherine was lying, and that I'd been knocked on the head.'

'What?' Edward stared.

'Drugged, chloroformed—starved . . .'

Edward cast a sharp glance around.

'Good Lord! I never dreamed—look here, I don't like talking out here. All these windows. Can't we go to your room?'

'All right. Did you bring my luggage?'

'Yes, I dumped it all with the porter.'

'Because when one hasn't had a change of clothes for a fortnight—'

'Victoria, what *has* been happening? I know—I've got

the car here. Let's go out to Devonshire. You've never been there, have you?'

'Devonshire?' Victoria stared in surprise.

'Oh, it's just a name for a place not far out of Baghdad. It's rather lovely this time of year. Come on. I haven't had you to myself for years.'

'Not since Babylon. But what will Dr Rathbone and the Olive Branch say?'

'Blast Dr Rathbone. I'm fed up with the old ass anyway.'

They ran down the stairs and out to where Edward's car was parked. Edward drove southwards through Baghdad, along a wide avenue. Then he turned off from there; they jolted and twisted through palm groves and over irrigation bridges. Finally, with a strange unexpectedness they came to a small wooded copse surrounded and pierced by irrigation streams. The trees of the copse, mostly almond and apricot, were just coming into blossom. It was an idyllic spot. Beyond the copse, at a little distance, was the Tigris.

They got out of the car and walked together through the blossoming trees.

'This is lovely,' said Victoria, sighing deeply. 'It's like being back in England in spring.'

The air was soft and warm. Presently they sat down on a fallen tree trunk with pink blossom hanging down over their heads.

'Now, darling,' said Edward. 'Tell me what's been happening to you. I've been so dreadfully miserable.'

'Have you?' she smiled dreamily.

Then she told him. Of the girl hairdresser. Of the smell of chloroform and her struggle. Of waking up drugged and

251

sick. Of how she had escaped and of her fortuitous meeting with Richard Baker, and of how she had claimed to be Victoria Pauncefoot Jones on her way to the Excavations, and of how she had almost miraculously sustained the part of an archaeological student arriving from England.

At this point Edward shouted with laughter.

'You are marvellous, Victoria! The things you think of—and invent.'

'I know,' said Victoria. 'My uncles. Dr Pauncefoot Jones and before him—the Bishop.'

And at that she suddenly remembered what it was she had been going to ask Edward at Basrah when Mrs Clayton had interrupted by calling them in for drinks.

'I meant to ask you before,' she said. 'How did you know about the Bishop?'

She felt the hand that held hers stiffen suddenly. He said quickly, too quickly:

'Why, you told me, didn't you?'

Victoria looked at him. It was odd, she thought afterwards, that that one silly childish slip should have accomplished what it did.

For he was taken completely by surprise. He had no story ready—his face was suddenly defenceless and unmasked.

And as she looked at him, everything shifted and settled itself into a pattern, exactly as a kaleidoscope does, and she saw the truth. Perhaps it was not really sudden. Perhaps in her subconscious mind that question: How did Edward know about the Bishop? had been teasing and worrying, and she had been slowly arriving at the one, the inevitable, answer . . . Edward had not learned about the Bishop of

Llangow from her, and the only other person he could have learned it from, would have been Mr or Mrs Hamilton Clipp. But they could not possibly have seen Edward since her arrival in Baghdad, for Edward had been in Basrah then, so he must have learned it from them *before* he himself left England. He must have known all along, then, that Victoria was coming out with them—and the whole wonderful coincidence was not, after all, a coincidence. It was planned and intended.

And as she stared at Edward's unmasked face, she knew, suddenly, what Carmichael had meant by Lucifer. She knew what he had seen that day as he looked along the passage to the Consulate garden. He had seen that young beautiful face that she was looking at now—for it was a beautiful face:

Lucifer, Son of the Morning, how art thou fallen?

Not Dr Rathbone—*Edward!* Edward, playing a minor part, the part of the secretary, but controlling and planning and directing, using Rathbone as a figurehead—and Rathbone, warning her to go while she could . . .

As she looked at that beautiful evil face, all her silly adolescent calf love faded away, and she knew that what she felt for Edward had never been love. It had been the same feeling that she had experienced some years earlier for Humphrey Bogart, and later for the Duke of Edinburgh. It had been glamour. And Edward had never loved *her*. He had exerted his charm and his glamour deliberately. He had picked her up that day, using his charm so easily, so naturally, that she had fallen for it without a struggle. She had been a sucker.

It was extraordinary how much could flash through your mind in just a few seconds. You didn't have to think it out. It just came. Full and instant knowledge. Perhaps because really, underneath, you had known it all along . . .

And at the same time some instinct of self-preservation, quick as all Victoria's mental processes were quick, kept her face in an expression of foolish unthinking wonder. For she knew, instinctively, that she was in great danger. There was only one thing that could save her, only one card she could play. She made haste to play it.

'You knew all along!' she said. 'You knew I was coming out here. You must have arranged it. Oh Edward, you are *wonderful*!'

Her face, that plastic impressionable face, showed one emotion—an almost cloying adoration. And she saw the response—the faintly scornful smile, the relief. She could almost feel Edward saying to himself, 'The little fool! She'll swallow anything! I can do what I like with her.'

'But *how* did you arrange it?' she said. 'You must be very powerful. You must be quite different from what you pretend to be. You're—it's like you said the other day—you're a King in Babylon.'

She saw the pride that lit up his face. She saw the power and strength and beauty and cruelty that had been disguised behind a façade of a modest likeable young man.

'And I'm only a Christian slave,' thought Victoria. She said quickly and anxiously, as a final artistic touch (and what its cost was to her pride no one will ever know), 'But you *do* love me, don't you?'

His scorn was hardly to be hidden now. This little

fool—all these fools of women! So easy to make them think you loved them and that was all they cared about! They had no conception of greatness of construction, of a new world, they just whined for love! They were slaves and you used them as slaves to further your ends.

'Of course I love you,' he said.

'But what is it all *about*? Tell me, Edward? Make me understand.'

'It's a new world, Victoria. A new world that will rise out of the muck and ashes of the old.'

'Tell me.'

He told her and in spite of herself she was almost carried away, carried into the dream. The old bad things must destroy each other. The fat old men grasping at their profits, impeding progress. The bigoted stupid Communists, trying to establish their Marxian heaven. There must be total war—total destruction. And then—the new Heaven and the new Earth. The small chosen band of higher beings, the scientists, the agricultural experts, the administrators— the young men like Edward—the young Siegfrieds of the New World. All young, all believing in their destiny as Supermen. When destruction had run its course, *they* would step in and take over.

It was madness—but it was constructive madness. It was the sort of thing that in a world, shattered and disintegrating, could happen.

'But think,' said Victoria, 'of all the people who will be killed first.'

'You don't understand,' said Edward. 'That doesn't matter.'

It doesn't matter—that was Edward's creed. And suddenly for no reason, a remembrance of that three thousand years old coarse pottery bowl mended with bitumen flashed across Victoria's mind. Surely those *were* the things that mattered— the little everyday things, the family to be cooked for, the four walls that enclosed the home, the one or two cherished possessions. All the thousands of ordinary people on the earth, minding their own business, and tilling the earth, and making pots and bringing up families and laughing and crying, and getting up in the morning and going to bed at night. *They* were the people who mattered, not these Angels with wicked faces who wanted to make a new world and who didn't care whom they hurt to do it.

And carefully, feeling her way, for here in Devonshire she knew that death might be very near, she said:

'You *are* wonderful, Edward. But what about *me*? What can *I* do?'

'You want to—help? You believe in it?'

But she was prudent. Not sudden conversion. That would be too much.

'I think I just believe in *you*!' she said. 'Anything *you* tell me to do, Edward, I'll do.'

'Good girl,' he said.

'Why did you arrange for me to come out here to begin with? There must have been some reason?'

'Of course there was. Do you remember I took a snap of you that day?'

'I remember,' said Victoria.

(You fool, how flattered you were, how you simpered! she thought to herself.)

'I'd been struck by your profile—by your resemblance to someone. I took that snap to make sure.'

'Whom do I resemble?'

'A woman who's been causing us a good deal of trouble—Anna Scheele.'

'Anna Scheele.' Victoria stared at him in blank surprise. Whatever she had expected, it was not this. 'You mean—she looks like *me*?'

'Quite remarkably so side view. The features in profile are almost exactly the same. And there's one most extraordinary thing, you've got a tiny mark of a scar on your upper lip, left side—'

'I know. It's where I fell on a tin horse when I was a child. It had a sharp ear sticking up and it cut quite deep in. It doesn't show much—not with powder on.'

'Anna Scheele has a mark in just the same place. That was a most valuable point. You're alike in height and build—she's about four or five years older than you. The real difference is the hair, you're a brunette and she's a blonde. And your style of hairdressing is quite different. Your eyes are a darker blue, but that wouldn't matter with tinted glasses.'

'And that's why you wanted me to come to Baghdad? Because I looked like her.'

'Yes, I thought the resemblance might—come in useful.'

'So you arranged the whole thing . . . The Clipps—who are the Clipps?'

'They're not important—they just do as they're told.'

Something in Edward's tone sent a faint shiver down

Victoria's spine. It was as though he had said with inhuman detachment, 'They are under Obedience.'

There was a religious flavour about this mad project. 'Edward,' she thought, 'is his own God. *That's* what's so frightening.'

Aloud she said:

'You told me that Anna Scheele was the boss, the Queen Bee, in *your* show?'

'I had to tell you something to put you off the scent. You had already learnt too much.'

'And if I hadn't happened to look like Anna Scheele that would have been the end of me,' thought Victoria.

She said:

'Who is she really?'

'She's confidential secretary to Otto Morganthal, the American and international banker. But that isn't all she is. She has the most remarkable financial brain. We've reason to believe she's traced out a lot of our financial operations. Three people have been dangerous to us—Rupert Crofton Lee, Carmichael—well they're both wiped out. There remains Anna Scheele. She's due in Baghdad in three days' time. In the meantime, she's disappeared.'

'Disappeared? Where?'

'In London. Vanished, apparently, off the face of the earth.'

'And does no one know where she is?'

'Dakin may know.'

But Dakin didn't know. Victoria knew that, though Edward didn't—so where *was* Anna Scheele?

She asked:

'You really haven't the least idea?'

'We've an idea,' said Edward slowly.

'Well?'

'It's vital that Anna Scheele should be here in Baghdad for the Conference. That, as you know, is in five days' time.'

'As soon as that? I'd no idea.'

'We've got every entry into this country taped. She's certainly not coming here under her own name. And she's not coming in on a Government service plane. We've our means of checking that. So we've investigated all the private bookings. There's a passage booked by BOAC in the name of Grete Harden. We've traced Grete Harden back and there's no such person. It's an assumed name. The address given is a phony one. It's our idea that Grete Harden is Anna Scheele.'

He added:

'Her plane will touch down at Damascus the day after tomorrow.'

'And then?'

Edward's eyes looked suddenly into hers.

'That's up to you, Victoria.'

'To me?'

'You'll take her place.'

Victoria said slowly:

'Like Rupert Crofton Lee?'

It was almost a whisper. In the course of that substitution Rupert Crofton Lee had died. And when Victoria took her place, presumably Anna Scheele, or Grete Harden, would die . . . But even if she didn't agree, Anna Scheele would still die.

And Edward was waiting—and if for one moment Edward doubted her loyalty, then she, Victoria, would die—and die without the possibility of warning any one.

No, she must agree and seize a chance to report to Mr Dakin.

She drew a deep breath and said:

'I—I—oh, but Edward, I couldn't do it. I'd be found out. I can't do an American voice.'

'Anna Scheele has practically no accent. In any case you will be suffering from laryngitis. One of the best doctors in this part of the world will say so.'

'They've got people everywhere,' thought Victoria.

'What would I have to do?' she asked.

'Fly from Damascus to Baghdad as Grete Harden. Take to your bed immediately. Be allowed up by our reputable doctor just in time to go to the Conference. There you will lay before them the documents which you have brought with you.'

Victoria asked: 'The real documents?'

'Of course not. We shall substitute our version.'

'What will the documents show?'

Edward smiled.

'Convincing details of the most stupendous Communist plot in America.'

Victoria thought: 'How well they've got it planned.'

Aloud she said:

'Do you really think I can get away with it, Edward?'

Now that she was playing a part, it was quite easy for Victoria to ask it with every appearance of anxious sincerity.

260

'I'm sure you can. I've noticed that your playing of a part affords you such enjoyment that it's practically impossible to disbelieve you.'

Victoria said meditatively:

'I still feel an awful fool when I think of the Hamilton Clipps.'

He laughed in a superior way.

Victoria, her face still a mask of adoration, thought to herself viciously, 'But *you* were an awful fool, too, to let slip that about the Bishop at Basrah. If you hadn't I'd never have seen through *you*.'

She said suddenly: 'What about Dr Rathbone?'

'What do you mean "What about him?"'

'Is he just a figurehead?'

Edward's lips curved in cruel amusement.

'Rathbone has got to toe the line. Do you know what he's been doing all these years? Cleverly appropriating about three-quarters of the subscriptions which pour in from all over the world to his own use. It's the cleverest swindle since the time of Horatio Bottomley. Oh yes, Rathbone's completely in our hands—we can expose him at any time and he knows it.'

Victoria felt a sudden gratitude to the old man with the noble domed head, and the mean acquisitive soul. He might be a swindler—but he had known pity—he had tried to get her to escape in time.

'All things work towards our New Order,' said Edward.

She thought to herself, 'Edward, who looks so sane, is really mad! You get mad, perhaps, if you try and act the part of God. They always say humility is a Christian

261

virtue—now I see why. Humility is what keeps you sane and a human being . . .'

Edward got up.

'Time to be moving,' he said. 'We've got to get you to Damascus and our plans there worked out by the day after tomorrow.'

Victoria rose with alacrity. Once she was away from Devonshire, back in Baghdad with its crowds, in the Tio Hotel with Marcus shouting and beaming and offering her a drink, the near persistent menace of Edward would be removed. Her part was to play a double game—continue to fool Edward by a sickly dog-like devotion, and counter his plans secretly.

She said: 'You think that Mr Dakin knows where Anna Scheele is? Perhaps I could find that out. He might drop some hint.'

'Unlikely—and in any case, you won't be seeing Dakin.'

'He told me to come to see him this evening,' said Victoria mendaciously, a slightly chilly feeling attacking her spine. 'He'll think it odd if I don't turn up.'

'It doesn't matter at this stage what he thinks,' said Edward. 'Our plans are made.' He added, 'You won't be seen in Baghdad again.'

'But Edward, all my things are at the Tio! I've booked a room.'

The scarf. The precious scarf.

'You won't need your things for some time to come. I've got a rig-out waiting for you. Come on.'

They got in the car again. Victoria thought, 'I ought to have known that Edward would never be such a fool as to let me get in touch with Mr Dakin after I'd found him out. He believes I'm besotted about him—yes, I *think* he's sure of that—but all the same he isn't going to take any chances.'

She said: 'Won't there be a search for me if I—don't turn up?'

'We'll attend to that. Officially you'll say goodbye to me at the bridge and go off to see some friends on the West Bank.'

'And actually?'

'Wait and see.'

Victoria sat silent as they bumped over the rough track and twisted round palm gardens and over the little irrigation bridges.

'Lefarge,' murmured Edward. 'I wish we knew what Carmichael meant by that.'

Victoria's heart gave a leap of anxiety.

'Oh,' she said. 'I forgot to tell you. I don't know if it means anything. A M. Lefarge came to the Excavations one day at Tell Aswad.'

'What?' Edward almost stalled the car in his excitement. 'When was this?'

'Oh! About a week ago. He said he came from some dig in Syria. M. Parrot's, would it be?'

'Did two men called André and Juvet come while you were there?'

'Oh yes,' said Victoria. 'One of them had a sick stomach. He went to the house and lay down.'

'They were two of our people,' said Edward.

'Why did they come here? To look for me?'

263

'No—I'd no idea where you were. But Richard Baker was in Basrah at the same time as Carmichael. We had an idea Carmichael might have passed something on to Baker.'

'He said his things had been searched. Did they find anything?'

'No—now think carefully, Victoria. Did this man Lefarge come before the other two or afterwards?'

Victoria reflected in a convincing manner, as she decided what movements to impute to the mythical M. Lefarge.

'It was—yes, the day *before* the other two came,' she said.

'What did he do?'

'Well,' said Victoria, 'he went over the Dig—with Dr Pauncefoot Jones. And then Richard Baker took him down to the house to see some of the things in the Antika Room there.'

'He went to the house with Richard Baker. They talked together?'

'I suppose so,' said Victoria. 'I mean, you wouldn't look at things in absolute silence, would you?'

'Lefarge,' murmured Edward. 'Who *is* Lefarge? Why have we got no line on him?'

Victoria longed to say, 'He's brother to Mrs Harris,' but refrained. She was pleased with her invention of M. Lefarge. She could see him quite clearly now in her mind's eye—a thin rather consumptive-looking young man with dark hair and a little moustache. Presently, when Edward asked her, she described him carefully and accurately.

They were driving now through the suburbs of Baghdad. Edward turned off down a side street of modern villas built in a pseudo-European style, with balconies and gardens round them. In front of one house a big touring car was standing. Edward drew up behind it and he and Victoria got out, and went up the steps to the front door.

A thin dark woman came out to meet them and Edward spoke to her rapidly in French. Victoria's French was not sufficiently good to understand fully what was said, but it seemed to be to the effect that this was the young lady and that the change must be effected at once.

The woman turned to her and said politely in French: 'Come with me, please.'

She led Victoria into a bedroom where, spread out on a bed, was the habit of a nun. The woman motioned to her, and Victoria undressed and put on the stiff wool undergarment and the voluminous medieval folds of dark stuff. The Frenchwoman adjusted the head-dress. Victoria caught a glimpse of herself in the glass. Her small pale face under the gigantic (was it a wimple?) with the white folds under her chin, looked strangely pure and unearthly. The Frenchwoman threw a rosary of wooden beads over her head. Then, shuffling in the over-large coarse shoes Victoria was led out to rejoin Edward.

'You look all right,' he said approvingly. 'Keep your eyes down, particularly when there are men about.'

The Frenchwoman rejoined them a moment or two later similarly apparelled. The two nuns went out of the house and got into the touring car which now had a tall dark man in European dress in the driver's seat.

'It's up to you now, Victoria,' said Edward. 'Do exactly as you are told.'

There was a slight steely menace behind the words.

'Aren't you coming, Edward?' Victoria sounded plaintive. He smiled at her.

'You'll see me in three days' time,' he said. And then, with a resumption of his persuasive manner, he murmured, 'Don't fail me, darling. Only you could do this—I love you, Victoria. I daren't be seen kissing a nun—but I'd like to.'

Victoria dropped her eyes in approved nun-like fashion, but actually to conceal the fury that showed for a moment.

'Horrible Judas,' she thought.

Instead she said with an assumption of her usual manner: 'Well, I seem to be a Christian slave all right.'

'That's the girl!' said Edward. He added, 'Don't worry. Your papers are in perfect order—you'll have no difficulty at the Syrian frontier. Your name in religion, by the way, is Sister Marie des Anges. Sister Thérèse who accompanies you has all the documents and is in full charge, and for God's sake obey orders—or I warn you frankly, you're for it.'

He stepped back, waved his hand cheerfully, and the touring car started off.

Victoria leaned back against the upholstery and gave herself up to contemplation of possible alternatives. She could, as they were passing through Baghdad, or when they got to the frontier control, make an agitation, scream for help, explain that she was being carried off against her will—in fact, adopt one or other variants of immediate protest.

What would that accomplish? In all probability it would mean the end of Victoria Jones. She had noticed that Sister

Thérèse had slipped into her sleeve a small and businesslike automatic pistol. She would be given no chance of talking.

Or she could wait until she got to Damascus? Make her protest there? Possibly the same fate would be meted out, or her statements might be overborne by the evidence of the driver and her fellow nun. They might be able to produce papers saying that she was mentally afflicted.

The best alternative was to go through with things—to acquiesce in the plan. To come to Baghdad as Anna Scheele and to play Anna Scheele's part. For, after all, if she did so, there would come a moment, at the final climax, when Edward could no longer control her tongue or her actions. If she could continue to convince Edward that she would do anything he told her, then the moment would come when she was standing with her forged documents before the Conference—and Edward would not be there.

And no one could stop her then from saying, 'I am not Anna Scheele and these papers are forged and untrue.'

She wondered that Edward did not fear her doing just that. But she reflected that vanity was a strangely blinding quality. Vanity was the Achilles heel. And there was also the fact to be considered that Edward and his crowd had more or less got to have an Anna Scheele if their scheme was to succeed. To find a girl who sufficiently resembled Anna Scheele—even to the point of having a scar in the right place—was extremely difficult. In the Lyons Mail, Victoria remembered, Dubosc and Lesurque had the extraordinary coincidence of both having a scar above one eyebrow and also of having a distortion, one by birth and one by accident, of the little finger of one hand. These coincidences must be very rare. No, the Supermen needed Victoria Jones, typist—and to that extent Victoria Jones had them in her power—not the other way round.

The car sped across the bridge. Victoria watched the Tigris with a nostalgic longing. Then they were speeding along a wide dusty highway. Victoria let the beads of her rosary pass through her fingers. Their click was comforting.

'After all,' thought Victoria with sudden comfort. 'I *am* a Christian. And if you're a Christian, I suppose it's a hundred times better to be a Christian martyr than a King in Babylon—and I must say, there seems to me a great possibility that I *am* going to be a martyr. Oh! well, anyway, it won't be *lions*. I should have hated lions!'

CHAPTER 23

The big Skymaster swooped down from the air and made a perfect landing. It taxied gently along the runway and presently came to a stop at the appointed place. The passengers were invited to descend. Those going on to Basrah were separated from those who were catching a connecting plane to Baghdad.

Of the latter there were four. A prosperous-looking Iraqi business man, a young English doctor and two women. They all passed through the various controls and questioning.

A dark woman with untidy hair imperfectly bound in a scarf and a tired face came first.

'Mrs Pauncefoot Jones? British. Yes. To join your husband. Your address in Baghdad, please? What money have you . . .?'

It went on. Then the second woman took the first one's place.

'Grete Harden. Yes. Nationality? Danish. From London. Purpose of visit? Masseuse at hospital? Address in Baghdad? What money have you?'

269

Agatha Christie

Grete Harden was a thin, fair-haired young woman wearing dark glasses. Some rather blotchily applied cosmetic concealed what might have been a blemish on her upper lip. She wore neat but slightly shabby clothes.

Her French was halting—occasionally she had to have the question repeated.

The four passengers were told that the Baghdad plane took off that afternoon. They would be driven now to the Abbassid Hotel for a rest and lunch.

Grete Harden was sitting on her bed when a tap came on the door. She opened it and found a tall dark young woman wearing BOAC uniform.

'I'm so sorry, Miss Harden. Would you come with me to the BOAC office? A little difficulty has arisen about your ticket. This way, please.'

Grete Harden followed her guide down the passage. On a door was a large board lettered in gold—*BOAC office*.

The air hostess opened the door and motioned the other inside. Then, as Grete Harden passed through, she closed the door from outside and quickly unhooked the board.

As Grete Harden came through the door, two men who had been standing behind it passed a cloth over her head. They stuffed a gag into her mouth. One of them rolled her sleeve up, and bringing out a hyperdermic syringe gave her an injection.

In a few minutes her body sagged and went limp.

The young doctor said cheerfully, 'That ought to take care of her for about six hours, anyway. Now then, you two, get on with it.'

He nodded towards two other occupants of the room.

They were nuns who were sitting immobile by the window. The men went out of the room. The elder of the two nuns went to Grete Harden and began to take the clothes off her inert body. The younger nun, trembling a little, started taking off her habit. Presently Grete Harden, dressed in a nun's habit, lay reposefully on the bed. The younger nun was now dressed in Grete Harden's clothes.

The older nun turned her attention to her companion's flaxen hair. Looking at a photograph which she propped up against the mirror, she combed and dressed the hair, bringing it back from the forehead and coiling it low on the neck.

She stepped back and said in French:

'Astonishing how it changes you. Put on the dark spectacles. Your eyes are too deep a blue. Yes—that is admirable.'

There was a slight tap on the door and the two men came in again. They were grinning.

'Grete Harden is Anna Scheele all right,' one said. 'She'd got the papers in her luggage, carefully camouflaged between the leaves of a Danish publication on "Hospital Massage". Now then, Miss Harden,' he bowed with mock ceremony to Victoria, 'you will do me the honour to have lunch with me.'

Victoria followed him out of the room and along to the hall. The other woman passenger was trying to send off a telegram at the desk.

'No,' she was saying, 'P A U N C E foot. Dr Pauncefoot Jones. Arriving today Tio Hotel. Good journey.'

Victoria looked at her with sudden interest. This must

be Dr Pauncefoot Jones' wife, coming out to join him. That she was a week earlier than expected did not seem to Victoria at all extraordinary since Dr Pauncefoot Jones had several times lamented that he had lost her letter giving the date of arrival but that he was almost certain it was the 26th!

If only she could somehow or other send a message through Mrs Pauncefoot Jones to Richard Baker . . .

Almost as though he read her thoughts, the man accompanying her steered her by the elbow away from the desk.

'No conversation with fellow travellers, Miss Harden,' he said. 'We don't want that good woman to notice that you're a different person from the one she came out from England with.'

He took her out of the hotel to a restaurant for lunch. As they came back, Mrs Pauncefoot Jones was coming down the steps of the hotel. She nodded without suspicion at Victoria.

'Been sight-seeing?' she called. 'I'm just going to the bazaars.'

'If I could slip something into her luggage . . .' thought Victoria.

But she was not left alone for a moment.

The Baghdad plane left at three o'clock.

Mrs Pauncefoot Jones' seat was right up in front. Victoria's was in the tail, near the door, and across the aisle sat the fair young man who was her gaoler. Victoria had no chance of reaching the other woman or of introducing a message into any of her belongings.

The flight was not a long one. For the second time,

Victoria looked down from the air and saw the city outlined below her, the Tigris dividing it like a streak of gold.

So she had seen it less than a month ago. How much had happened since then.

In two days' time the men who represented the two predominant ideologies of the world would meet here to discuss the future.

And she, Victoria Jones, would have a part to play.

'You know,' said Richard Baker, 'I'm worried about that girl.'

Dr Pauncefoot Jones said vaguely:

'What girl?'

'Victoria.'

'Victoria?' Dr Pauncefoot Jones peered about. 'Where is—why, God bless me, we came back without her yesterday.'

'I wondered if you'd noticed it,' said Richard.

'Very remiss of me. I was so interested by that report of the excavations at Tell Bamdar. Completely unsound stratification. Didn't she know where to find the lorry?'

'There was no question of her coming back here,' said Richard. 'As a matter of fact, she isn't Venetia Savile.'

'Not Venetia Savile? How very odd. But I thought you said her Christian name was Victoria.'

'It is. But she's not an anthropologist. And she doesn't know Emerson. As a matter of fact, the whole thing has been a—well—a misunderstanding.'

'Dear me. That seems very odd.' Dr Pauncefoot Jones

273

reflected for some moments. 'Very odd. I do hope—am I to blame? I know I am somewhat absent-minded. The wrong letter, perhaps?'

'I can't understand it,' said Richard Baker, frowning and paying no attention to Dr Pauncefoot Jones' speculations. 'She went off in a car with a young man, it seems, and she didn't come back. What's more, her baggage was there and she hadn't bothered to open it. That seems to me very strange—considering the mess she was in. I'd have thought she'd be sure to doll herself up. And we agreed to meet here for lunch . . . No, I can't understand it. I hope nothing's happened to her.'

'Oh, I shouldn't think so for a moment,' said Dr Pauncefoot Jones comfortably. 'I shall start going down in H. tomorrow. From the general plan I should say that would be the best chance of getting a record office. That fragment of tablet was very promising.'

'They've kidnapped her once,' said Richard. 'What's to prevent their having kidnapped her again?'

'Very improbable—very improbable,' said Dr Pauncefoot Jones. 'The country's really very settled nowadays. You said so yourself.'

'If only I could remember the name of that man in some oil company. Was it Deacon? Deacon, Dakin? Something like that.'

'Never heard of him,' said Dr Pauncefoot Jones. 'I think I shall change over Mustafa and his gang to the north-east corner. Then we might extend Trench J—'

'Would you mind awfully, sir, if I went into Baghdad again tomorrow?'

Dr Pauncefoot Jones, suddenly giving his colleague his full attention, stared at him.

'Tomorrow? But we were there yesterday.'

'I'm worried about that girl. I really am.'

'Dear me, Richard, I had no idea there was anything of *that* kind.'

'What kind?'

'That you'd formed an attachment. That's the worst of having women on a Dig—especially good-looking ones. I really did think we were safe with Sybil Muirfield the year before last, a really distressingly plain girl—and see what came of it! I ought to have listened to Claude in London—these Frenchmen always hit the nail on the head. He commented on her legs at the time—most enthusiastic about them. Of course this girl, Victoria, Venetia, whatever her name is—*most* attractive and such a nice little thing. You've got good taste, Richard, I will admit that. Funny thing, she's the first girl I've ever known you take any interest in.'

'There's nothing of that kind,' said Richard, blushing and looking even more supercilious than usual. 'I'm just—er—worried about her. I *must* go back to Baghdad.'

'Well, if you *are* going tomorrow,' said Dr Pauncefoot Jones, 'you might bring back those extra picks. That fool of a driver forgot them.'

Richard started into Baghdad at early dawn and went straight to the Tio Hotel. Here he learnt that Victoria had not returned.

'And it was all arranged that she was to have special dinner with me,' said Marcus. 'And I kept her a very nice room. It is odd, is it not?'

'Have you been to the Police?'

'Ah no, my dear, it would not be nice, that. She might not like it. And *I* certainly would not like it.'

After a little inquiry, Richard tracked down Mr Dakin and called upon him in his office.

His memory of the man had not played him false. He looked at the stooping figure, the indecisive face and the slight tremor of the hands. This man was no good! He apologized to Mr Dakin if he was wasting his time but had he seen Miss Victoria Jones?

'She called on me the day before yesterday.'

'Can you give me her present address?'

'She's at the Tio Hotel, I believe.'

'Her luggage is there, but she isn't.'

Mr Dakin raised his eyebrows slightly.

'She has been working with us on the excavations at Tell Aswad,' explained Richard.

'Oh I see. Well—I'm afraid I don't know anything that can help you. She has several friends in Baghdad, I believe—but I don't know her well enough to say who they are.'

'Would she be at this Olive Branch?'

'I don't think so. You could ask.'

Richard said: 'Look here. I'm not leaving Baghdad until I find her.'

He frowned at Mr Dakin and strode out of the room.

Mr Dakin, as the door closed behind Richard, smiled and shook his head.

'Oh Victoria,' he murmured reproachfully.

Fuming into the Tio Hotel, Richard was met by a beaming Marcus.

'She's come back,' cried Richard eagerly.

'No, no, it is Mrs Pauncefoot Jones. She arrives by plane today I have just heard. Dr Pauncefoot Jones, he told me she was coming next week.'

'He always gets dates wrong. What about Victoria Jones?'

Marcus's face went grave again.

'No, I have heard nothing of her. And I do not like it, Mr Baker. It is not nice. She is so young a girl. And so pretty. And so gay and charming.'

'Yes, yes,' said Richard, flinching. 'I'd better wait over and greet Mrs Pauncefoot Jones, I suppose.'

What on earth, he wondered, could have happened to Victoria.

'You!' said Victoria with undisguised hostility.

Ushered up to her room in the Babylonian Palace Hotel, the first person she saw was Catherine.

Catherine nodded her head with equal venom.

'Yes,' she said. 'It is I. And now please go to bed. The doctor will soon arrive.'

Catherine was dressed as a hospital nurse and she took her duties seriously, being obviously quite determined never to leave Victoria's side. Victoria, lying disconsolately in bed, murmured:

'If I could get hold of Edward—'

'Edward—Edward!' said Catherine scornfully. 'Edward

has never cared for you, you stupid English girl. It is *me* whom Edward loves!'

Victoria looked at Catherine's stubborn fanatical face without enthusiasm.

Catherine went on:

'Always I have hated you from that first morning you came in and demanded to see Dr Rathbone with such rudeness.'

Searching about for an irritant, Victoria said:

'At any rate I'm much more indispensable than you are. *Anybody* could do your hospital nurse act. But the whole thing depends on me doing mine.'

Catherine said with prim smugness:

'Nobody is indispensable. We are taught that.'

'Well, *I* am. For goodness' sake order up a substantial meal. If I don't get something to eat, how do you expect me to give a good performance of an American banker's secretary when the time comes?'

'I suppose you might as well eat while you can,' said Catherine grudgingly.

Victoria took no notice of the sinister implication.

Captain Crosbie said:

'I understand you've got a Miss Harden just arrived.'

The suave gentleman in the office of the Babylonian Palace inclined his head.

'Yes, sir. From England.'

'She's a friend of my sister's. Will you take my card up to her.'

He pencilled a few words on the card and sent it up in an envelope.

Presently the boy who had taken it returned.

'The lady is not well, sir. Very bad throat. Doctor coming soon. She has hospital nurse with her.'

Crosbie turned away. He went along to the Tio where he was accosted by Marcus.

'Ah, my dear, let us have a drink. This evening my hotel is quite full. It is for the Conference. But what a pity, Dr Pauncefoot Jones went back to his Expedition the day before yesterday and now here is his wife who arrives and expects that he will be here to meet her. And she is not pleased, no! She says she told him she was coming on this plane. But you know what he is like, that one. Every date, every time—he always gets it wrong. But he is a very nice man,' finished Marcus with his usual charity. 'And I have had to squeeze her in somehow—I turn out a very important man from UNO—'

'Baghdad seems quite mad.'

'All the police they have drafted in—they are taking great precautions—they say—have you heard?—there is a Communist plot to assassinate the President. They have arrested sixty-five students! Have you seen the Russian policemen? They are very suspicious of everybody. But all this is very good for trade—very good indeed.'

The telephone bell rang and was promptly answered.

'American Embassy.'

'This is the Babylonian Palace Hotel. Miss Anna Scheele is staying here.'

Anna Scheele? Presently one of the Attachés was speaking. Could Miss Scheele come to the phone?

'Miss Scheele is ill in bed with laryngitis. This is Dr Smallbrook. I am attending Miss Scheele. She has some important papers with her and would like some responsible person from the Embassy to come and fetch them. Immediately? Thank you. I will be waiting for you.'

Victoria turned from the mirror. She was wearing a well-cut tailored suit. Every blonde hair was in place. She felt nervous but exhilarated.

As she turned, she caught the exultant gleam in Catherine's eyes and was suddenly on her guard. Why was Catherine exultant?

What was going on?

'What are you so pleased about?' she asked.

'Soon you will see.'

The malice was quite unconcealed now.

'You think you are so clever,' said Catherine scornfully. 'You think everything depends on you. Pah, you are just a fool.'

With a bound Victoria was upon her! She caught her by the shoulder and dug her fingers in.

'Tell me what you mean, you horrible girl.'

'Ach—you hurt me.'

'Tell me—'

A knock came on the door. A knock twice repeated and then after a pause, a single one.

'Now you will see!' cried Catherine.

The door opened and a man slipped in. He was a tall man, dressed in the uniform of the International Police. He locked the door behind him and removed the key. Then he advanced to Catherine.

'Quickly,' he said.

He took a length of thin cord from his pocket and, with Catherine's full co-operation, bound her swiftly to a chair. Then he produced a scarf and tied it over her mouth. He stood back and nodded appreciatively.

'So—that will do nicely.'

Then he turned towards Victoria. She saw the heavy truncheon he was brandishing and in a moment it flashed across her brain what the real plan was. They had never intended that she should play the part of Anna Scheele at the Conference. How could they risk such a thing? Victoria was too well known in Baghdad. No, the plan was, had always been, that Anna Scheele should be attacked and killed at the last moment—killed in such a way that her features would not be recognizable . . . Only the papers she had brought with her—those carefully forged papers—would remain.

Victoria turned away to the window—she screamed. And with a smile the man came at her.

Then several things happened—there was a crash of broken glass—a heavy hand sent her headlong down—she saw stars—and blackness . . . Then out of the blackness a voice spoke, a reassuring English voice.

'Are you all right, Miss?' it asked.

Victoria murmured something.

'What did she say?' asked a second voice.

The first man scratched his head.

'Said it was better to serve in Heaven than reign in Hell,' he said doubtfully.

'That's a quotation,' said the other. 'But she's got it wrong,' he added.

'No, I haven't,' said Victoria and fainted.

The telephone rang and Dakin picked up the receiver. A voice said:

'Operation Victoria successfully concluded.'

'Good,' said Dakin.

'We've got Catherine Serakis and the medico. The other fellow threw himself off the balcony. He's fatally injured.'

'The girl's not hurt?'

'She fainted—but she's OK.'

'No news still of the real A. S.?'

'No news whatever.'

Dakin laid down the receiver.

At any rate Victoria was all right—Anna herself, he thought, must be dead . . . She had insisted on playing a lone hand, had reiterated that she would be in Baghdad without fail on the 19th. Today was the 19th and there was no Anna Scheele. Perhaps she had been right not to trust the official set-up—he didn't know. Certainly there had been leakages—betrayals. But apparently her own native wits had served her no better . . .

And without Anna Scheele, the evidence was incomplete.

A messenger came in with a piece of paper on which was written Mr Richard Baker and Mrs Pauncefoot Jones.

'I can't see anybody now,' said Dakin. 'Tell them I am very sorry. I am engaged.'

The messenger withdrew, but presently he returned. He handed Dakin a note.

Dakin tore open the envelope and read:

'I want to see you about Henry Carmichael. R. B.'

'Show him in,' said Dakin.

Presently Richard Baker and Mrs Pauncefoot Jones came in. Richard Baker said:

'I don't want to take up your time, but I was at school with a man called Henry Carmichael. We lost sight of each other for many years, but when I was at Basrah a few weeks ago I encountered him in the Consulate waiting-room. He was dressed as an Arab, and without giving any overt sign of recognition, he managed to communicate with me. Does this interest you?'

'It interests me very much,' said Dakin.

'I formed the idea that Carmichael believed himself to be in danger. This was very soon verified. He was attacked by a man with a revolver which I managed to knock up. Carmichael took to his heels but before he went, he slipped something into my pocket which I found later—it didn't appear to be important—it seems to be just a "chit"—a reference for one Ahmed Mohammed. But I acted on the assumption that to Carmichael it *was* important.

'Since he gave me no instructions, I kept it carefully, believing that he would one day reclaim it. The other day I learnt from Victoria Jones that he was dead. From other things she told me, I have come to the conclusion that the right person to deliver this object to is you.'

He got up and placed a dirty sheet of paper with writing on it on Dakin's desk.

'Does this mean anything to you?'

Dakin drew a deep sigh.

'Yes,' he said. 'It means more than you can possibly imagine.'

He got up.

'I'm deeply obliged to you, Baker,' he said. 'Forgive my cutting this interview short, but there is a lot that I have to see to without wasting a minute.' He shook hands with Mrs Pauncefoot Jones, saying, 'I suppose you are joining your husband on his Dig. I hope you have a good season.'

'It's a good thing Pauncefoot Jones didn't come into Baghdad with me this morning,' said Richard. 'Dear old John Pauncefoot Jones doesn't notice *much* that goes on, but he'd probably notice the difference between his wife and his wife's sister.'

Dakin looked with slight surprise at Mrs Pauncefoot Jones. She said in a low pleasant voice:

'My sister Elsie is still in England. I dyed my hair black and came out on her passport. My sister's maiden name was Elsie Scheele. *My name, Mr Dakin, is Anna Scheele.*'

CHAPTER 24

Baghdad was transformed. Police lined the streets—police drafted in from outside, the International Police. American and Russian police stood side by side with impassive faces.

Rumours were spreading the whole time—neither of the Great Ones was coming! Twice the Russian plane, duly escorted, landed—and proved to contain only a young Russian pilot!

But at last the news went round that all was well. The President of the United States and the Russian Dictator were here, in Baghdad. They were in the Regent's Palace.

At last the historic Conference had begun.

In a small ante-room certain events were taking place which might well alter the course of history. Like most momentous happenings, the proceedings were not at all dramatic.

Doctor Alan Breck of the Harwell Atomic Institute contributed his quota of information in a small precise voice.

Certain specimens had been left with him for analysis by the late Sir Rupert Crofton Lee. They had been acquired

285

in the course of one of Sir Rupert's journeys through China and Turkestan through Kurdistan to Iraq. Dr Breck's evidence then became severely technical. Metallic ores . . . high uranium content . . . Source of deposit not known exactly, since Sir Rupert's notes and diaries had been destroyed during the war by enemy action.

Then Mr Dakin took up the tale. In a gentle tired voice he told the saga of Henry Carmichael, of his belief in certain rumours and wild tales of vast installations and underground laboratories functioning in a remote valley beyond the bounds of civilization. Of his search—and of the success of his search. Of how that great traveller, Sir Rupert Crofton Lee, the man who had believed Carmichael because of his own knowledge of those regions, had agreed to come to Baghdad, and of how he had died. And of how Carmichael had met his own death at the hands of Sir Rupert's impersonator.

'Sir Rupert is dead, and Henry Carmichael is dead. But there is a third witness who is alive and who is here today. I will call upon Miss Anna Scheele to give us her testimony.'

Anna Scheele, as calm and composed as if she were in Mr Morganthal's office, gave lists of names and figures. From the depths of that remarkable financial brain of hers, she outlined the vast financial network that had drained money from circulation, and poured it into the financing of activities that should tend to split the civilized world into two opposing factions. It was no mere assertion. She produced facts and figures to support her contention. To those who listened she carried a conviction that was not as yet fully accorded to Carmichael's wild tale.

Dakin spoke again:

'Henry Carmichael is dead,' he said. 'But he brought back with him from that hazardous journey tangible and definite proofs. He did not dare to keep those proofs on him—his enemies were too close on his track. But he was a man of many friends. By the hands of two of those friends, he sent the proofs to the safe keeping of another friend—a man whom all Iraq reveres and respects. He has courteously consented to come here to-day. I refer to Sheikh Hussein el Ziyara of Kerbela.'

Sheikh Hussein el Ziyara was renowned, as Dakin had said, throughout the Moslem world, both as a Holy Man and a poet of renown. He was considered by many to be a Saint. He stood up now, an imposing figure with his deep brown hennaed beard. His grey jacket edged with gold braid was covered by a flowing brown cloak of gossamer fineness. Round his head he wore a green cloth head-dress which was bound with many strands of heavy gold *agal* and which gave him a patriarchal appearance. He spoke in a deep sonorous voice.

'Henry Carmichael was my friend,' he said. 'I knew him as a boy and he studied with me the verses of our great poets. Two men came to Kerbela, men who travel the country with a picture show. They are simple men, but good followers of the Prophet. They brought me a packet which they said they had been told to deliver into my hands from my friend the Englishman Carmichael. I was to keep this in secrecy and security and to deliver it only to Carmichael himself, or to a messenger who would repeat certain words. If in truth you are the messenger, speak, my son.'

287

Dakin said, 'Sayyid, the Arabic poet Mutanabbi, "the Pretender to prophecy", who lived just one thousand years ago, wrote an Ode to Prince Sayfu 'l-Dawla at Aleppo in which those words occur: *Zid hashshi bashshi tafaddal adni surra sili.*'*

With a smile Sheikh Hussein el Ziyara held out a packet to Dakin.

'I say as Prince Sayfu 'l-Dawla said: "You shall have your desire . . ."'

'Gentlemen,' said Dakin. 'These are the microfilms brought back by Henry Carmichael in proof of his story . . .'

One more witness spoke—a tragic broken figure: an old man with a fine domed head who had once been universally admired and respected.

He spoke with a tragic dignity.

'Gentlemen,' he said. 'I shall shortly be arraigned as a common swindler. But there are some things that even I cannot countenance. There is a band of men, mostly young men, so evil in their hearts and aims that the truth would hardly be believed.'

He lifted up his head and roared out:

'Antichrist! I say this thing must be *stopped*! We have got to have peace—peace to lick our wounds and make a new world—and to do that we *must* to try to understand each other. I started a racket to make money—but, by God, I've ended in believing in what I preach—though I don't advocate the methods I've used. For God's sake, gentlemen, let's start again and try to pull together . . .'

---

* Add, laugh, rejoice, bring nigh, show favour, gladden, give!

There was a moment's silence, and then a thin official voice, with the bloodless impersonality of bureaucracy said:

'These facts will be put forthwith before the President of the United States of America and the Premier of the Union of Soviet Socialist Republics . . .'

CHAPTER 25

'What bothers me,' said Victoria, 'is that poor Danish woman who got killed by mistake in Damascus.'

'Oh! she's all right,' said Mr Dakin cheerfully. 'As soon as your plane had taken off, we arrested the French woman and took Grete Harden to hospital. She came round all right. They were going to keep her drugged for a bit until they were sure the Baghdad business went off all right. She was one of our people, of course.'

'Was she?'

'Yes, when Anna Scheele disappeared, we thought it might be as well to give the other side something to think about. So we booked a passage for Grete Harden and carefully didn't give her a background. They fell for it—jumped to the conclusion that Grete Harden must be Anna Scheele. We gave her a nice little set of faked papers to prove it.'

'Whilst the real Anna Scheele remained quietly in the nursing home till it was time for Mrs Pauncefoot Jones to join her husband out here.'

'Yes. Simple—but effective. Acting on the assumption

that in times of stress the only people you can really trust are your own family. She's an exceedingly clever young woman.'

'I really thought I was for it,' said Victoria. 'Were your people really keeping tabs on me?'

'All the time. Your Edward wasn't really quite so clever as he thought himself, you know. Actually we'd been investigating the activities of young Edward Goring for some time. When you told me your story, the night Carmichael was killed, I was frankly very worried about you.

'The best thing I could think of was to send you deliberately into the set-up as a spy. If your Edward knew that you were in touch with me, you'd be reasonably safe, because he'd learn through you what we were up to. You'd be too valuable to kill. And he could also pass on false information to us through you. You were a link. But then you spotted the Rupert Crofton Lee impersonation, and Edward decided you'd better be kept out of it until you were needed (if you should be needed) for the impersonation of Anna Scheele. Yes, Victoria, you're very very lucky to be sitting where you are now, eating all those pistachio nuts.'

'I know I am.'

Mr Dakin said:

'How much do you mind—about Edward?'

Victoria looked at him steadily.

'Not at all. I was just a silly little fool. I let Edward pick me up and do his glamour act. I just had a thoroughly schoolgirl crush on him—fancying myself Juliet and all sorts of silly things.'

'You needn't blame yourself too much. Edward had a wonderful natural gift for attracting women.'

'Yes, and he used it.'

'He certainly used it.'

'Next time I fall in love,' said Victoria, 'it won't be looks that attract me, or glamour. I'd like a real man—not one who says pretty things to you. I shan't mind if he's bald or wears spectacles or anything like that. I'd like him to be interesting—and know about interesting things.'

'About thirty-five or fifty-five?' asked Mr Dakin.

Victoria stared.

'Oh thirty-five,' she said.

'I am relieved. I thought for a moment you were proposing to me.'

Victoria laughed.

'And—I know I mustn't ask questions—but was there really a message knitted into the scarf?'

'There was a name. The *tricoteuses* of whom Madam Defarge was one, knitted a register of names. The scarf and the "chit" were the two halves of the clue. One gave us the name of Sheikh Hussein el Ziyara of Kerbela. The other when treated with iodine vapour gave us the words to induce the Sheikh to part with his trust. There couldn't have been a safer place to hide the thing, you know, than in the sacred city of Kerbela.'

'And it was carried through the country by those two wandering cinema men—the ones we actually met?'

'Yes. Simple well-known figures. Nothing political about them. Just Carmichael's personal friends. He had a lot of friends.'

'He must have been very nice. I'm sorry he's dead.'

'We've all got to die some time,' said Mr Dakin. 'And if there's another life after this which I myself fully believe, he'll have the satisfaction of knowing that his faith and his courage have done more to save this sorry old world from a fresh attack of blood-letting and misery than almost anyone that one can think of.'

'It's odd, isn't it,' said Victoria meditatively, 'that Richard should have had one half of the secret and I should have had the other. It almost seems as though—'

'As though it were meant to be,' finished Mr Dakin with a twinkle. 'And what are you going to do next, may I ask?'

'I shall have to find a job,' said Victoria. 'I must start looking about.'

'Don't look too hard,' said Mr Dakin. 'I rather think a job is coming towards you.'

He ambled gently away to give place to Richard Baker.

'Look here, Victoria,' said Richard. 'Venetia Savile can't come out after all. Apparently she's got mumps. You were quite useful on the Dig. Would you like to come back? Only your keep, I'm afraid. And probably your passage back to England—but we'll talk about that later. Mrs Pauncefoot Jones is coming out next week. Well, what do you say?'

'Oh, do you really *want* me?' cried Victoria.

For some reason Richard Baker became very pink in the face. He coughed and polished his pince-nez.

'I think,' he said, 'we could find you—er—quite useful.'

'I'd love it,' said Victoria.

'In that case,' said Richard, 'you'd better collect your

luggage and come along back to the Dig now. You don't want to hang about Baghdad, do you?'

'Not in the least,' said Victoria.

'So there you are, my dear Veronica,' said Dr Pauncefoot Jones. 'Richard went off in a great state about you. Well, well—I hope you'll both be very happy.'

'What does he mean?' asked Victoria bewildered, as Dr Pauncefoot Jones pottered away.

'Nothing,' said Richard. 'You know what he's like. He's being—just a little—premature.'